The Hundred-Year Storm

A Novel

Thomas Hofstedt

"The past is never dead.
It's not even past."

William Faulkner, *Requiem for a Nun*

Table of Contents

The Storm

Five Years Ago

Not all cataclysms are apparent at the time.

Later, it would be known as "The Hundred-Year Storm" and subsequent storms would be measured against it, always falling short. That night, however, it was just an exceptionally intense rainstorm that had gone on much too long, exhausting the thin stocks of patience and hopefulness that buffer ordinary people from a run of bad luck. It caused some to change their plans, to stay home with vague forebodings and worry about whether the roof would leak or the power fail. For those who ventured out, the storm provided a rare sense of adventure, a sense of overcoming larger forces in their lives.

None of them, however, knew of the coming tragedy that – in the retelling – would recast the storm as an omen, a fitting and ominous backdrop for mundane evil.

From the road, the McKay house first appeared as a soft-edged yellow glow whose shape and intensity changed as waves of rain swept through the inadequate headlights. As one came closer, the rain kept the outlines blurry, until the glow devolved into individual squares and rectangles associated with windows or the cones of outside lights. Even the parking attendants in their hooded yellow slickers with their black umbrellas seemed not quite real, shrouded creatures of the storm. It was only when the guests entered the brightly-lit ballroom with its distinctly human noise and physical contact that people felt and began to act as though they were once more in control; although even then they were quicker to seek out others, to stand a little closer and talk louder than usual.

The ballroom, with its two huge chandeliers and mirrored surfaces, amplified both light and sound; its vastness diminished only by the two hundred or so guests that formed distinct clusters, each with its own epicenter, but with enough ebb and flow between them that the ballroom seemed full of motion and people. The far wall was mostly glass, a series of large French doors opening onto the veranda overlooking the lawn and river, although anyone looking outside would see only his or her own reflection. The thin vertical barrier of glass sharply separated the interior light from the outer darkness and drenching rain, emphasizing the feeling of sanctuary that one felt on first coming in from the storm.

Edith, the woman with only a short time to live, was at the center of one of the clusters at the far end of the room. She probably would have been at the center even if she had not been the hostess for the evening. She was young, not yet thirty, but she exuded the assurance and presence that comes from good schooling and old money. She was animated and unaffectedly beautiful in a way that attracted men without seeming to threaten other women. In conversation, she impressed people as being someone completely natural, without any agenda and open to different points of view.

That impression was utterly wrong. Edith McKay had stronger passions and many more secrets than others of her age and class; secrets that were more dramatic, more capable of damage if disclosed. Unknown to those dozen or so individuals standing close to her, one of those secrets had just risen to the surface in a way that caused her to reimagine the trajectory of her life. Looking back, it is remarkable that none of those individuals noticed the change in Edith as she abruptly stopped being the gregarious hostess and withdrew into herself to envision the new possibilities.

She stood on tiptoe to find those few others who needed to know about the new world she was still visualizing. Typically, she did not worry about how her own transformation would require those others to adapt their own lives to new circumstances, nor was she aware that that very unconcern would condemn her.

She quickly located Marcus, partly because he was looking directly at her with that expression that she knew so well. She smiled. How fitting that he should be the first to know!

Marcus was halfway listening to Nathaniel talk about the rain, but devoted most of his attention to watching Edith. He thought once more how controlled she was, remarkable when one knew of the passions that were so close to the surface, and he wondered at her sudden change in intensity and obvious emotional withdrawal from those around her. He saw her purposeful scan of the crowd and her change in expression when they made eye contact across the room. He was not surprised when she abruptly broke away from her small group and started toward them.

He glanced at Nathaniel, who was also watching Edith approach and looking quite horrified by the prospect. A barely disguised panic was becoming more and more evident, a panic whose source was well known to Marcus. *Well, it's been a long seven years since the three of us have talked. Should be quite interesting.*

Given the possibilities, Marcus felt strangely detached, only mildly curious about her intentions. He was aware of and faintly surprised about his lack of curiosity. *Maybe I'm conditioned. I wonder if you can build up immunity to surprise, like you can with measles or loud noises? Or – more likely, after the last few years as a cop – maybe it's just harder to expect something good to happen.*

For some reason, he recalled his last conversation with his father. Cooper, in his usual awkward parental way, had suggested that Marcus had an annoying habit of over-analyzing things; that he should just go with his emotions for once. When Marcus said sarcastically, "I should follow your example?" Cooper just looked at him, then turned and walked away. It was their typical father-son encounter.

Then Edith was directly in front of them. She gripped his and Nathaniel's arms tightly enough that Marcus knew that this was not going to be the typical "Hi. Long time, no see" kind of cocktail party encounter.

Edith's husband Robert stood alone at the far end of the ballroom, alternating between watching her and checking his reflection in the mirrored wall facing him. It was not vanity, merely a reflex response to a mirror. He knew himself to be attractive and felt no compulsion to reconfirm it. Everything fit nicely – the salt and pepper hair, blue eyes, and broad shoulders. Central casting would place him as a CEO, a senator or a commanding general in a war zone. He was one of the few men wearing a tuxedo, consistent with his usual formality. In fact, he was rarely seen in public without a tie. If you asked him why, he would be puzzled by the implication that one's image should be variable or left to the perceptual whims of others. The combination of his good looks, carefully concealed cynicism, and dedication to image made him an occasional but ideal politician.

His main concern at the moment was that he was insufficiently intoxicated by his own cocktail party standards. He had yet to reach that exact tipping point where the alcohol triggered a burst of extroversion, enabling him to talk and behave as though he cared about whomever he was talking to at the moment.

He shifted his preoccupation from himself to his second wife Edith, looking down the length of the room at her. He viewed her objectively, accepting her animation and abundant sensuality without any particular pleasure or sense of ownership; more interested in the way those around her were affected by those very features. As always, she was at the center of a small group. He was surprised to see that she did not have her usual public half-smile, but was tight-lipped, obviously not interested in whatever was being said. She was clearly bothered by something, looking for someone.

He watched her as she walked directly to Nathaniel and Marcus, clearly noting Marcus's raised eyebrows and Nathaniel's visible uneasiness as they watched her approach.

Seeing Nathaniel made him wonder where Maria was. She was easy to find, standing by herself, a few steps up the staircase and elevated from the crowd. Outwardly, she seemed composed. But Robert also noted the extreme rigidity in her posture and the way her eyes followed Edith's progress through the crowd toward Marcus and Nathaniel. He wondered how much longer she could hold herself together and what form the meltdown might take on ... and how Simon would handle it.

Maria's husband Simon -- his brother – was standing near the veranda doors. Robert was surprised to see Simon watching Edith quite overtly and with some obvious concern. *Careful, Simon! The two of you need to be a little more cautious. You're a pretty obvious pair of adulterers.* When Edith abruptly left Nathaniel and Marcus and moved with clear purpose toward Simon, Robert was amused to see him stand straighter and adjust his expression, putting on an appearance of polite expectancy, something appropriate for just another casual encounter with the hostess. Robert laughed to himself.

Until five minutes ago, Maria had been standing in the exact center of the ballroom, trying to stay precisely equidistant from the four walls and feeling pleased with her self. She'd negotiated the entire first hour of the cocktail party without incident. *Simon will be pleased.* But her awareness of the storm and the press of smiling people were beginning to erode her self-control. The lights were too bright and her face felt too tight, her smile more and more forced. She wanted to slap the silly woman that insisted on telling her about the book she was reading. She began to feel that she was being watched, that everyone in the ballroom was waiting for her to lose control.

Where was Simon? He'll cover for me, like he always does ... with that little grimace of discontent that I know so well.

She abruptly walked away from the annoying woman, moving several steps up the staircase, to the point where she could see the entire ballroom. She scanned the room until she saw Simon talking with a couple she didn't know, and her son Nathaniel, standing with his friend Marcus. As she watched, she saw Edith approach the two of them, talk for only a minute or so, although with an intensity that was apparent even to her.

What does that woman want with Nathaniel?

Don't go, Nathaniel! By then, she wasn't sure if it was merely a thought or if she had screamed it. Nothing changed in the people around her, so she assumed that she had not.

She watched as Edith left Nathaniel and Marcus and went directly to Simon, leaning into him to talk. Maria easily detected Simon's sharp reaction but could not say whether it was surprise, anger, or some combination. He said something to Edith, who turned and walked away without responding, toward the veranda door. Maria watched her until she was lost amid the crowd at the far end of the ballroom.

She looked again for Nathaniel but could not see him. *Nathaniel! Where are you? Don't go with that woman again ... she's evil!*

Maria felt the room getting smaller, the lights brighter, and the voices louder, creating a pressure wave that seemed to be swirling around her in ever-smaller circles. Then the lights went out, and as the familiar terrifying blackness descended on her there on the staircase, she did scream.

Simon, as always, was at the epicenter of a small group, albeit that group consisted of the "A-List" invitees – the socialites, power brokers and opinion leaders whose status depended on "access" to the inner circles that he inhabited. He was halfway listening to one of the mainline dowagers of Stanton semi-ranting about the "new people" and how they were ruining the city.

He watched Edith coming toward him. As always, in the last few seconds before she was near enough to touch, he felt both anticipation and guilt, simultaneously and with equal intensity. In public, as they were tonight, he also felt an almost continuous and pleasurable tingle of excitement, brought on by the need to play a role in front of watchful and critical eyes. He acknowledged and welcomed the way it intensified their coming together once out-of-sight, without the need for pretense or clothing. In quieter times, he wondered how much of their mutual and intense attraction arose from their shared need for risk taking.

He felt the sudden tension in the woman that was doing all of the talking, and the pulling away, both physical and emotional as Edith approached. He briefly marveled at how the very quality of the air seemed to change when two alpha females – rivals for something, usually but not always a man -- met in public, polite to a fault.

He saw Maria on the staircase, and then Robert at the other end of the room, their eyes quite clearly following Edith as she crossed the ballroom.

My wife and my brother. I wonder if they know? I wonder if I even care?

He almost laughed out loud when he thought about how much they did not know. For the thousandth time, he marveled at his own recklessness, at the secrets-within-secrets that he was juggling. *Deception squared, practiced on everyone around me … including this woman.*

Edith reached him. She smiled distractedly at the couple he was talking with and tugged at Simon's sleeve to break him free for a moment. Simon could feel the intensity radiating from her. She started to speak, then stopped, stood on tiptoe, leaned against him and whispered in his ear.

Simon heard the words clearly. The formal syntax was clear; nouns and verbs were everyday and straightforward. But what she said did not make sense.

He stood rigidly in place as she stepped back. She smiled again at the couple standing patiently, gave Simon's arm a very hard squeeze, and then turned away, as though anxious to get away. She walked rapidly toward the far entrance, a woman with somewhere to be.

Then the lights went out. Maria screamed. And the world shifted.

Damn this rain!

Nathaniel was standing at the edge of the lawn under the overhang of the veranda, just outside of the ballroom and just short of the wall of rain. The rain seemed impenetrable; the light streaming from the massive house behind him simply bounced off. The noise – from the storm outside and from the house -- drowned out everything else.

Nathaniel's steadfast belief that everything had a purpose, that nothing happened by accident, was being severely tested by the series of events – more like mini-disasters – looming around him.

He had avoided them for seven years, with great care. At first, he was fatalistic. Consequences must surely follow actions. His mother's insistence on a just and vengeful god – the contradiction never occurred to her – overwhelmed his innate sense of entitlement. But as time passed and he perfected his rationalizations, his fear of consequences receded.

When Edith McKay came back two years ago, Nathaniel assumed total exposure would follow. When weeks passed without any retribution, he accepted the gift but knew that it could be retracted at any time. He avoided any contact with her, difficult in a city the size of Stanton and for people with their habits. Again, the passage of time and her apparent lack of interest lulled him. The secret seemed safe.

His peace of mind was helped considerably by the various pills. "Softeners" was how he thought of them, keeping the world at bay. Until tonight. Now the once far-off consequences loomed over him, like a series of advancing great waves.

What in the hell was she going to do? Tell the world?

She had come looking for Marcus and him, purposefully, a straight line through the milling crowd, ignoring several of those trying to engage her. As soon as he saw her heading for them, he knew that his life was about to change.

The encounter lasted only thirty seconds. He would never forget the tightness of her grip on his forearm or her expression, alternating between excitement, determination & supplication. Her words confirmed his fears. "It's time to talk. Something has changed."

Where's Marcus? Damn him!

Then the house – ablaze with light -- went instantly dark, and the blackness was complete, somehow made moreso by the roar of the falling rain..

Nathaniel stood facing the dark house, his back to the rain, unmoving, waiting. He heard a door open and close and felt rather than saw a presence move past him into the wall of rain, toward the river. Then another.

End of an Affair

The world was made of water.

The rain seemed part of the ink-black sky, so continuous and dense that Edith felt herself to be swimming rather than walking. She knew it as rain only through the persistent downward pressure on her head and shoulders.

Even the ground seemed liquefied, as though the rain had simply chosen to move horizontally rather than vertically. The earth had become a non-dimensional surface that she walked in or through rather than on; a medium that offered little resistance when she pushed herself forward toward the river.

Reference points did not exist in such a world, neither physical nor moral.

The physicality of the water was emphasized by its sound, a continuous roar punctuated by drumming tones as the heavy drops struck Edith's rubberized black poncho. Mini-cascades and rivulets running haphazardly across the uneven ground added an overlay of constantly changing sub-rhythms. The sound was made complete and overwhelming by the unseen river below, the seemingly vocal protest of tons of water being forced through a rocky gorge, creating currents, rapids and eddies across the jutting rock surfaces, adding tonal variation to the underlying roar.

Edith stood in the water and the sound, slowly turning in circles looking for her lover, her mind racing with images of what could be.

She felt the approaching shape before it was visible, as if preceded by an aura. She sensed a small rift in the grayness to her right, away from the river, confirmed by a faint variation in the sound of the falling rain. She turned to see a phantasmagoric figure emerge, first as a mere discoloration in the overall grayness, then as a three-dimensional object. It took shape -- a peaked rain hat and a poncho – seemingly a black pyramid shrouded in waterfalls, somehow sinister.

They stood side by side, facing the river just short of the point where the lawn sloped steeply downward, apparently content with their expectant silence accented by the surrounding din of water.

Edith spoke first, raising her voice to a near-shout against the rain. "I wasn't sure you would come."

There was a pause, and then the response, "I should have spoken long ago. This needs to end, here and now."

The shape that was Edith jerked backward, as though by electrical impulse. It turned toward the other, shouting, "No! It can't end!" in a voice that was both angry and pleading. "We have … we are … something special. You can't change that with a few words … what we mean to each other… all that's happened. Not now! Not when --" The disjointed phrases tumbled out of her with a rising volume.

The other form came closer to Edith, reached out a hand, and said accusingly, "What about those that you're hurting … people you say you love and care about? Don't we … they … have rights too? Or is that just 'collateral damage', as the military likes to say?"

Edith's response began haltingly, barely audible. "I do think about them, and I wish …." She paused, seemed to shake herself. She slapped away the hand reaching out to her and her voice became shrill, "I don't care! And you can't stop me from doing this!"

Both stood still, water all around them. The rain somehow intensified in both pitch and volume, as though in concert with their rising passions, as if searching for a suitably dramatic setting for what was being played out within the rain.

The figure moved even closer and stood very still, not touching Edith, and said quite calmly, "I will stop you! And the consequences are yours, not mine."

Edith laughed, "You're crazy! There's nothing we can do to change what we are!" and she turned away, toward the sharp edge where the lawn began its steep descent to the edge of the rapids.

The ominous pyramidal figure seemed to become taller in the rain. It moved jerkily, merging with Edith's silhouette. A black-clad arm emerged, strangely elongated as it rose high above the pair and then descended rapidly with a sound that was different than that of the rainfall, punctuated by a cry that was not quite human.

The silhouettes parted, one slipping downward and the other simply fading to nothing in the grayness of rain, back toward the faint residual glow of candles and flashlights beginning to dot the McKay house.

Water was everywhere. Edith felt herself enveloped within it, falling encased in a gray waterfall. The sound changed and overrode all other sensation. It transformed into a rhythmic chant in time with all of the varying sounds of water: "It's all wrong!" "Not now!" "It's all wrong!" "Not now!"

Then the sounds blurred and faded to simple white noise. Then silence. The gray became black.

And the rain continued to fall, indifferent.

Cooper

(The Present - Five Years Later)

Cooper pushed the "end call" button and thought about the call. His first reaction was dismay, at his inability to just say "No." *You haven't learned a thing, have you? A dozen years of triaging calls that begin "I need your help", and you still think that this one will be different.*

At first glance, Cooper was your average fifty-year-old white male, the type to easily blend in at Starbucks in mid-morning on a weekday. He was a little taller, leaner and had more scars than most of his contemporaries; but when dressed in his standard khakis and sport coat, he did not seem particularly remarkable. Up close, he had an aura of stillness about him that was often unsettling to those who were not quite sure of themselves, who were prone to mistake it for implied judgment. Dmitri insisted that it was an aura that all cops carried around with them, a variant of the body language instinctive to urban gang members. When Cooper protested mildly on the grounds that he was an ex-cop, one who had turned in his attitudes and auras along with his gun and badge, Dmitri extended his theory, claiming that the aura was permanent, like a birthmark.

Basically, Cooper was an observer. He couldn't help it, and he had stopped trying to decide whether it was a blessing or a curse.

However, Cooper spent most of his time observing and thinking about his own self rather than others. Not in the narcissistic way that so many middle-aged, divorced males tended to adopt. And not in the manner of graduates of modern self-help programs, the sort that subscribe to the doctrine "know thyself" as a way of life. Cooper's habitual introspections were driven by simple curiosity. *Why did I do that? Why do I feel that way? How did I get this way? These* were the themes that occupied most of his inner-directed thoughts.

The idea of asking others to help him think about these questions never occurred to him. If it did, he would reject it as a violation of the self-reliant philosophy that he lived by. And the elusiveness of the answers ensured a continuously fresh outlook on his recent past. He did not think very much about the future.

For Cooper, history was binary, a "before" and "after" time series, distinctive time segments with little to do with one another, separated as cleanly as if he had entered a Witness Protection Program. He was the only continuing character, and sometimes he thought of his earlier self in the second person, as "he" rather than "I."

The "before" phase covered everything up to September 11, 2001. It featured childhood, the army, college, a wife, child, job; all the trappings of normalcy for the late twentieth-century American male. It was also characterized by a free-floating trajectory sustained by an alcohol-fueled buzz for most of his waking hours.

For a long time, he was able to sustain the illusion that his drinking was a necessary antidote to normalcy, a more manly form of anti-depressant for someone who – in his self-view -- was limited by his milieu rather than by any lack of talent or character. He did not use this belief to defend himself to others. He did not whine or become paranoid, nor did he invent local conspiracies to justify his small but continuing failures. He accepted that he was imperfect and was content.

He did not have any particular ambitions during the "before" phase. Each day presented itself and he responded to people and events as they arose. He asked for nothing from others and expected nothing, mistaking his own contentment for an endorsement or at least a tacit acceptance of his life style. He noted but did not respond to the ever-widening gap between himself and those few people he permitted into his life. He was incapable of expectations for either himself or others and, therefore, was not subject to the resentments so typical of those with ambitions or prospects.

His first and only wife lasted fifteen years, sustained by the irrational conviction common to good-hearted women who marry alcoholic men – that the problem is the liquor, not the underlying person -- and the even more unlikely belief that the person is fixable. She never got the chance to test the validity of either proposition. Cooper simply wore her out with his passivity. One morning, she simply said, "*I quit. I just can't do this any more.*" There was no argument or even discussion. Each of them knew quite well everything that was implied by those few words. Cooper suspected that she was having an affair but just did not care enough to be bothered. His apathy was helped by his conviction that she was entitled to a better person than him.

She stayed in Stanton and Cooper heard occasional reports. He knew that she had not remarried and had a flourishing career as a commercial real estate broker. Their last formal contact was four years ago, a Christmas card whose only notation was "*Hope you're well ... Natalie.*"

His son Marcus was less accepting of his shortfalls. The divorce accelerated the estrangement between father and son that had been building through Marcus's adolescence. Marcus chose sides early and, not surprisingly, allied with his mother. But unlike her retreat into sheer indifference and occasional sadness where Cooper was concerned, Marcus opted for outright hostility. Or indifference; it was hard to tell the difference. That still defined their relationship to the present time, with Marcus's antagonism muted only by the reality that they did not see one another and rarely talked on the telephone.

Ironically to Cooper, Marcus was now a cop, working closely with Dmitri, Cooper's old partner on the Stanton police force. Cooper thought a lot about the ironic forces at work but accepted them as too complex to fully understand, involving a three-way dynamic flow of shifting emotions.

Dmitri was once his best friend and had been an uncle-like figure for Marcus during his late adolescence. He was unmarried and had no children, but Cooper knew that he had been part of a sprawling and contentious family back in Russia.

He also knew that Dmitri was deeply emotional about relationships and family and he strongly suspected that Dmitri harbored a plan – dormant at the moment -- to restore Marcus and Cooper to some kind of mutually caring state.

A dozen years ago, Cooper was disciplined for "unprofessional behavior as a police officer" and was ordered to a session with a psychiatrist on contract with the department. At about the same time, he agreed to see a marriage counselor "to work on some of his issues" in a last-ditch effort to stay married. He found the two therapeutic programs to be remarkably similar; concurrent monologues rather than the dialogue that he was actually looking forward to. He was disappointed that the shrinks were not very much interested in his self-analysis. They wanted to talk about "feelings" as if they obeyed some hard-to-understand cause-and-effect relationship visible only to a licensed priesthood. An unexpressed feeling was an oxymoron in their world.

To their credit and to his surprise, the shrinks did zero in on his drinking habits. Although they did not quite say it, he felt that they agreed with him that *"Let's face it. You're an asshole when you're drinking."* As therapists, however, they tended to focus on his childhood to explain his adult pathology. Cooper had read some of the literature on adult children of alcoholics and noted that he exhibited most of the characteristic traits. Foremost among them was the motto that Cooper would have emblazoned on his family coat-of-arms if he had one: *"Never complain. Never explain."* This among other things made him a poor subject for brief psychiatric interventions, and he did not go back after the first mandatory sessions.

His marriage and his law enforcement career ended at the same time and for the same reasons, mostly to do with alcoholism, inattention and chronic moroseness. The three important personal relationships in his life terminated at about the same time, those with his wife, son and his friend and partner Dmitri.

He continued to drink, rationalizing it as a necessary antidote to problems he could not name. He was a quiet, amiable drunk in neighborhood bars, living off his cashed-in police pension and savings, thinking about himself and how he'd screwed up his and other lives. He developed a small reputation and made some money as a "problem solver," somewhere in the murky interface between the citizenry and the law. His tasks were simple -- finding a balky adolescent, tracking through documents to see who really owned what, escorting zonked-out celebrities into hush-hush treatment programs, using their money to paper over their sins. He was part of a highly specialized underground economy, calling for experience and skills that aren't transmitted through college courses or internships.

He floated through each day, finding liquor, TV and books to be sufficient for his needs. He had little interest in women, and the occasional relationship was brief and unsatisfying. He was becoming a morose monastic, addicted to himself and booze.

Then everything changed, all at once and all over the country. The "after" phase of Cooper's history began on September 11, 2001. Like the rest of the country, he awoke to the inconceivably obscene images of planeloads of people being used as unwilling firebombs against tall buildings of unforgiving steel and concrete. The beginning of the end of Cooper's prior history was catalyzed by the sight of individuals jumping from the tops of the towers to escape the flames. Even though they appeared as mere falling dots filmed from far off, lacking personality or gender, he could not stop himself from imagining their state of mind, choosing between incineration or stepping off into space on a sunlit morning when they had gone to work as though nothing was about to change. He could not imagine himself facing such a choice.

He did not understand why, but the falling dots changed him. Perhaps it was the starkness of their choice, contrasted with his passive, drifting existence. He became bored with himself, and he stopped drinking. Later, when the AA crowd or some puzzled addict with multiple failed attempts to stop pressed him on how or why he did it, he always responded,

"I just stopped" and was always surprised when that answer was insufficient or -- for some -- somehow offensive.

The semantics were troublesome. The typical reformed drunk talked a lot about "sobriety," a comprehensive term that Cooper would use to describe a Scandinavian or a personality defect. He simply thought of it as "not drinking."

His life style didn't change, other than the absence of booze. He still frequented a neighborhood bar, finding something pleasurable in nursing a cup of coffee in the late afternoon ambience.

He discovered that he was a natural loner. It wasn't the alcohol that had exiled him, but a built-in predisposition to self-sufficiency, to a benign sociopathy that he came to think of as an aversion to being needed. At the most mundane level, it showed up as a profound inability to simply *chat*. He found himself to be an outlier, searching for something to say in perfectly ordinary contexts – elevators, cocktail parties, picking up his laundry – the kind of social situations that make up the bulk of human relationships. His ex-wife had complained that he was "judgmental," but he thought it more likely that he could not help analyzing rather than simply responding. Maybe Dmitri was right; perhaps it really was a trained incapacity that infected cops.

His social life was superficial. Friends from what he viewed as "his prior life" – when he was married, working and mostly drunk – had been few and had fallen away.

He was equally awkward with men and women, but it bothered him more with the women. Men accepted taciturnity as an identifying mark, a sort of emotional tattoo. Women seemed to view it first as a challenge, something to be overcome and corrected; then – when it persisted -- as an affront to their femininity, a public sign of some failure on their part.

After he stopped drinking, he had semi-serious relationships with two women. The women were quite different from one another, but the dynamics of the relationships were depressingly similar. The first – Emily – was a forty-year-old forensic psychologist, sneaky-smart and a major believer in AA.

She was followed by Daniela, a pharmaceutical sales rep and a physical fitness addict, a few years older. Both relationships began as a mutual experiment, showed some promise of permanence, and then drifted into a routine marked by increasing disinterest. Each relationship ended amicably, a fact that Cooper viewed as confirmation of their sterility.

Other men in the same situation complained about the lack of what they called "companionship." Cooper was not sure what that entailed, but he did know that he missed the sex; the sheer *fun* that came with shedding the inhibitions that go with culture and clothing and lighted rooms. The incredible, unspeakable intensity of skin on skin, of friction and crescendo, of shared breathing and breathlessness, where wanting and giving were indistinguishable, of the always-too-short interlude between the oneness and the return to being separate people.

But as Daniela told him, "Good sex does not a relationship make." Eventually, each of the women in his life went away for the same reason. His ex-wife said it best: "You don't make enough of yourself available for others to share." Cooper understood the emotion, but did not know how to change; or, more likely, was unwilling to undergo the psychic surgery that would have been prescribed.

Cooper also knew that part of his relational difficulties stemmed from his over-developed sense of right and wrong, a binary world-view that worked only because it carried no expectations and did not assign responsibility. It was not exercised as the moralistic small-minded judgment of the religious fanatic, and he had no illusions about his own flaws. He recognized his inability to change people, even if he wanted to. However, one of its many dysfunctional manifestations was a resistance to authority, especially if exercised without a moral focus, as is so often the case in police work.

For the past year, Cooper had reconciled himself to his solitary state, convincing himself that it was a tolerable existence. He seemed to have reached a point where he could meet an attractive, smart woman for the first time without automatically assessing her as a prospective "relationship."

One of the consequences was that he was working more. That "work" had just surfaced in the form of a phone call from a man named Simon Radner. They talked for three or four minutes, with Cooper looking unhappier as the call went on. He looked at the few notes he had jotted down from the call he had just finished. And thought again, *This is not likely to be a happy venture. And you know that, don't you?*

A Conflicted Client

I don't need this! The unvoiced thought had become a refrain in Cooper's mind, beginning with the phone call and continuing through the afternoon traffic to his meeting with Simon Radner. He spent most of the twenty minute transit time running through his own memories of Simon Radner from a dozen years ago. They had met a couple of times. Nothing more than a perfunctory handshake that failed to bridge the multiple social and cultural gaps between them.

Why am I doing this? Wearing a tie and about to be polite to some sanctimonious stuffed shirt in trouble; some indignant rich guy who's just been rousted by the cops but still thinks he can make it go away if he throws enough money at it. His internal monologue had run through numerous variations on this theme, until he realized that his characterizations of the client were really projections of his own dissatisfaction with his own drifting existence. He couldn't fool himself about his real discontent: *I'm tired of this crap. I would like to stay home and read books.*

Cooper's uncharacteristic self-pity ended abruptly when the elevator stopped at the top floor of the tallest building in the city. He stepped out into a reception area that seemed to be composed of about equal parts fabric, glass and chrome. The nameplate said *Simon Radner - Attorney,* and Cooper asked himself again, *why am I doing this?* The client was also a lawyer, not a happy combination in Cooper's experience. And judging by the office décor and Cooper's own recollections, he was also a very important lawyer. Cooper was intrigued despite himself. *So, we've got a real upper crust attorney who needs an investigator on his own account ... and it's not for some sleazy reconnaissance job on a wayward wife. I wonder what his problem is?*

To his further surprise, the receptionist was a man, older than Cooper. That was a definite first in Cooper's experience with big-city law firms and it ratcheted up his interest level another notch.   The receptionist was expecting him and immediately ushered him into a corner office with floor-to-ceiling glass on two sides and a 180° view of gigantic cumulus clouds hovering over a sun-streaked downtown. The lone shirt-sleeved occupant came from behind the desk. Its surface was bare, except for a laptop computer and a single neatly aligned stack of paper.

The man smiled and extended his hand. "I'm Simon Radner. Thanks for coming on short notice."

So, he either doesn't remember me or – more likely – chooses not to.

Radner was in his fifties, obviously fit, and seemingly untroubled. He had startling blue eyes and the kind of creases around them that suggested someone who laughed a lot. Cooper guessed that he had a lot of men friends who went on golfing and fishing trips together and that women would find him to be good-looking, in a rumpled sort of way.

He shook Radner's hand. "No problem. But I don't think I've ever auditioned under such conditions. I know nothing about why you think you need an investigator, except that it's for you and it's a criminal matter."

"I guess it is an audition, isn't it?" Simon said, and then added, "But for which one of us?"

Cooper shrugged. "You're buying the product, so that makes me the one to show my stuff, I think."

While they were talking, Simon led them to a pair of leather-upholstered swivel chairs near the far window and they sat facing one another with the sunlit cumulus clouds as backdrop. When both were seated, he continued. "But from what I've heard about you, you set very high acceptance standards for clients. The colleague who referred you – actually, a police officer – said that I shouldn't take you for granted, even if I hired you! Made you sound like some kind of knight errant."

Cooper grimaced. "Whoever he was, he's been reading too much Dashiell Hammett. I just don't want to spend my time or moral energy on other people's problems unless I can help."

Simon said, "Sounds like the doctor's mandate -- Do no harm....."

Cooper sat up a little straighter. *So far, this is not the usual client in trouble!* He added out loud, "I don't know about the medical profession, but my experience is that harm is inevitable.   It's the distribution of it across various parties – including you and me – that worries me."

Simon gazed out of the window with an unseeing stare, obviously tuning out of the small talk. He was seeing Edith's face as he had last seen it, disappearing into a black vinyl body bag, with a last forlorn blond tendril of her hair caught in the zipper. The five-year-old image was still vivid and it brought him back to the present with a jolt.

"I think I'm about to be charged with murder." Simon said abruptly. "And I've been told I need your help."

Cooper's response was instantaneous, and harsher than he'd intended. "Did you do it? Murder someone?"

"No," Simon said flatly, with absolutely no hesitation. And then he asked, clearly curious, "You know, you're the first person that's asked me that question outright. It's kind of refreshing."

He paused, looked intently at Cooper and asked, "How much would it matter to you if I said 'yes'?" Everything about the way he asked – his posture and voice – signaled Cooper that it was an important question.

Cooper took some time to think about it. Not the answer, which was easy, but about the kind of person that would ask such a question. He said, "I wouldn't work for you. I long ago rejected this high-minded stuff about how 'everybody deserves a defense ....' I keep seeing the victim -- "

Whap!

The sound startled both men and was followed by a very faint vibration in the air around them. They spun in their chairs, instinctively crouching, to see a gray feathery blob slide down the vertical length of the window glass. It left a very slight trail of blood at intervals along its path and thudded to rest on the narrow ledge at the bottom, shapeless and unalterably still.

Some few seconds passed. Then Simon said, almost as if talking to himself, "That happens all the time. The birds can't see the glass. They think it's all air and all for them."

Cooper was still staring at the bundle of feathers, recalling the wet sound of the impact. He said very softly, "I used to feel the same way about certain spaces. And came close to the same end a couple of times."

When he noticed Simon's puzzled look, he said "Sorry. That's overly melodramatic. The good news is that it must be a great way to go out – doing something that you want to do and then an instant, permanent and painless exit."

"Yes, I suppose," Simon responded. "But should we be bothered by the omen? I had just denied committing murder. And then a very live creature is immediately and emphatically killed in front of us. It's just a little too spooky for me."

Cooper turned away from the window.

"I'm just an ex-cop trying to make a living. Can't do incantations and don't believe in omens. I'm a great believer in randomness, actually."

He went on, "If you need atonement, make a donation to the Audubon Society or paint big neon X's on your windows."

"We all need atonement," Simon said. "Some of us more than others."

If he's a murderer, he's a very reflective one! Enough philosophy! Cooper pivoted away from the view, leaned back in his chair and crossed his arms. "So. Give me the Cliff Notes version. Why do the cops think you're a killer? And what is it you think I can do for you?"

Simon hesitated. He was very much out of his comfort zone. First, the incident with the bird really did disturb him. Beyond that, he was for the moment cast in the role of a supplicant; a role that he was unfamiliar with and one that made him uncomfortable. He was accustomed to being in control, telling others what to do. And the person opposite him apparently didn't like being told what to do. He radiated disinterest, a seller of services who didn't really care if you bought his product. Even more unsettling, however, was the dawning realization that Simon didn't have the slightest idea what he was about to ask for.

I should be good at this. Nathaniel and I have done this dance a thousand times. In holding cells, kitchens, on sidewalks, loading docks and ski lifts. Me wanting something that I could not express and him walled off behind an expression that conveyed an immense weariness with whatever it was that I was about to say.

Cooper waited with growing skepticism as Simon visibly receded into his own thoughts. After a moment, he took a small notebook from his jacket pocket and flipped it open to a blank page. This seemed to rouse Simon.

"It's a long sad story --"

Cooper winced and barely suppressed a retort. *No. It's not. It will be a completely ordinary and sordid little story. Important only because it disturbs the routine that is important to you.*

Before Radner could go on, Cooper said. "This is not a literary contest. Just stick with the main story line for now. We'll get to all of the sub-plots later."

Simon answered, almost wistfully, "I suspect even the main story line may be a bit more, shall we say, lurid than you are used to. Its got adultery, runaway egos, murder, greed ... power ... all of the elements for a made-for-TV melodrama."

"Sounds like most of my other family law cases to me," Cooper said. "Never underestimate our capacity for screwing up our perfectly ordinary lives."

Simon stood up abruptly, taking the pile of papers off his desk and dropping it on the coffee table in front of Cooper, making a sound remarkably like the sound of the bird striking the window. The stack of paper was about four inches high and divided into about twenty sections separated by small multi-colored tabs, each labeled with a word or phrase.

"I asked my attorney to put this together for you. It's a chronological summary of what we know leading up to my possible arrest. It's got every public record that we think is pertinent. That's the best way to bring you up to speed. But everything in there is old stuff. What's changed – and why I need you – is what's happened in the last week."

Typical! Why is it that clients – particularly the guilty ones – want to communicate with paper rather than face-to-face? I wonder what's left out of that pile?

He said as neutrally as he could, "That's great; I'll read through it once – and if -- we decide to go ahead." He put a lot of stress on the word "if". "But I'd like to hear your version. Unexpurgated, as the book blurbs say."

Radner visibly relaxed, settling back into the chair like someone getting comfortable for a long session. "OK. First, the alleged murder took place five years ago. In Stanton – that's about 30 miles down the river from here."

Cooper said, "I know Stanton. My ex-wife is from there."

He didn't add that he had lived in Stanton and worked there for fifteen years on the Stanton police force, or that his son Marcus was now on the force. He knew the omissions were deliberate, and wondered about his motivation. He suspected that it was due to simple embarrassment over his screwed-up life during those years.

"So why has somebody dying five years ago become a headline murder case today? Has a witness popped up?"

"No witnesses, either then or now. The cops – and almost everybody else – thought Edith died in an accident. It happened during the big storm and flood that hit Stanton five years ago. She was near the river gorge when the storm was at its peak and was reported missing when she failed to come home. Her body was found the next day a mile downriver with a massive head injury. The riverbank was washed out in several places and the conjecture at the inquest was that she slipped, struck her head on a rock, drowned and was carried by the current."

Cooper prompted, "Edith?" But he now knew where this was going. *And I don't think I like it!*

"Edith McKay. It was her land."

"So how does a simple accident become a murder case five years later?" Cooper asked.

Simon said, "They just found what they think may be a murder weapon … a hammer … with some tissue and blonde hairs on it. The lab tests are due in within a day or so, but I'm sure they'll match up with Edith."

"I know some of the cops in Stanton," Cooper said. *Now there's a massive understatement!* "They're not bad. From what you've told me, they would have scoured the area to rule out a homicide. How could they have taken five years to find such an obvious clue?"

Simon said, "They did search. Really hard, in fact. Frankly, the DA was convinced at the time that it was a murder. But the flooding had taken out the entire riverbank where she would have been walking, exposing a lot of rocks. It was underwater for a couple of weeks and then silted up. There was nothing to go on, and the DA had nothing except his suspicions."

"Hammers don't float. Why didn't it turn up when the water receded?"

"It was buried in the silt. It was found just last week, purely by accident. Edith's land sat for years, tied up in litigation. They finally got the legal stuff settled and development began last week. One of the first bits excavated was near the site where she was thought to have gone in the river. A worker found it and called the cops , probably someone who was around five years ago and had some idea of what it might mean."

Cooper interrupted, "How do they know it wasn't thrown there just recently?"

Simon held up two fingers. "First, it's a special kind of hammer. A ceremonial thing. It had a date on it and it was in a sealed display case, not the kind of thing you could buy at your local hardware store. Second, it was dropped or thrown into a crevice that quickly silted up. It was preserved as though in a plaster-of-paris cast. The DA has a soils expert and we think that he will testify that the hammer and case have been in place since approximately the night Edith died. The clincher is that the DA is sure that the hairs and tissue on the hammer will match Edith's. They're running DNA comparisons now."

Cooper had not glanced at his notebook while Simon was talking. He asked "And exactly why are you a 'person of interest', as the British would put it?"

Simon hesitated. "The hammer has my name on it."

He looked away from Cooper and added, "And I think the lab will also find my fingerprints on it."

This last statement was delivered with such calmness that Cooper suspected that there was more to come. He said, "I get the feeling that there may be other reasons why you're at the head of the suspect list?"

Simon actually grinned. "Well, there were rumors at the time that I was having an affair with Edith ... one that – according to the rumors – wasn't going very well."

Cooper asked instantly, "Were you? And was it?"

When Simon hesitated, Cooper thought, *He may be a great attorney, but he'd make a lousy poker player!* As if to confirm this, Simon's response was stilted, as though he was in a witness box reciting.

"Edith was not the kind of woman to have covert affairs. She was the proverbial straight arrow. To the point where she irritated people around her. As for me, I am – and always have been – happily married."

Cooper noted but didn't pursue the evasive non-answer. He went on, "Let's see if I've got this so far. We have a probable murder weapon with your name and prints on it. We have motive – the kind that newspapers and juries love, with sex, scandal and famous people!"

Simon nodded.

"Ah! But I know! You have an ironclad alibi?"

Simon ignored the sarcasm. "Nope. I was there. Along with at least a couple of hundred people who were within fifty yards of where Edith disappeared that night. She was hosting a major community event in spite of the storm. Then the lights went out. It was a wild scene ... rain, noise, a lot of confusion, people coming and going. As far as I know, any number of people can put me at the general scene. But no one noticed Edith – or anybody else -- leave. Her husband didn't even realize that she was missing until early in the morning. And remember, all this happened five years ago!"

Cooper continued probing. "You said that a couple of hundred people were there. Any other suspects that you know of? People with possible motives?"

For the second time, Simon hesitated and Cooper knew that he was about to lie.

"None that make any sense ..."

Cooper pressed him. "If I were your lawyer, I'd sure try to dig some up. And you don't sound very sure of yourself on this one."

Simon went on, somewhat reluctantly. "Edith's land was quite valuable – a thousand acres of riverfront, with old growth trees, wildlife and scenery from another century. She inherited it from her father who in turn got it from his father – a very crusty widower who owned most of Stanton at one time."

Cooper interrupted, "Aha! So now the 'greed' factor enters in. Forgive the obvious question, but who inherited the land when she died?"

"Her husband. She had no family and they were childless, so he's the sole heir. But they seemed to have a model marriage. And there was another reason the land may have been a motive. A number of Stanton bigwigs – politicians & businessmen mostly – wanted to develop the land for housing and commercial purposes. It would have been worth tens of millions if put to commercial use. But Edith was adamant that it should be kept as it was. At the time of her death, she was actually holding talks with the State Conservancy to have the land put into a perpetual trust and preserved in its present form."

"Doesn't sound like the DA will have any trouble finding motive all over the place."

"Oh. Well, that's another complication ... the DA ..."

Cooper leaned back and waited. He had the distinct impression that Simon was embarrassed.

Simon went on, "Her name's Joan Martine. She's been in place about a year. She isn't very objective about this case." He paused and looked past Cooper, out the window. "In fact, she hates me."

"And not just because she thinks you're a murderer?"

"Let's just say that she has – thinks she has -- other reasons. But they have nothing to do with Edith or her killing."

Cooper still had not taken a single note.

"You really aren't making this up, are you?"

"I know. It must sound like a pilot script for a soap opera. Edith's death was a tragedy … But five years is a long time to get over …. things … I don't want to revisit any of that again."

Beyond the wall of windows, the cumulus clouds had darkened, faintly lit from below as downtown lights came on. Cooper looked again at the dead bird. Simon saw the direction of his glance and said, "He'll be there until the next round of window washing … a couple of months probably."

Cooper grimaced. *He's dead … no problem for him.* To his own surprise, his next thought was *I wonder if he had a family?* He turned away from the window thinking, *Some impression I'm making … tough guy grieving over dead bird!*

But Simon was paying no attention. He moved to his office door, opening it and saying, "Take a look at that pile of paper. If nothing else, it's a fascinating story. Then let's talk about what you might do to help. If you want to, of course."

Cooper said, "I'll read it. And I'll ask around my acquaintances in Stanton. But, frankly, I still don't see what I can do to help you. Based on what you've told me, it looks like this is for the police and your attorney to fight about."

Simon pushed the door half shut and turned to Cooper, saying, "I need help with two things. I believe that Edith was in fact murdered … this was not an accident … and that I am… with reasonable cause … about to become a prime suspect. The first thing I need your help with is to find me some evidence to convince a jury that I didn't kill her."

Cooper shrugged. "I understand that. It's my usual role in a murder case. And I'm reasonably good at it. But given what you've told me I just don't see that there's much I can do. What is there to find this long after the fact?"

He went on. "Look. You must have had a course in criminal law while you were planning your genteel future in the refined arts of corporate law, intellectual property and high finance. You must know that your best defense – and one that is already teed up for you by Edith's circumstances – is to point to an even more likely villain; one with more motive, opportunity & passion than you."

Simon began shaking his head and started to say something, but Cooper overrode him. "What you need is 'reasonable doubt'! For that, you need a really eloquent attorney in a five-thousand-dollar suit, a gifted storyteller with credentials. What you don't need is some grubby investigator with a telephoto lens and a non-existent moral threshold!"

Simon grinned briefly but quickly sobered and said, "Forgetting for the moment your overly-cynical self-assessment, there's also the second reason I need your help ... an area where the police and my glib attorney in an expensive suit not only can't help but will probably be working against what I want.

"Oh, and by the way, my attorney does have expensive suits. And she is in fact an excellent storyteller. I think you know her and how good she is ... Ellen Pastore?"

When Cooper simply looked blank, Simon added, "That's her married name. I think you knew her as Ellen Ballard."

Cooper winced when he heard the name, and thought, *Another person that I would prefer to remain in the past! I should get out of this now.* Instead, he shifted the stack of papers to his other arm, walked across the hall & pushed the elevator button. He asked, "And exactly what is it that you want where she is working against your interests?"

Simon said, quite formally, as though reciting, "I have two quite serious priorities. The first one: I want to be found innocent of murder. The second? I don't want the other most likely suspects to be found guilty either."

Cooper leaned his head back and looked down at Simon through half-closed eyes, thinking to himself that he should drop the papers on the floor, turn and walk away. For the first time since he left the elevator, the phrase *this sucks!* came unbidden to his mind. Instead, he sighed and asked with some bemusement, "And what if these priorities are mutually exclusive?"

He did not need to add, "and I think they are."

"Which one will you go with?"

But Simon was done with the conversation. The elevator doors opened, but he held the doors open for Cooper and said, "That's an interesting moral – and hypothetical – question. I believe that Dickens wrote an entire novel around just that dilemma. You know ...'Tis a far, far better thing I do ...' etc., etc."

However, when he saw Cooper's darkening expression, he quickly added, "I don't know. I haven't faced that possibility yet. But what you need to know is that the next most likely suspect is my brother."

With that, he released the elevator doors and stepped back. The last words Cooper caught were, "Read the docs, then call Ellen Pastore, and then me."

Simon stood staring at the blank elevator doors after they had closed behind Cooper, thinking about all of the things he had left out of their conversation.

A good man, I think. I feel sorry for him. It's too bad he's about to take on a client with so many secrets that can't be shared. Especially with him!

Old Friends

Cooper had to be reminded to leave the elevator when it reached the lobby, still thinking about Radner's parting comment.

What in the hell kind of game was Radner playing?

He replayed their conversation in his mind, recalling mostly the omissions and inconsistencies. It was complicated by the realization that he liked Simon. He had already accepted that he wanted the job. The question of *"Why?"* was for later analysis, although he suspected the dead bird had something to do with it.

His ex-wife had flat-out nailed him on his weakness for quirky types: "Your clients all have one common trait, and it's not that they're either guilty or innocent. It's that they actually believe they're some of each! You seek irony, mistaking it for justice."

Cooper protested, even though he knew it was true. Part of his protest was because he suspected that this same flaw, in its various forms, was the single feature that his then-wife found most irritating. It clashed in every way with her binary view of conflicts, both large and small. While Cooper struggled with ambivalence, especially when rights and wrongs were being asserted, she was forever unequivocal. In her world, if there was a problem, then some unique person was at fault; and there always was a single, obviously superior solution. Cooper often thought that she would have made a great malpractice attorney ... and a really lousy judge.

Cooper recalled Simon's wistful "We all need atonement." That put him clearly in the mainstream of past clients. He wanted Simon to be truly innocent of murder, but he knew himself well enough to reserve judgment. There were too many unanswered questions.

He drove through the early evening traffic, running through what he recalled about Stanton that might have some bearing on the case. It was a painful act of recollection. During most of his time in Stanton, he had been in an alcoholic fog and on a decidedly downward trajectory, systematically destroying his marriage, alienating his son, and dragging his partner Dmitri down with him.

Dmitri Akov was a Russian Jew, a thoroughly cynical ex-police detective from Moscow who emigrated to Stanton when the Soviet Empire collapsed of its own weight. He was fifty-three years old when he arrived and from that first moment on American soil through today, he thanked his ill-defined god for, as he frequently put it, "... getting me out of that sinkhole and putting me in a place where a policeman can do what he's supposed to do!" Dmitri was simultaneously the most cynical and the most patriotic American that Cooper had ever met.

They met when Cooper was assigned as Dmitri's partner on the Stanton police force. But they really bonded because of their shared affinity for vodka and books. They were the most productive and the most decorated pair of officers in the department, until the vodka became a problem too big to be ignored. They were suspended for six months after they systematically worked over a local insurance agent who tried to bribe them to commit perjury so that he could stiff his ex-wife on alimony.

Dmitri sobered up first and went back to the department, using AA's *"90 meetings – 90 days"* as a mantra. He continually nagged Cooper about quitting, as only a reformed alcoholic could. But AA didn't take with Cooper. *Probably not enough moral ambiguity*, he thought wryly. They parted amicably and still talked occasionally.

On a whim, Cooper opened his "contacts" list on his cell phone. He was faintly surprised to find that he still had Dmitri on "speed dial." He dialed and was surprised again when Dmitri's gruff *"Hello"* pleased him inordinately. *Good grief! Do I have so few friends that I get choked up when someone answers their phone?*

Dmitri apparently felt somewhat the same. They talked for a few minutes in the fashion that men adopt with what they term "friends"; circling around the personal zones, hinting about self-doubts and then deflecting any follow-up questions back into safe territory. Cooper learned that Dmitri was still patriotic, still dry, and beginning to contemplate retirement.

When Dmitri pressed Cooper as to what he was doing with his time, Cooper didn't answer, but instead asked, "Have you heard anything about a reopened investigation into the death of a woman named Edith McKay? She drowned about five years ago, during your infamous Hundred Year Storm."

Dmitri said something in Russian, clearly a curse, and went on, "Heard anything! That's all we're talking about! We've got national TV crews and reporters here. Stanton is about – I think – to experience its promised fifteen minutes of fame. I'm sure ... Hey! Hold on! Are you working on this?"

Cooper deflected the question. It wouldn't help if he admitted to working for a client who was about to become a primary suspect.

"I've been approached. But I'm not sure if I want to be involved. It sounds more like a soap opera than a murder case. C'mon! A five year old accidental death?"

Dmitri laughed. "Ah! But the DA is all over this one. She's going for a Murder One charge. McKay's death is going to be her springboard from Stanton to the state capitol. She's got this magical clue appearing from the earth and she's going to build a case around it. She's holding a press conference about every twenty minutes!"

Cooper remembered Radner's description: 'She's not very objective about this case." *Wonder how Dmitri would put it? Let's find out.* "Sounds like it's almost personal with her ... I think I remember her – Joan something-or-other. Very intense lady as I recall."

"She's a politician; it's always personal with them!" snapped Dimitri. "And it's Joan Martine. Whatever! But she almost-but-not-quite accused the downtown crowd of offing McKay to prevent the land from being sequestered."

Cooper suggested, "And you're shocked? You're from Russia. Isn't that a standard way of doing business?"

"I've stopped drinking vodka, so I'm no longer Russian. Anyway, she's got better suspects to choose from."

"Like who?"

"A boatload. Try a jealous husband, or the inheritor of her millions, or the main advocate for commercial development of her property, or a reputed and highly unauthorized lover .... "

Cooper said, "Sounds like a crowd. Your Stanton citizens must be a murderous lot!"

Dmitri snorted. "No more than your average resentful suburbanite behind on his bills. But in this case, it's easy to sort them out. Conveniently, all of the likely suspects are named Radner!"

Cooper jerked to attention, thinking angrily, "Simon's version is more than a little incomplete." He forced his voice to a normal tone. "Sounds like the charge should be incest rather than murder. Who are all these characters?"

"Actually, they roll up into only two. Robert Radner is the jealous husband, the inheritor, and her main opponent as to the use of the land. Simon Radner is the odds-on favorite for lover. Oh? And for your soap opera fans? Simon and Robert are fraternal twins. But there's not much fraternity between them, if you catch my drift."

He paused and than added, "Y'know, that's one of your quaint American expressions I never understood. How do you catch a drift?"

Cooper ignored this last question. He had learned long ago that Dmitri was more fluent in American idioms and slang than any sixth-generation native.

"I'm sure you'll work it out, Dmitri."

He went on, "I see that our old friend Ellen Ballard – now known as Pastore -- is going to be working for Simon Radner. From what I remember about her, she'll probably treat murder as a personal affront."

"You're more right than you know," Dmitri responded. "She and Edith McKay were good friends from way back. And they both were off-the-scale treehuggers. Dedicated themselves to keeping the developers' mitts off of the McKay property so that the owls & eeldarters wouldn't be disturbed."

"I think you mean snaildarters," Cooper said mildly.

"Who cares!" snapped Dmitri. "Whatever!"

"One more question: What we Americans used to call 'the $64,000 question' ..."

Dmitri interrupted dryly: "Only very old Americans ... Today we say, 'This one's for all the marbles.' "

Cooper ignored the dig, "What's your take? You know Stanton better than anyone, especially the really seamy stuff. Do you think McKay was killed for cause? And what's the streetwise odds on who did it?"

Dmitri was silent for twenty seconds or so, and Cooper realized that he was pushing too obviously. Dmitri spoke, with some coolness that wasn't there before. "There's an American colloquialism that doesn't translate into Russian very well ... This is your classic clusterfuck. I don't know who your client is, but – as your friend and ex-partner – I would advise you to run like hell the other way!"

Cooper badly wanted to restore the call to the same nostalgic note where it began, but before he could speak, Dmitri said, "One more little family-oriented tidbit. Your son... you do remember Marcus, don't you? ... is on the investigative team that's trying to answer the questions you just asked!"

And the phone went dead.

Dmitri

Dmitri pushed the "end call" button on his desk phone but didn't remove his finger from the button, as though the conversation could be resumed as long as he maintained contact. *Like playing chess. The move isn't official until you let go.* Finally, he sighed, laced his fingers together behind his head, leaned back in his leather chair, and thought about Cooper and his call.

Everything about Dmitri was rumpled – his clothing, his thick grey hair, the papers on his desk; even the flower pots on his window sill seemed disordered. The effect was as though a severe windstorm had just blown through the office. When they worked together, Cooper occasionally wondered whether Dmitri had not consciously modeled himself after Lieutenant Colombo, the TV detective. When he suggested that, Dmitri simply smiled and said, "More like Clouseau than Columbo."

The rumpled exterior was probably natural to him, but it also served to give Dmitri an edge that he liked, to be perceived as dumber, more naïve, than he was. Cooper – and a number of overly complacent felons -- quickly learned that Dmitri's mind was decidedly uncluttered, combining the logic of a championship chess player with an intuitive sense for people and their flaws.

Dmitri was a detective lieutenant on the Stanton police force, head of a small department responsible for "major crimes." These days and in a city the size of Stanton, that meant mostly homicide cases, which was fine with him. He liked the clarity, the lack of ambiguity. Somebody was unequivocally dead. Find the killer. Let the courts fit the punishment to the crime. He often thought that the worst possible assignment would be "white collar" crime, where it wasn't clear whether there was even a victim, or whether a crime had actually been committed.

He also liked the essential equality of murder victims; how, with a few uniquely American exceptions, the victim –

whether man, woman, adolescent, poor, rich, or any of the other possible dimensions of dead Americans – was accorded a degree of outrage that made Dmitri's job both easier and more of a moral quest than other crimes. Once, when he was a simpler man, Dmitri believed that it was the sheer rightness of the sixth commandment – "Thou shalt not kill" – that left no room for vagueness. But he no longer believed in simplicity. Long ago, he himself had killed for reasons that he did not trust, for a society he did not value.

He was fond of revisionist history books these days and he sometimes speculated about where he would be and what he and his world would be like if Marx, Lenin, Trotsky and the First World War had not launched Russia on its seventy-year-long social engineering experiment. The fictional possibilities were limitless. *Assuming I survived the pogroms!* He came from a long line of Muscovite Jewish academics, whose ability to adapt to the times enabled them to survive and to pass on their quintessentially Russian love of languages, poetry, music, art and literature to Dmitri and his siblings. However, in his view, the moral plasticity that enabled their survival also guaranteed their hypocrisy.

When he finished University, he made a dramatic departure from family tradition by joining the Moscow police force. He no longer analyzed his reasons, but had long ago recognized that part of it was youthful idealism. But the much larger part was his need to clearly mark his rejection of his family.

His training and early experiences on the Moscow force eliminated his idealism once and for all. He quickly learned that there were two classes of justice: one for the Party and one for everyone else. The former did not require any real police skills. The only prerequisite called for discretion, a selective blindness to crimes committed by certain people. Dmitri saw serial killers go free and overly ambitious journalists die "accidental" deaths with multiple gunshot wounds.

In the case of justice for the general public, Dmitri was free to try. However, in the declining days of Soviet aspirations, the police force was riddled by indifference, corruption, and incompetence; afflicted with a lack of resources that was laughable. He once transported a corpse to the morgue in the trunk of his personal car. Dmitri became a rogue – a police officer operating outside of the system according to his own code. He became a vigilante, finding it both easy and satisfying to simultaneously be policeman, judge, jury and – sometimes – executioner.   To everybody's puzzlement, he did not become corrupt.

He left Russia eighteen months after the Berlin Wall came down. It took that long for him to accept that the "new" Russia would be worse than the old, with the same tsar-like leaders, but – this time – without even the slightest pretense of the "one-for-all, all-for-one" idealism of the communists. Ironically, his extended family was now prospering, operating in the shadier niches between the oligarchs, relabeled communist bosses, and the mafia. Dmitri, by his own rough count, had two nephews and a brother that were probably close to becoming billionaires in the new Russia.

He found it surprisingly easy to leave his family and Russia. He found ways to avoid the usual red tape, in part because his superiors were glad to be rid of him, finding his incorruptibility to be a handicap to their own goals. He wound up in Stanton for no particular reason other than it was on a river and had advertised for "experienced police officers." He smiled when he thought of his naiveté in applying. However, he was fortunate; his first interviewer was Cooper. He remembered their initial encounter quite well.

Cooper was sitting at a desk, looking bored and unhappy. Dmitri was his seventh and last interview of the day.

"I see you have twenty years of police experience in Russia. Do you think what you learned there is relevant here?"

"I hope not."

He was pleased to see Cooper sit up straighter and begin to pay attention.

"What do you see as different here?"

"Aside from the balmy climate? You have this strange preoccupation with this thing you call 'due process'. That's a very un-Russian concept."

Dmitri was gratified to see Cooper put down the ten-page application form that Dmitri had filled out, finally paying real attention rather than preparing to check off boxes. But he was surprised by Cooper's next comment.

"I read Dostoyevsky once. I remember thinking that his Russian policeman – I forget his name – was a really lousy detective. His murderer – Raskolnikov, wasn't it -- would have confessed much sooner here."

"The detective's name is Porfiry Petrovich, and you obviously missed the point of the entire book."

"Do you drink?"

"Of course! I'm Russian!"

They continued the "interview" at one of Cooper's bars, long into the evening. During the next few days, Cooper coached Dmitri on how to present himself and guided him through the hiring process. The clincher for the Chief was Cooper's volunteering to take Dmitri on as his partner for an extended probationary period.

They were partners for seven years during which time Cooper taught Dmitri to be an American policeman. They found that they shared old-fashioned views about high-minded concepts such as *right* and *wrong* and *justice*, as well as some specific preferences for vodka, novels and argumentation. Off the job, Dmitri became a virtual member of Cooper's family, even as it was disintegrating around them. He and Cooper's son Marcus developed a very close relationship, and Dmitri became his surrogate father during his college years and first year or so on the Stanton police force. The role developed gradually and by default, because Cooper was either in the "before" phase of his personal history or gone to the big upriver city.

Like Cooper, Dmitri was highly introspective. In his prior life as a Russian policeman, such a habit would have been a dangerous and thoroughly non-constructive luxury. In America, people seemed to expect it of him, as though his nationality required him to be representative of the overwrought protagonists of Tolstoy and Dostoyevsky. Unlike Cooper, however, Dmitri was not bothered by ambiguity. In his world, you made your choice and you moved on. What did bother him was Cooper's inability to do the same, and his own helplessness to change that.

What he did know, however, was that Cooper had been his best friend and that he owed him something that he could neither define nor repay.

An Official History

Damn it! Cooper realized that he was gripping the phone as if it was his only hold on Dmitri's attention. In his preoccupied state, he drove two exits past his usual turnoff. Their talk unsettled him, partly because of his ambiguous past relationship with Dmitri, but also because it raised serious new doubts about Simon's motivations. And the parting shot about Marcus was the final touch.

Dmitri is angrier about what I did to Marcus than what I did to him. Well, he's got a right ... he's closer to Marcus than I am.

Ten minutes later, Cooper opened his door to his apartment, empty as always. And, as always, he stood for a few seconds thinking quite objectively and without any self-pity -- *How sad!*

For the next several hours, he immersed himself in an uncomfortable past. He placed Simon's stack of paper on the table in front of his couch. On the couch alongside him, he placed a blank writing tablet and a ballpoint pen. He took the top sheet from the stack, read it, and then placed it face-down in a new stack alongside the original. Then he repeated the process. Occasionally he made a note.

For Cooper, it was like opening a time capsule, a painful one.

His first reminder of that past was triggered by the very first document, a simple transmittal memo from *Defense Attorney Ellen Pastore.* Cooper forced himself to call up her image from a past that had been carefully suppressed. His last involvement with her was highly official and unpleasant. She was legal advisor to Internal Affairs of the Stanton police department when Dmitri and Cooper went off the rails. She more than anyone else was responsible for them being suspended for their beating of the sleazy insurance agent.

Cooper thought back to the hearings and Pastore's righteous indignation. It more than overwhelmed their simpleminded defense, which was basically "He had it coming to him!" They even had tape recordings of the bastard trying to bribe them to commit perjury, but she got the tapes thrown out. He remembered her saying "You just arrest them. The courts punish them!"

Some punishment! The city paid the son-of-a-bitch fifty thousand bucks so that he wouldn't sue them!

The suspension was a turning point. Dmitri quit drinking and returned to the department. Over the next dozen years, he worked himself up to become a highly respected and senior member of the police force. Cooper stayed on the booze for a few more years, drifted away from Dmitri, and never went back to the cop business.

When the two stacks of paper – the read and the unread – were approximately of equal height, he stood for the first time, stretched, got two sodas and a jar of peanuts from the kitchen, and went back to reading. The only breaks in his reading came when he would jot a note on the tablet. Three hours later, he had read everything and made a handful of cryptic notes on a single page of the tablet.

He stood, stretched, and thought about what he had learned. *One thing that Simon had right: it was a fascinating story.*

A lot of the papers in the stack were newspaper clippings from the few weeks after the death of Edith McKay. The circumstances of her death in what they called "the hundred year storm," the prominence of the McKay family, and the quite public suspicions of the DA made the case front page material for a surprisingly long time. It made the national TV news and the major papers. Between them, they gave a surprisingly full account.

Edith McKay was the third and last generation of a mini-dynasty. Her grandfather was the founder of Stanton. The town itself emerged in the late nineteenth century, centered on the farming/ranching operations of her ancestor. The term "robber baron" was used frequently in describing him. By the end of the second world war, he owned, controlled or intimidated almost every significant aspect of life in Stanton. He died rich, disliked and alone. His only child, James – Edith's father and a widower for most of his life – acted out the clichéd role of the son of an empire builder. Over time and with care, he sold off the original McKay properties and businesses and used the money to create real institutions – newspapers, schools, museums, parks; the kind of community assets that, according to a couple of national surveys, made Stanton one of the *"Ten Most Desirable Small Cities in America"* by the year 2000.

From a few of the feature articles from local papers, it was clear that Edith was intelligent, pretty and highly self-willed. Cooper found himself envisioning a cross between Scarlett O'Hara and an early Margaret Thatcher. Even after discounting for the inevitable journalistic bias that creeps into stories about home-grown dynasties, Cooper could easily picture an out-of-the-ordinary person. She grew up in Stanton and lived there through her second year at the local university. She apparently left abruptly after her sophomore year. There was little mention of her in local papers for the next five years, until she returned to be near her dying father. When he died, the robber baron's image had been transformed into that of a philanthropist and Edith McKay inherited three major assets: a good name, a hundred million dollars, and a thousand acres of prime riverside land.

Based on the local press – including in about equal parts the news section, the society pages, and the editorials – Edith was a virtual whirlwind. She put all of her inherited assets into a family foundation and reentered Stanton life as though determined to make up for lost time. If small cities in America could be said to have a "first lady," she was it.

Cooper soon encountered another curious key omission from Simon's narrative in his office. A year before her death, Edith married Robert Radner, Simon's fraternal twin. The society pages were full of it – *Beautiful heiress marries most eligible bachelor* -- and similar tabloid stuff. From other articles, Cooper could piece together the main threads of what seemed to be a storybook romance.

Robert was fifty when they married, Edith twenty years younger. Each had the obvious advantages – wealth, reputation, good looks and the other elusive intangibles that drive *eligibility*. The courtship was very low-key. They were thrown together frequently because of their respective roles – she as large landowner and civic activist and him as Mayor of Stanton and (before and after his mayoralty) the biggest and most important real estate developer in Stanton.

Edith retained her maiden name – McKay. From what Cooper could tell, her mix of activities did not change following her marriage, other than to move out of her family home – now formally retitled as "Riverbend" -- to live in Robert's downtown condo.

The question of Riverbend's future apparently was the biggest single problem within an otherwise satisfactory marriage. Edith wanted to put the Riverbend property -- the thousand-acre core of the McKay estate -- in its present pristine and undeveloped form in a trust for future generations. She was working with the State Conservancy to finalize the paperwork at the time of her death. Robert, on the other hand, was the leader of a business coalition that wanted to develop the site – adding homes, businesses, parks, and increased property taxes for Stanton. Shortly after her death, the dispute was being fought bitterly on all fronts – lawsuits, full-page ads, petitions, zoning.

Cooper noted that their opposing views on developing the property must have made Robert and Edith's relationship more contentious than it would have been. *Unless they were exceptionally skilled at compartmentalizing.*

Cooper's reading also revealed that Simon – to put it mildly – had been less than forthcoming about the extent of his relationship with Edith McKay. He had spent a lot of time with her in the year before her death. It was clear from newspaper clippings that the two of them were often associated with major community projects. They were on two boards together – the historical society and a low-income housing project – and several stories featured the two of them, describing them in one case as *"... shirtsleeve activists confronting entrenched interests in Stanton."* Interestingly, there was little mention of Robert and Simon together, despite their obvious prominence as individuals. Cooper remembered Dmitri's conjecture about their lack of fraternal feelings.

There was nothing whatsoever in the stack of documents that referred to or even hinted at any scandal surrounding Edith McKay. Although there was one tab labeled 'Rachel' that had nothing after the tab. *Someone has been censoring the original stack that Pastore put together. Simon? I wonder why?*

Cooper concentrated on the dozens of items in the file that focused on the events around the night of Edith's death. These were mostly news clippings, with some annotations (probably added by Pastore, thought Cooper).

On the night she died, McKay was hosting a major awards ceremony at her father's house, the original and sprawling McKay main house on the Riverbend property. The invitation read, *"To recognize those who have significantly contributed to the quality of life in Stanton."* It was mailed to five hundred citizens of the city well in advance.

Nature did not cooperate. The rainstorm started two days before the scheduled event, with steadily increasing intensity. It would become known as "the hundred year storm" in local history. It was still raining on the appointed evening, but approximately two hundred and thirty of the invited guests did attend. Two last minute touches were to change the dress requirement from *"Black tie or business attire"* to *"weather appropriate attire"* and to put a sign over the entrance door -- *Welcome to Noah's Ark."*

The newspaper coverage of the actual event became sketchy at this point, driven out by the sensationalism of Edith's disappearance and coverage of the storm itself, which continued for another two days. Simon found himself reading transcripts from the various hearings and related public documents, which went into considerable detail. Apparently, everybody in attendance was interviewed.

The evening went according to schedule until the lights went out. The cocktail hour was loud and animated, lasting longer than usual because of late arrivals due to the rain and deteriorating road conditions.   Edith and Robert moved through the crowd easily as co-hosts, apparently at ease with each other. The formal award ceremony was scheduled to begin at about nine, well after dark and – according to several witnesses – when the storm seemed to reach a peak. A glossy program was circulated, identifying the awardees, the reason for their selection, and a description of the award they were to receive.

Cooper focused on the printed program's description of one award particularly.

To Simon Radner ... For his unstinting effort on behalf of the Stanton Housing Coalition, as reflected in hundreds of hours of uncompensated legal work, a dozen Saturdays of highly unskilled physical labor dedicated to moving dirt and building actual houses, and an infinite amount of encouragement and support to make the Stanton Housing Coalition a reality.

He opened a large manila envelope containing about a dozen 8x10 black & white photos. Several of them were the classic society page poses of beautiful people holding wine glasses and smiling fixedly at the camera. Simon appeared in two or three, Robert in another three or four, always with other guests and never together. With hindsight, it is clear that, by prearrangement, each of the four awardees was photographed with Edith. In these pictures, she has an ethereal air, although Cooper distrusted his judgment on this point. It may be that it is her unawareness that she has only an hour or so to live that made her stand out as she did to Cooper.

In Simon's case and one other, the award was to be given by Edith McKay. The other two awards were to be announced by Robert Radner. The other awardees were a local teacher retiring after forty years in a Stanton middle school; a city councilman who singlehandedly managed the campaign that earned Stanton its *"Ten Best"* status, and a stockbroker who funded the construction of a facility for unwed mothers and their children. The program included a description of the four awards, each symbolizing the nature of the respective contributions. For the other three nominees, the awards were a crystal paperweight, a plaque signed by the Governor of the state, and a scale replica of the new clinic.

In Simon's case, the award was a carpenter's framing hammer, engraved with his name, the date and the words *"Stanton Housing Coalition"* on the steel shaft.

The power failed just as the formal program was to begin, effectively ending the evening's planned activities. The blackout was an area-wide power failure, clearly not part of any premeditated murder plot. It created mass confusion. A few flashlights, candles & cigarette lighters only amplified the blackness until someone organized several cars in the drive to direct their headlights at the house. This provided enough light to quell a rising nervousness and to encourage an exodus. The county sheriff was one of the guests and he used a megaphone to tell those still milling around that the outage would last at least for a couple of hours and to advise everyone to go home. He also cautioned that some flooding was being reported.

No one recalls seeing Edith McKay at any time after the power failed. She was reported missing by her husband Robert at three AM – when power was restored -- and family members and a sheriff's team began a search on the McKay property shortly afterward. Her body was discovered late the next morning, among some flood debris about a mile downriver from Riverbend.

For about three days, the presumption was that her death was a tragic accident. The newspaper stories were subdued and elegiac. However, the amount and the nature of the coverage changed dramatically when the DA announced that he was unable to rule out foul play and began to conduct a very public investigation into a possible murder charge. The stories were sensationalistic, hinting at unrevealed secrets.

The preliminary hearings revealed nothing that would support an indictment. The coroner's ruling was *"Accidental death by drowning,"* probably abetted by a severe blow to her head. The skull was fractured by *"a single sharp contact by an unknown object,"* and was deemed consistent with *'a slip-and-fall scenario,"* bringing her into contact with the rocks on the riverbank or in the river. The coroner opined that the blow rendered her unconscious, and that it could well have been fatal even if drowning had not intervened. No physical evidence was discovered despite an exhaustive search at the McKay home and the downstream riverbank.

All witnesses agreed that Edith's behavior during the evening was completely in character with her usual style and her role as hostess. She was visible throughout the evening, but was not observed in any unusually close conversations with any single person. No one noticed Edith leaving the house. This was also true for all of the Radner's – Robert, Simon, Maria, and Nathaniel.

Cooper found very few documents pertaining to the five years after her death. They mostly described the contentious unwinding of the McKay estate. Robert inherited everything, but was limited by the legal agreements that Edith had partially completed prior to her death. Once all hurdles were cleared, Robert immediately launched the first stage of commercial development on the Riverbend estate.

Cooper was startled to encounter a short article featuring his ex-wife – under her maiden name, "Benson". The article noted how her firm would be the primary commercial and residential broker for the planned development. It included a grainy picture of her and Robert Radner sitting side-by-side at a zoning hearing. The picture was not good, but she looked younger than he remembered her, causing him to wonder if the act of shedding him had somehow arrested the aging process.

Heavy equipment began work two weeks ago on the riverbank next to the McKay home and, on the second day, a hammer was found, *"in a plastic display case, encrusted in a cocoon of dried mud as though awaiting an archeologist from the future"* as described by a reporter apparently fresh from a creative writing course.

The final and most recent item in the stack was a two-paragraph news item in the local paper that reported the suspension of development work on the Riverbend Project due to the discovery of *"an unidentified object that may be connected with the mysterious drowning of Edith McKay."* The chronology ended at that point.

Cooper looked at his single sheet of paper and his scrawled notes:

1. Who had access to the hammer that night?
2. Why would the killer replace the hammer in its case?
3. What was Edith McKay doing in the five years she was away from Stanton?
4. Why are Robert and Simon estranged from one another?
5. Was Edith happily married? Robert? Simon?
6. Why did she go out into the storm?
7. Why didn't Robert report her missing until three the next morning?
8. Who's 'Rachel'?

Cooper sat back on the couch, staring at the innocent looking stack of paper that had pulled him back in time and place to somewhere he didn't want to be.

If I do this – and I'm going to – it's going to be painful.

Then he realized that he wasn't alone; that Simon Radner was about to enter a new world as well.

Simon's had it his way for a long time. High-powered lawyer, hot-shot philanthropist ... never met a problem he couldn't money-whip. Wants to control the narrative. Life as a murder suspect is going to be a real shock to him!

The Attorney

Cooper wondered how many times he'd been in a courtroom, probably hundreds. But this was the first time when he had nothing at stake himself. He was there purely as an observer, sitting in the main Stanton courtroom for the first time in years. The last time he had been in this building was on the occasion of his suspension from the Stanton police force. He was only partly sober at the time and there were few people in the courtroom. This time, the courtroom was almost full and he was stone cold sober.

He hadn't planned on being there. He and Ellen Pastore had agreed to meet in a conference room at the courthouse. But when he checked in for their three o'clock meeting, he was told she would be in court for another hour. He decided to go watch.

When he walked into the almost full room, Cooper was surprised to see that his son Marcus was sitting in the second row. He picked out a seat as far out of Marcus's line of sight as he could and slumped down as far as the hard bench allowed. He noted that Marcus was in the standard sport coat and slacks that all detectives seem to wear when they're asked to testify in court, like they'd all been watching the same Hollywood detective. *Harry Callahan, or maybe Sergeant Friday. No, they're from an earlier generation. Who the hell knows who the current role models are!* He thought that Marcus looked good. *A little too young, maybe.* He was handsome, self-assured and looked to Cooper like he'd be a good cop. *I hope he is.*

The case seemed to involve a middle-aged Hispanic male accused of armed robbery. Apparently, Marcus was in attendance as the arresting officer. About twenty minutes after Cooper came into the courtroom, the Assistant DA sat down and Pastore stood to begin the presentation for the defense. Cooper leaned forward and watched attentively.

He had last seen Ellen Pastore – then Ballard -- in this same courtroom. Her job then was as Legal Counsel to the

Internal Affairs Department of the Stanton Police Department, and her specific task that day was to get him fired. She was his nemesis, and she disassembled him piece by piece. He recalled an aggressive, asexual and irritating woman of indeterminate age, wearing bad pants suits. Perhaps time and a shift in roles was the cause, but the woman he was watching was quite different, even from Cooper's last-row perspective in the room. His first thought when she stood and walked to the bench was *I'd like to have a lawyer like that!* Later in the day, when he deconstructed that thought, he admitted to himself that it was blatantly sexist, but didn't feel guilty about it.

Dmitri had warned him. "Forget what you think you remember about her. That was a long time ago and we were all different people then. She's a really good criminal defense attorney. You need to see today's version."

Cooper asked, "So why would she meet with me? I'm pretty sure she thought I was just above pond scum on the evolutionary ladder."

Dmitri said, "Two reasons. The obvious one: because you're both working for Simon. Second, because she's the old-fashioned kind of lawyer. She wants to be in control and she wants the right people doing time. And between you and me, I'm not sure she's quite sure about Simon."

Her court session finished at about four and they met in a conference room looking out on a parking lot. When Cooper got there, the door was open and she was talking on her cell phone. Cooper knocked to get her attention and she waved him to a chair. Up close, the years showed. She was harder, more confident than he remembered. She somehow managed to be simultaneously more feminine and less approachable. She ended her phone call, rose and shook his hand, quite firmly, using a slight pressure to direct him to a hard chair opposite her at the conference table.

Pastore was tall, only an inch or so less than Cooper. She wore her dark hair long and was dressed simply – dark slacks, a very tailored jacket over a white blouse. She had a distinctive intensity about her. Much of that intensity went with her eyes – dark with flecks – that seemed to challenge, to maintain contact slightly longer than was polite. But it was more than that. The intensity was accented by a stillness, a kind of poised readiness that an athlete or actor might cultivate. Cooper had the feeling that if only it was quiet enough, she might give off a detectable low hum.

Daunting! was the single best one-word descriptor that came to Cooper's mind.

Cooper did not like attorneys generally and he particularly disliked criminal defense attorneys. As an ex-cop, he remembered too well all the times that they had tried to humiliate him in court and, too often in his opinion, subverted both the letter and the spirit of the law so that predators could stay on the street.

Pastore, however, was an intriguing mixture. Cooper knew very few female criminal defense attorneys, and none of them so unsettling at first glance. But it was more than that. For the first time in a long time, Cooper realized that he was strongly aware of a woman as a woman. He knew that part of it was voyeuristic in nature, from watching her – spying on her -- in court, probably stirring up some primitive section of the male brain stem. Another part was their current setting – in a small space, with late afternoon light and a sense of isolation that heightened his awareness of her. But the far larger part was the barely-implied sexuality that she carried with her. Cooper was uncomfortably aware of the contrast between her dark hair and her white collar, of the way her hand had touched his …

He realized that neither of them had said a word since sitting down. She was staring at him quite intently, and he suddenly felt quite sure that she knew exactly what he was thinking. Cooper felt like a fool. She must have had many chances to assess the reactions of over-awed men at first contact.

Cooper flushed, and then said, "I don't know if you remember me, but we've met before."

"Yes. I remember quite well."

And then she surprised him. "I really was an officious little bitch, wasn't I?"

Cooper tried not to show his surprise. *How should one respond to that? This could be a very short interview!*

He hoped the pause was imperceptible and went on to say, "I admit that I did think something along those lines at the time. Although I would say *ambitious* instead of officious. But then, I was a self-righteous drunk cop with too much testosterone ... the kind that assaults civilians ... not the one to be making judgments about straight arrows like you."

Her eyes widened ever so slightly. Cooper went on, "Internal Affairs is a tough assignment. You did the right thing for the right reasons. My partner-in-crime would say the same thing, and he's now one of the most respected officers on the force."

It was her turn to pause. She chose safer ground: "I know Dmitri well. If we could clone cops like him --"

He interrupted. "You'd have an entire colony of overly-introspective, highly cynical, poetry-spouting, flag-waving career police officers who are very good at their profession."

She smiled, and said, "I hear you've dried out."

So much for small talk. "Hit bottom ... and bounced a couple of times. Had to learn the hard way."

Pastore smiled, more sadly, and said, "Some people say that's the most effective form of learning ..."

Cooper had the distinct feeling that she may have been talking more about herself than him. He responded, "Effective? Maybe. But neither efficient nor pain-free!"

Somehow, their conversation had veered off into a different, more personal tone and both of them sensed it. As though choreographed, they each looked away at the same time, simultaneously cleared their throats, and then spoke at precisely the same instant. They each laughed, at themselves.

Ellen felt like she was playing catch-up. *He's not what I remember. No surprise there. A dozen years ago, both of us with demons ... alcohol for him, husbands for me. We didn't like each other very much, for reasons that had probably had very little to do with us.*

Her distaste for what she was envisioning showed on her face, causing Cooper to imagine that it was about him and what he had been to her in that courtroom. He could not know how hard she tried to avoid revisiting those days; a time that she thought of as "the dark period."   To suppress her own memories, she took a very close look at Cooper.

Fifty maybe?   Good looking, like someone you see in a book jacket photo. Looks like someone that would really rather be somewhere else, and I'll bet that's true wherever he is. Wary ... cautious ... maybe a little bit nervous.   Like he doesn't expect anything good to come out of this. Whatever 'this' is.

She said, "OK. Let's review the ground rules. You need to know that I argued against hiring you. I agreed to meet with you only as a favor to Simon."

"Yep. And I appreciate it. I really do." Cooper said. "I know that everything you say is off the record, and I also know that you're probably not sure you can trust me with anything pertaining to the ongoing case."

Pastore leaned forward, and her voice hardened. "Frankly, I wouldn't have caved in to Simon. But he also said that he thought you could help us. That got my attention. I mean, I'm trying to defend the guy on a murder charge ... and he wants me to talk to an unknown quantity who's related to the chief investigator – that's Marcus -- and old friends with the head homicide guy – that'll be Dmitri! I feel like I should read you your rights .... You know? the part about anything you say can and will be used against you?"

Cooper leaned forward in response, bringing them close together, like two friends sharing a secret. "I'll waive my rights for the moment, thank you. First, I don't know any more about Simon or what he did -- or didn't do -- than you do, so there's nothing I can do to hurt his case. Second, I thought the lawyer's job was to insure that justice is done? Means justify ends, and all that stuff?"

She sat back, clearly amused. "Justice? Somewhere I read that when defendants plead for justice, what they're really asking for is mercy."

"Don't you think Simon is innocent?   You're his attorney!"

"I'll defend him as well as I can. But the evidence strongly suggests that he's guilty as hell. Or, as the euphemism goes, 'We've working with bad facts'." She paused, clearly thinking. "Frankly, that's why I agreed to meet with you. You sure you don't know something I don't?"

"Nope. I like the man and I don't think he killed anyone. But I've been wrong before. The only information he's given me is stuff that's been in the newspapers and he has yet to tell me what he expects me to do on his behalf."

That's not quite true, but I'm not going to share that until I understand it myself!

"Curiouser and curiouser! So, what do you want to talk about ... other than to reminisce about our common life in the good old days of the Stanton PD?"

"I'd like to know more about Edith McKay. Dmitri told me that you knew her. Not just as a victim, but as a friend. She was clearly an exceptional person, based on the usual ways we keep score. I never met her during my time in Stanton, she's been dead for five years, and she apparently fell off the world for five years before she showed up here again. I've never seen one of these high-profile murder cases where so little was known about the victim."

Pastore said, clearly curious: "You've got it backward. The person we need to understand is her killer."

Cooper shook his head. "If she was murdered – and it looks like she was – then there's a connection between her and her killer. It doesn't mean that she's bad, or that she deserved to die, or that guilt gets redistributed. But my experience is that what you call 'motive' can be understood only in the context of two people – the killer and the victim."

She literally snorted. "That's the most ridiculous thumbnail psychobabble I've heard in a long time! My last case was a gangbanger that held up a McDonald's and shot three kids that were sitting there drinking vanilla milkshakes! Do you want their personal life stories so that you can sort out motive?"

Cooper waited a moment, then said, "That's not fair, and you know it. Most people – maybe not your milkshake drinkers, but people like Edith McKay -- get killed for a reason that has something to do with who they are or what they do. Who was she? What was she like? Why did someone want to get rid of her? In Edith's case, knowing why she was killed will probably tell you who killed her."

"In my experience, an extra-marital affair is loaded with motives." Ellen retorted instantly.

"You're focusing on the obvious! We've got almost too many possibilities, don't you think? We have an unidentified lover, maybe even more than one, greedy real estate developers, and a jealous husband...."

Their exchanges were sharper, more closely spaced and their voices were rising. Pastore stood up abruptly, Cooper more slowly. They looked at one another for a long moment. Then she sat back down and – very visibly – took a deep breath.

Cooper sat. He smiled in a sad way, saying, "We seem to have picked up where we left off in that Internal Affairs hearing."

As he said it, he realized that he was slightly afraid, aware that he did not want to alienate this woman; that it was somehow important to him to make her believe that he was not who she remembered.

He tried to make his voice as casual as possible. "Look, Dmitri said that you were a personal friend of hers. Can we talk about that?"

She looked at him really hard for a long few seconds, clearly thinking about his question.

"OK," Pastore said with a forced calm. "She and I met when she was in college, before she took off from Stanton. She spent a couple of years at the local university while I was taking a couple of post-graduate courses. We both inhabited the same café late at night, studying and drinking coffee. She was younger, more idealistic than me, but the two of us found ourselves in the same protest movement ... one of those 'Save the Whales' kind of things."

Cooper asked, "What was she like, other than young and pretty?"

"She was both of those, with a vengeance. But she was also smart, ambitious and ... to be truthful ... more than a little wild. I know that she drank, smoked a little dope and she clearly had no shortage of males around her.

"She just flat took off after her second year of college, and I didn't see her again for five years. No word at all, which surprised me a bit. She was quite different when she came back ... much more serious, grown up. By then, I was a working lawyer and she was her father's nurse and then, after he died, the town benefactress. But we got together some, mostly superficial do-gooder kind of stuff, but even then I had the feeling I was her best friend. It was kinda sad."

Cooper asked, "Do you know why she took off from Stanton in the first place? It sounds pretty abrupt."

"It was. Surprised everybody ... including her father. James McKay was blindsided as much as the rest of us. There was a lot of speculation. Several of her friends – including me – thought she'd been different, kind of depressed, the last couple of months before she left. But no one knew anything."

"What about the five years she was gone?"

"Same story. No clue whatsoever. She had her own trust fund, so there were no strings to Stanton.She gave me the impression that she'd been through some heavy stuff, but never talked about it. When people asked, her father would say something about graduate school on the east coast, or a tour of Europe, or interning at some big-name medical foundation in California. It was always pretty vague. At times, I wondered if he even knew where she really was.

"When her father James was diagnosed with cancer, she came back. The last couple of years before she was killed, her life's the proverbial open book. Giving away money, setting up the Land Conservancy, a whirlwind relationship and marriage to Robert Radner. She still traveled a lot, but she clearly intended to make Stanton her home."

"Enemies?"

"She was twenty-nine years old, hardly enough time to accumulate serious enemies. But I presume you've read the local paper and the files that I put together at Simon's request. So you know that the business community thought she was evil incarnate for trying to sequester the Riverbend property. But they're hardly the type to bludgeon a woman for the sake of a real estate project."

"What about the love angle? Or its close counterpart, adultery?"

"Rumors only. But she did attract lots of attention from men. If Stanton had tabloids, she'd be their favorite celebrity. She was seen a lot with Simon, and the DA will clearly play that card. But that could be put down to their boards and other common interests. Everybody involved – that is, both sets of Radners – seemed content with their respective spouses."

"How about money? The granddaddy of all motives?"

"The husband -- Robert Radner -- comes up big on that one. She had no surviving relatives, so he inherits everything – cash, land, the whole ball of wax. And with hindsight, we now know that he acquires what he wants most – the right to develop Riverbend. It took almost five years of litigation, but he finally got the Conservancy deal unwound."

She thought for a moment and then continued, "On the other hand, Robert already had lots of money of his own. And other than developing Riverbend, he and Edith seemed to pretty well agree on where and how to spend money. The same will had been in place the entire time they'd been married; a straightforward community property arrangement since there were no children or ex-spouses on either side."

"Witnesses?"

"Not one that does either us the DA any good. Ironically, there were a couple of hundred people within a few yards of her when she left the house, but no one saw her actually go outside. No one saw anyone go. Remember, it was pitch black, the power was off and it was mass confusion. The cops literally interviewed everybody on the guest list. No one saw anything that Edith or anyone else did that evening that seemed unusual in any way."

Cooper sat thinking for a moment, then said, "So. We've got a tragic death; a beautiful young woman dies in semi-mysterious circumstances on – please forgive me – a 'dark and stormy night', for heaven's sake! We have two or three contending but unprovable motives, and we lack both witnesses and weapon to make a reasonable homicide case. Seems like a straightforward case of 'death by misadventure'."

"That was the decision five years ago, and quite fair-minded it was…. then. But fast-forward to today. Today, we have not just a weapon; we have *the* weapon … with Edith's brain tissue and Simon's fingerprints all over it. That makes it murder."

She paused, clearly visualizing something. "And whoever did it is still walking around out there."

It was late afternoon and the sunlight had left the conference room. Ellen walked over to the door and turned on a harsh overhead light. The effect changed the atmosphere that was building between them and was a clear signal that the meeting was over.

Cooper stood and said, "One more question. Simon said – implied – that the DA isn't very objective … that she intends to make him a special case. Any idea what that's about?"

"I know she really doesn't like him. And it's not just righteous indignation aimed at a possible murderer. There's something else."

"Any theories about what that is?"

"Nope. As far as I know, they didn't meet until she showed up about a year ago. And when I asked him about it, Simon said that he had no idea why she might harbor any particular hostility toward him."

"Simon is being very coy… clearly keeping some things to himself. That's usually a bad idea. Do you think he's playing straight with you?"

She thought carefully before answering. "I obviously believe it's a bad idea to lie to your attorney. I also think that he was seriously in love with Edith McKay. And I think that she wanted to change the game."

"How?"

"That I don't know. But I am absolutely sure of two other things."

Pastore's voice had shifted. It was throatier, more personal, hinting of strong feelings damped down. Cooper once more was acutely aware of the woman beneath the professional veneer.

He asked, "What are they? Those two other things?"

Pastore smiled, "Oh, your usual attorney fantasies. I want to get Simon acquitted. And I want to nail the bastard that killed Edith!"

Cooper thought of the irony. *Simon's fine with the first of those, but I don't think he's in agreement on the second one. I wonder if she knows that?*

He said the same thing he had said to Simon. "I hope those are not incompatible objectives."

She simply smiled and extended her hand. They shook hands and Cooper walked away. From across the anteroom, he turned and looked back. Pastore was reading a document she had just picked up, standing in the doorway to the conference room, one hand absentmindedly stroking her hair. Cooper watched her and tried to imagine her naked, but the image would not come into focus. Then he realized that she was looking at him, and he knew once more that she knew exactly what he was thinking.

She held her gaze until he turned and walked out the door.

Ellen

There goes a mistake looking for a place to happen!

Cooper made her somehow sad, and then angry with herself for being sad. The seesawing emotions annoyed her, because she knew the cause, and it had far more to do with her than with Cooper.

Damn Simon anyway! All the investigators out there and he has to pick the one that brings out the worst in me!

She had easily picked him out in the courtroom that afternoon. Her case didn't require much of her attention – her client was guilty as hell, going through a hearing with a preordained outcome – and she quickly became aware of being watched. She easily identified Cooper as the source. Interestingly, he was spending equal amounts of his attention on Marcus. *Not so surprising given their history.*

Her first thought was *he's different... in a good way.* That troubled her, because she was predisposed to dislike him. When Simon told her that he was thinking of hiring Cooper, she had protested, citing his prior history as a drunk and failed cop. But he insisted, so emphatically that Ellen wondered about his real motivations.

Simon told her, "I want him. He knows Stanton and he comes very highly recommended."

She tried but failed to keep her skepticism from showing when she asked, "Recommended? By whom?"

"You don't need to know." And Simon cut off the discussion.

Their small dispute triggered a recurrent and troubling question in Ellen's mind. *Why am I defending this man? He may have murdered a close friend of mine, someone that I really cared about and that needed me ... in ways I needed to be needed.* She had thought long and hard about various answers to the question, but a satisfactory answer had eluded her until Cooper had said simply, "I like the man. And I don't think he killed her." *Nor do I. And there's more. He loved Edith.*

Standing in the doorway of the conference room watching Cooper as he left, she was struck by a sudden certainty. *I'll bet it was Dmitri that recommended him, one way or another. It's just the kind of behind-the-scenes game that he loves to indulge in.*

That thought triggered a sudden memory. During her preparation for the Internal Affairs hearing, she remembered being impressed – against her will -- that Cooper and Dmitri had been a very close pair of friends.

Like most successful trial attorneys, and probably like most women, Ellen enjoyed being watched when she was in public and doing something she was good at. She accepted that about herself. And she also knew that part of the reason for the man/woman tension that ran through her subsequent meeting with Cooper was that awareness – for both of them – beginning when he walked into that courtroom. Since then, they had been consciously engaged in foreplay of a most subtle type.

That tension was sharpened by their past experience with one another. She had savaged him in open court. She had changed his outward life dramatically. They had been enemies.

He is different. He didn't care what happened to him then. Now he does. And he cares about Simon. And Dmitri.

And then another certainty … *He cares about Edith McKay too. He really wants to get the person that killed her.*

Another cause of her anger and sadness was that her meeting with Cooper brought back a series of memories that she had hoped to suppress; memories about what she was like at their last meeting more than a decade ago.

Officious little bitch, I said. That pretty well captures my miserable professional side. Of course, it's an incomplete description. It leaves out the personal dimension. How about 'emotionally stunted, vindictive and insecure woman in a bad marriage' for a start? No wonder I attacked Cooper in court! He was a handy surrogate for men in general and Tony in particular.

She didn't like herself very much in those days. She was working in Internal Affairs, dealing with incompetent and/or corrupt police officers that detested her. The even harder part was the distrust and outright dislike on the part of the "good" officers who viewed her as an obstacle and threat, one with the potential to ruin them. Understandably, she acquired a shell. Unfortunately, it deflected everything, including the overtures and ordinary social gestures that make up much of the everyday world.

She was continually appalled by her marriage, even as she was in the process of ending it. The fact that she had voluntarily entered into a legal commitment and – what was worse, much worse -- an intimate relationship with Anthony Pastore made her wonder about both her judgment and her needs.

Even now, she shuddered when she thought about what she had done. *It's like a play co-written by Neil Simon and Alfred Hitchcock!* She was new in town, fresh out of law school, and Tony looked like the most eligible bachelor in Stanton. He put on a full blitz and she was swept up in a torrid high-intensity affair, the kind of courtship where massive amounts of attention and money overwhelm common sense. Six months into the marriage, she knew she had made a colossal mistake. Tony was incapable of loving anyone except himself; the irony being that he had no particularly attractive aspects to love. He was cruel, superficial, arrogant, insecure, and greedy.

Their divorce was a long-running, scorched earth battle, contested on every front. It used up her financial and emotional resources, leaving her with little interest in men.

Her relationship with Edith McKay provided a much-needed outlet for her. Their joint interest in environmental issues in general and the preservation of the Riverbend property in particular bonded them and enabled them to share hidden parts of themselves.

I was her best friend. That's sad. I was ten years older, hating men and feeling trapped far away from the bright city lights. The exact opposite of her in so many ways. But she needed me. Her father dying, everything landing in her lap. Marrying Robert! So wrong for her! Any man would have been wrong; she needed men, not a man.

Her best friend, but I know nothing about what matters to finding her murderer. Why she left Stanton? What she did for the five years she was gone? Who her lovers were? What she really wanted?

Ellen shook herself. At some point, she had returned to her chair at the conference table, staring blankly at the opposite wall.

I shouldn't have taken Simon's case. It will force me to go back to those times when I didn't much like myself, to revisit all the stupid mistakes I made ... count the wasted years.

Maybe that's good. Maybe it's time for some reminiscing about what might have been. Some constructive resolution of past issues that are still festering, blocking change.

That's what gets me about Cooper, I think. He's got the same problem ... a past that he wants to get rid of but can't. I wonder if he knows that about himself?

Family Affairs

Dmitri's office was on the third and top floor of the old county courthouse, a building that was one hundred and ten years old, built of massive limestone blocks and lacking both elevators and air conditioning. He would never admit it to the other cops, but Dmitri liked it. In his eyes, the sheer massiveness and austerity of the building seemed appropriate for something as solemn as "the law." The grandeur was all on the outside, however. His office was small enough that he and Marcus together made it feel crowded.

The architecture of the building also reminded him of his previous office in Russia, one of those pre-Soviet civic buildings that seemed impervious to the Communists' efforts to remove its class overtones. They made up for it by converting the interior into a warren of shoddy "offices," most of them with a backless wooden bench alongside the door to hold a seemingly constant pool of supplicants. For Dmitri, the simple act of coming to work every morning and seeing the same faces lined up on the same benches with the same expression of hopelessness was a reminder of his own futility. He still occasionally marveled at the air of expectancy that the Americans had when they came into the Stanton city offices, clearly anticipating that the wheels of government would work to solve their problem.

His phone rang, the line from the DA's office. He answered simply, "Akov."

"This is Martine. We have the official lab results on the hammer. The brain tissue and blood traces are Edith McKay's. The fingerprints are Simon Radner's."

"Is it time for an arrest?"

"No. I want the bastard to sweat a bit. And we're still waiting for the state crime lab on dating the soil samples. You

Thomas Hofstedt

might mention his name as a "person of interest" to any reporters asking around, though. That should mess up his do-gooder image just a bit!"

"Ms. Martine. You seem a little fixated on Simon Radner as suspect." *Worse than that: you are way too personal about him. Where's that icy detachment you're noted for?* "We've got other possibilities as well --"

"They're peripheral. I want to focus on Radner. He's dirty as all hell on this one!"

She hung up, leaving Dmitri staring thoughtfully at the dead phone in his hand.

Marcus knocked lightly on the open door and came in. Dmitri thought, as he always did, how much he looked like Cooper, and how different he was in other ways. Cooper would have taken Edith McKay's murder personally, as a "quest," in the old-fashioned sense; a quest with the goal of meting out punishment. Marcus viewed it as a puzzle, a lot of muddled facts and possibilities to be sorted through and "solved." Each of them, however, along with Dmitri, shared the view that premeditated murder is the worst of all crimes; and that understanding the killer's motive is important to the determination of guilt or innocence, but irrelevant to the sentencing.

Marcus stood patiently. He was accustomed to Dmitri's reveries and blank stares.

Dmitri waved him to a chair. "Your father called me yesterday."

Marcus looked at him for a few seconds. "Am I supposed to assume that's a coincidence?"

"Nope. He was fishing for some deep background on the McKay case. I think he's about to get a client named Simon Radner."

"Typical." Marcus snorted. "So he calls the police department for help! Did you explain the concept of 'private' investigator to him? Y'know ... privileged information, licensing requirements, and all that stuff?"

"C'mon, Marcus! You know him – and me – better than that! I think he was really trying to get a reading on Simon Radner ... whether he's worth the effort ... Christ! He should have been a priest!"

Half to himself, Marcus muttered, "He came close. He got the drunk part OK ... but never got to the pedophilia stage."

Dmitri glared. He stood up abruptly, took a deep breath and started to speak, "Look. You've got –"

Marcus held his hands up. "OK! OK! I'm out of line. I shouldn't put you in the middle of this. I'm sorry."

"I am in the middle. Always have been. You can't change that. But ...."

Dmitri sat down as abruptly as he had stood up and – with a perceptibly enforced calm – said, "You're both old enough by now to get along without a referee."

Dmitri moved some papers to the center of his desk. "Let's talk about lighter things. For instance, how about our high-profile homicide case?"

Marcus relaxed back into his chair. "At least it's now officially a homicide case. The lab has positively identified the bone fragments and hairs from the hammer as belonging to Edith McKay. The soils guy – I think -- will testify that the hammer and the case have been in place for at least a few years at that site. And they've got halfway decent partial prints of at least two people from the hammer, one of them being the deceased."

Dmitri gestured at the phone. "I just talked with Martine. Simon Radner's prints are definite. No surprise there. We know he handled it earlier in the evening as a run-up to the ceremony."

Marcus smiled, "So. We've got a weapon, a corpse, a potful of motives, and a handful of suspects, each of them with ample opportunity, and not one of them with an alibi. Should wind this up before lunch ..."

"We tried that five years ago, remember?" Dmitri said. "Nothing's changed, except now we know that it is in fact a homicide."

He smiled. "I suppose we could put the suspects on trial as a group, but the judge would probably want us to narrow it down a little. Maybe put 'em all in a locked room and let them vote on it."

"That's been done. I think it's been made into a reality show on Fox."

Marcus took a small notebook from his pocket and asked, "OK. Now that we know we've got a murder, where do you want me to start?"

"Two things. First, take a look at the interviews we did five years ago with people who were at the ceremony before McKay disappeared. Isolate those who actually talked with her before she walked out – probably no more than ten to twenty people. And that will include all of the Radners as well."

"And ...?" asked Marcus.

"Read the interviews. Then go back to each of them ... most of them are still around ... and tell them about the new evidence. Ask them if they can recall their conversations with McKay. See if you can find someone who was actually standing with either her or Simon Radner when the lights went out. Maybe if they know there's a murder involved, not just a slip-and-fall accident, they might come up with something new."

Marcus raised his eyebrows and said, "Pretty thin. And it's been five years ..."

"Got a better idea? And while you're at it, be sure to caution both Robert and Simon Radner about not leaving town. You know the drill. Oh, and take along these 8x10 glossies that the news guy took before the power failure. Ask your interviewees to take a look ... See if they see anything out of the ordinary."

Marcus took the envelope that Dmitri pushed across the desk, and asked, "OK. And what's your second thing?"

"The DA has zeroed in on Simon Radner as sole suspect. I don't know why and I worry that she's jeopardizing our case, but it's too soon to forget about the rest of the field, including some of our local fat cats. We need to check out this squabble between McKay-as-environmentalist and the pro-development crowd. See if there's anything that's happened since she died that bears on that motive."

Marcus did not hide his skepticism. "A more aggressive form of white collar crime? That's a stretch, particularly for the country club set in Stanton. Bashing a woman with a hammer over a zoning dispute requires more collective balls than they have between them."

"I agree, but you're forgetting about the trend toward outsourcing. A couple of our very respectable citizens have some interesting connections with some characters that make a nice living by bashing people. Think Tony Pastore, for example."

"Oh yeah, and be polite. There are some significant taxpayers in that set."

Marcus stood. "OK. I'll wear my best suit. Oh, and if my long-lost father calls again …"

Dmitri sighed, "Yeah?"

"Tell him that you make a lousy referee. Too much bias, not enough objectivity. You really need to be able to call a flagrant foul every now and then."

Marcus

Marcus was amused, as always, by Dmitri's continuous attempts to rehabilitate a father-son relationship that had never existed in the first place. Those attempts were as transparent as they were misguided, but Marcus had always played his part, a role he thought of as the hard-to-get embittered son. It was a risky game. Marcus knew better than to underestimate Dmitri's uncanny ability to see through the outer shells that serve as defense mechanisms for guilty parties. But it was a game that he enjoyed, and one that he could use to his advantage.

Marcus was crystal clear about his relationship with his father: he simply did not care. Dmitri's error was in assuming that he did care; or, if he did not now, that he once had, and could again. In fact, Marcus felt no particular resentment toward Cooper, his wayward parenting, or his episodic desertions. Such a feeling would be a weakness, implying a need that he did not feel.

He abhorred dependency in all of its forms, particularly in human relationships. He could not recall any single incident where he did not feel self-sufficient, and he was continually amazed by the absurd behaviors of individuals driven by other-centered motives – loyalty, love, duty, forgiveness – the ever-hopeful and forlorn lexicon of incomplete people.

He knew that he was different, defective in some way – a missing gene, a badly wired synapse, some biochemical imbalance – but he was comfortable with his particular self, and saw no need to worry about or try to "fix" the difference. If he thought about it very much – which he didn't – he would have put it down to simple genetic chance, rather than to any act of will or deliberation on his part. And he would have viewed it as a positive rather than negative trait.

He chose to be a cop because it reinforced his self-sufficiency, and it enabled him to control people and situations in ways that pleased him. Unlike Dmitri and Cooper – both of whom he studied carefully – Marcus saw his own emotional detachment amid the revealed squalor of other people's lives to be an affirming rather than dehumanizing side effect of "the job." He was a good cop, in the sense that he enforced the law efficiently and was incorruptible. The missing parts – compassion, empathy, etc. – were simply not part of the job description in his view.

His personal life was his own and entirely private. He did not fraternize with his colleagues, either up or down the chain of command. Dmitri was closest to him, but they had little to do with one another outside of the office, and Marcus was confident that neither Cooper nor Dmitri knew anything about what he had come to think of as his "other life."

Frequent and often kinky sex was the centerpiece of that other life. It was helped by the reality that Marcus was physically attractive and enjoyed manipulating others. He was – like his father – tall, lean and good looking, but where Cooper was indifferent or even averse to social contact, Marcus was receptive. He could make small talk and cloak his intense appraisals as a normal interest upon meeting someone for the first time. He was a charming sociopath who had discovered a long time ago that women and even the occasional man wanted to "be in love" with him, and that this desire was particularly strong among a certain subset of the rich and famous, the types of individuals that needed to be dominated or controlled to make up for something that neither they nor Marcus could articulate.

In some circles, he would be described as a predator, but the sad reality was that the counterparties sought him out.

His alliances with publicity-shy, eminent individuals seeking unconventional sexual outlets were natural for Marcus. In addition to his physical attractiveness, he offered two valuable and hard-to-find properties: complete discretion and the semblance of reciprocal passion. He chose those who wanted longer term, more conventional relationships with a partner that would humor their need to "be in love." Almost always, the relationships ended as his partners gradually recognized the poor bargain they had made, trading off their intense emotional needs for the cold satisfaction of his contingent approval. The endings were always anti-climactic and quiet, more of a withering away than a breaking up, featuring a lack of melodrama traceable to Marcus's policy of always choosing partners who had more to lose than him.

Marcus found the irony in the present situation to be exquisite. He was investigating the death of Edith McKay, the woman who – more than any of his liaisons – had come the closest to understanding him. She had once said to him, "You don't need anything from anybody. It makes you irresistibly attractive to those of us who cannot tolerate the notion that we could possibly be unimportant to someone we choose to fuck."

Joan Martine

Joan Martine was a thoroughly modern woman who happened to be missing some essential human component, perhaps a cornerstone gene or a biochemical trace element that acted as a governor of needs and wants; the kind of internal mood regulator that would trigger constructive disappointment rather than a mindless rage when those needs were not satisfied.

She was a sociopath, but she had mastered her public self, tamping down her contempt for others beneath a highly polished veneer that she displayed to the world at large. However, she understood and even felt a kinship with the all-too-frequent misfit – the gothic teenager, ostracized postal worker, religious fanatic or jilted lover – who used semiautomatic weapons to transform a supermarket, workplace, classroom or movie theatre into a charnel house. She was puzzled and disappointed that such distraught social jihadists were overwhelmingly male, feeling herself to be quite capable of mass murder. Nor did she understand why they ended their rampage by killing themselves, leaving their dramatic acts to be deconstructed by inane talking heads, always "shocked by this act of senseless rage."

Aside from that missing key element, genetics had been kind to her. She was what the psychologists called "a resilient child," overcoming abusive parents and a loveless, barren childhood to excel in everything that she undertook. She was president of her high school and college classes, editor of the law school review and the youngest District Attorney in the state as well as one of the very few women in such a position.

She was intelligent, with an affinity for detail but still able to keep the larger picture in focus. She could grasp complex ideas quickly and – important in her professional world – simplify and communicate those ideas to colleagues, judges and juries. She was also physically attractive, in the fashion of an early twenty-first century American professional woman. Her face was regular, with quite large brown eyes and a just-visible spray of freckles, framed by black hair that she kept short enough that she often forgot to comb it in the morning. She was smaller than she liked – just five feet, five inches tall – but all of the parts were proportionate, so that she exuded an air of muted sexuality in her day job, thoroughly professional but leaving the men around her intrigued and wondering.

At work, she was respected, even admired, by both bosses and peers. The fact that she was a woman was irrelevant except for a few good-old-boys just short of retirement, Neanderthals who could neither admit nor even acknowledge that gender no longer mattered very much. It helped that goals were clear and measureable – crime rates, conviction percentages, number of cases cleared. And cause-and-effect was well understood: attention to detail, rigorous pre-trial preparation, jury selection. Under Joan Martine, the Office of the District Attorney was not troubled with gender discrimination.

However, after dark and away from the office, she became more feminine, more complex and more insecure. She was baffled by the hopelessly ambiguous role demands. At age forty, she was part of the post-feminist generation that was still struggling to rewrite cultural and social norms. She had bypassed the "motherhood vs. career" debate that took up so much press time, rejecting the idea of children for as long as she could remember. Not because a child was a hindrance to a career, but because she just didn't like children – their deadweight dependence on her; their potential for rogue behavior.

But that still left the issues of companionship, relationship and – most troubling of all -- sex. She did not think of them as "needs," but rather as puzzles to be solved, treaties to be negotiated with counterparties whose motivations were unclear to her, with uncertain benefits. She was hampered by this transactional view, constantly running head-on into a demand for "compromise" or "accommodation" or "reciprocity," commodities that she could not bring herself to deal in.

Until law school, she adhered to a rigorous self-sufficiency, believing that she did not need another person in her life – either emotionally or professionally. This attitude was supported by her sense of superiority. She gauged everyone she encountered on physical, intellectual and philosophical scales, always relative to herself. She always found fatal flaws in the first meetings with those suitors who sought her out, flaws that loomed larger through time. She came to believe that she had no peer, in her mind a necessary condition for mating. She found this to be a completely satisfactory state of affairs.

The ultra-feminist views of the latter twentieth century were too strident for her taste, but they did force her to confront her sexual needs. She adopted what she thought of as a practical promiscuity during her college years, sleeping with whatever faintly appealing earnest boy came along but never for very long and always coming away thinking *what's the big deal?* A phrase from *Lady Chatterley's Lover* (required reading in Freshman English of that era) expressed her view nicely: *This ridiculous bouncing of buttocks!*

In the same spirit of experimentation, she declared herself to be lesbian and spent a semester sharing a house with four other women, each of them committed to the libertarian lifestyle and eager to instruct her. She found them to hopelessly banal and their brand of sex to be as self-centered and uninspiring as the men that they deplored. The oldest of the four told her, "You just don't like sex. It requires that you pay real attention to what someone else needs, and you can't do that." Joan thought that it summarized her views nicely.

Law school immediately challenged her calculated self-sufficiency. She found that a smart, self-confident --even aggressive – woman could do very well for herself, but that same woman would do even better if she was seen as attainable rather than intimidating and intent on existing entirely on her own merits. She crafted a new image, engaging in a pair of carefully chosen year-long relationships; first with the son of a senator one year ahead of her class and then with a professor of constitutional law. She developed an exquisite sense of the male ego and exited both relationships on her terms, with an enhanced reputation as the archetypical modern woman – expert in both the boardroom and the bedroom.

She met Simon Radner in the middle of her third year of law school. He was a guest lecturer in a two-day workshop on "Legal Ethics" and she was assigned as his on-campus guide. At first sight, she determined to seduce him, for no other reason than to demonstrate that she could. It helped that they were both attracted by the irony of fucking between sessions of a Legal Ethics workshop. They found themselves spending most of their time in bed together in the Marriott on campus and for the first time in her adult life she felt a glimmer of attachment to a man. The sense of possibility stayed alive in her until the next time they met – a dozen years later in Stanton and a few months before Edith's "accident" became a murder case.

The venue was a cocktail party at Robert Radner's house, a fundraiser for one of Robert's charities. There were seventy or eighty people circulating through the rooms and it was inevitable that she and Simon found themselves momentarily isolated, standing side-by-side looking out across the crowded room, close enough that he was acutely aware of the occasional pressure of her breast against his arm. He was quite sure that the pressure was deliberate, calculated in frequency and intensity.

"Simon. What an overdue treat!"

"Hello Joan. I heard you were in town."

"I've been here a year. Apparently, the news of my arrival didn't galvanize you into picking up the phone."

Simon looked pained, as if considering the first glimmer of a faint headache.

"I spend most of my time in the city now. Not much to do with Stanton." And after a pause, he added, "And I had no reason to call."

"You seemed eager enough when I last saw you. Maybe it's harder for you to talk when we both have clothes on?"

"Joan ... I --"

"I was just talking with your wife Maria. She's very attractive ... exotic, even. But she doesn't seem quite right. Something's off. I think I can see why you would be drawn to young law students."

"Joan ... I --"

"Relax, Simon. I'm not about to blow any whistles. It was fun. Really great sex. And I have much more to lose from scandal than you do."

Simon did seem to relax a bit. A strolling waiter stopped to refill her wine glass and for the first time, Simon looked directly at her, his expression shifting from one of tense watchfulness to a more speculative look.

When the waiter moved on, he said, "I'm with you on the 'fun' part. I still have flashbacks to that Marriott Inn. I'm glad it happened, but it was a long time ago and we were different people then. Let's let the past stay in the past, shall we?"

She smiled brightly, mostly for the benefit of a couple strolling by. When they were out of hearing range, the smile abruptly faded and she said, "Actually, I was hoping that we might pick up where we left off."

Simon's alarm was visible to anybody that happened to be watching. He stepped back, as though the added distance could negate her words. He started to speak but realized that he didn't know what to say. She continued while he was still trying to organize a response.

"Nothing flamboyant or indiscreet. Thoroughly clandestine. No talk of love or permanence. Just a few hours on the occasional afternoon ... maybe a weekend trip together to a mythical convention in a distant city."

Simon looked at her ... really looked at her ... for the first time. On the surface, he saw a quite attractive, well-dressed, youngish professional woman making bright conversation at a cocktail party. Beyond that, it was easy to conclude from her expression and posture that she was intelligent and self-assured, comfortable with her own self.

However, her eyes conveyed what mattered most about her. They were dark and unchanging, as though disconnected from the smile that seemed so sincere. They stayed fixed on him, as though challenging his own gaze. She did not blink. When the silence continued, he realized that she was amused by his confusion.

He held her gaze while scrolling through his limited options. *It's no use appealing to her for empathy. She doesn't possess any. It's impossible to do what she asks. So ...*

He spoke as matter-of-factly as he could. "I absolutely decline. I have no interest in occasional sex with another woman."

"I'm not just another woman. I can --"

He overrode her protest, raising his voice. "I know very well what you can do. But I particularly have no interest in you. As I said, that was a different time and place. You were attractive to me then, for reasons that no longer matter."

As he watched her expression freeze, he added, "I'm sure you can find someone suitable to meet your needs. Perhaps some older man who will be flattered by your diverseß appetites."

The transformation was astonishing to watch. She visibly shuddered, as though struggling to suppress waves of rage barely contained by her skin. Her face reddened and her mouth compressed into a single line. Her eyes narrowed, channeling pure fury and hatred. She seemed to expand and then shrink before him. She slammed her glass down onto the nearby table, splashing red wine onto the glass top.

He turned away. But she stopped him, gripping his forearm so tightly that it hurt. Leaning toward him as though to whisper a secret, she hissed, "Watch out for yourself, Simon! Whoever said hell hath no fury like a woman scorned knew what he was talking about!"

Simon put his hand over hers where it was imbedded in his forearm. To a casual observer, it might seem an affectionate gesture. His expression did not change, but he forcibly pried her index finger back until she released her grip. Leaning in as though for a parting kiss, the kind that substitutes for a handshake among the professional classes, He whispered, "You've got red wine dripping on your shoes."

And then he walked away.

Additional Information

Cooper rang the buzzer beside Simon's nameplate at about eight that evening. Simon's primary residence was in the city, but he maintained a second home in Stanton. It was located in the gentrified downtown area, in an old riverfront warehouse that had been converted into luxury condos with distant views. Once buzzed in, Cooper took the elevator to the sixth and top floor. When the doors slid open, he found himself in a furnished reception area facing Simon's door. His was the sole residence on this floor.

Simon's wife Maria opened the door, gesturing for him to come in. Cooper was immediately struck by her *presence*, as though she traveled with some form of radiant energy that extended beyond her physical self. Cooper tried to analyze it as they walked down the hall toward Simon's den. He decided that the emanation he was picking up was more sinister than it was benevolent, that something was "off." The impression was amplified by her silence; she had not said a word since opening the door. She preceded him down the hall, walking with a limp.

When Simon came out of the den to meet them in the hall, Cooper realized that Maria was not limping. She was wearing only one shoe. When she turned to leave, she smiled at Cooper, and he thought he saw an asymmetry in her face. Her eyes were somehow different or moved separately from one another. It was unsettling.

Simon didn't speak to Maria or comment after she had moved away. "Glad you could stop by. I don't have a lot of time, but it saves me a lot of explaining at the office."

I'll bet it does. High priced corporate attorneys don't usually entertain cops or questionable-looking private investigators.

Once again, Cooper was struck by Simon's apparent lack of concern. They could have been about to discuss the state of local politics rather than his possible indictment for murder.

Cooper said "I'll be as brief as I can; I've got four topics for the moment. Call them 'puzzles'."

They moved into the den and seated themselves in a pair of matching leather chairs on either side of a massive fireplace. Simon asked politely if Cooper wanted anything to drink and – when Cooper declined – settled back expectantly.

Cooper started. "For your information, I've read through all of the materials you provided and I've met with Ellen Pastore. I assume you know that she's not one of my biggest fans?"

Simon smiled. "She made that quite clear. Very colorful language."

Cooper looked at him, waiting for more, but Simon merely leaned back in his chair with that same polite smile.

Cooper shrugged. "OK. First topic, that hammer. How'd your fingerprints get on it, if they are?"

Simon was quick to respond. "Oh, they are! The hammer was going to be formally presented to me later that evening – the night Edith died. She would make a brief speech about all the good things I'd done for the housing coalition and then award me the hammer 'as a token of', etc., etc."

Cooper interjected, "But that never happened. The lights went out and the night ended without any speeches or awards."

Simon nodded. "True. But Edith had asked each of the award winners – there were four of us – to come a little early, so that we could take a photo for next morning's newspaper. I and one other recipient posed with Edith. In my case, we did a couple of pictures – one showing a handoff, and the other with me holding the hammer prominently in front of me. Ellen's got the glossies, so it's on the record."

Cooper said, "What happened to the hammer after the photos?"

Simon paused before responding and Cooper thought, *he's rehearsing his testimony.* His impression was confirmed when Simon began speaking in whole sentences, without a pause.

"By the time we finished the photo session, the crowd was starting to arrive. All four awards were placed on the speaker's table at the front of the ballroom, behind the little tabletop podium. The hammer was in a customized Lucite display case. I saw them there, and I think there's also a photograph of just the awards once they're arranged on the table."

"So anyone could have picked it up?"

"Easily. Especially in the dark and confusion."

"And afterward? Wasn't it missed?"

Again, Simon paused to think. "Nobody really knew about the awards except the nominees and Edith. Edith commissioned them herself. I suspect somebody delivered the other awards to their respective winners, but no other ceremony was ever scheduled and I know that I never gave the hammer another thought. Frankly, the last thing I needed was another memento from a needy not-for-profit agency."

As he spoke, he waved his hand at his bookshelf on the opposite wall. Cooper could easily see an entire row of plaques, certificates and various acrylic objects on the lower shelf.

That's handy. A murder weapon that nobody missed. But then, a startling thought occurred to Cooper. *Only a few people knew about the hammer and one of them was Simon.*

Cooper went on. "My second puzzle: There's something that makes no sense. The killer takes the hammer out of the case, uses it to kill Edith ... and then puts it back in the case before throwing it away? Why would they do that? It's almost as though they're trying to preserve the evidence!"

Simon is clearly intrigued by the question. Finally, he shook his head. "I agree. It makes no sense."

Cooper said, "Let's move on to my next puzzle. Why would Edith go outside, toward the river? She was the hostess, the awards are about to start, and the weather is atrocious."

Simon was quick to respond, "I don't know." *First mistake. That was too quick.*

"Think about it." Cooper pressed. "She stopped to put on heavy rain gear, so she wasn't running away from anybody in a state of panic; it was a deliberate outing. And she left at the exact time when she was most needed to deal with the confusion. So her going outside must have been in reaction to something that happened during the cocktail hour or right after the lights went out."

"That all sounds right. But I still don't know why – or exactly when -- she went outside."

Cooper deliberately shifted to an accusing tone. "You and/or Robert were with her most of the evening before she disappeared. Did she say anything unusual? Did anything seem to upset her?"

Simon looked down, as though he was about to lie. "I've thought about this a lot. And the cops asked this over and over back at the time. Something happened about ten minutes before the blackout. I don't know what it was. But I was watching her move around the room, talking with small clusters of people, dealing with caterers, all the sort of stuff you'd expect of a hostess. But she was behaving differently ... definitely more distracted ... seemed to be looking for somebody in particular. When she saw me looking at her, she came over and said she had to talk to me. She was clearly agitated about something. I assumed it was something about the ceremony, but before we could go any further, she was gone. Then the lights went out."

He knows more than he's telling. But before he could pursue it, Simon asked, "You said 'four puzzles'; what's the last one?"

One you'll hear a lot about when the cops come. But he simply asked, "How well did you know Edith?"

"It was strictly Platonic. We were good friends. We spent a fair bit of time together on boards and various civic projects. And, remember, she was my sister-in-law, my brother Robert's wife. But he and I haven't been seeing much of each other for awhile, so there wasn't much social time together from that angle."

"You were spending a lot of time in Stanton while she was growing up there. Did you have anything to do with her then?"

Simon was quick to smile at Cooper's unspoken implication. "She was a kid ... I think she left town when she was about twenty or twenty-one years old."

Cooper allowed a silence to build, lasting thirty seconds or so.

Simon smiled again, without much humor, and said, "OK. Everyone in town knew her. She was a McKay. And she was one of those high achievers that society manages to turn out every now and then. But my contact with Edith at that time was meeting her maybe three or four times, usually while she was accompanying her father James to some civic function of some sort. We shook hands and smiled and that's about all I recall."

"What about the five years she was gone? Any contact at all?"

Simon said flatly, clearly losing patience, "None whatsoever. I didn't know where she was, nor did I care. And I wasn't much around Stanton myself at that time."

"What about '—"

"Look, Cooper. Let me save you a lot of time. I had nothing – I repeat, *nothing* – to do with Edith McKay until about a year before she was killed. And then it was nothing more than a friendship and common interests."

Fifty-percent of that is true. Maybe all of it – if "common interests" is defined liberally...

Cooper stood and moved toward the hallway door. "OK. That fills in some of the blanks for me. But I still have a lot of questions."

He turned for the door, but then stopped and said, "We both know you're not telling me everything you know. I don't know why, but that's OK for the moment --"

"How about if I used that famous phrase 'need-to-know', like in the spy movies?"

Cooper said sharply, "Doesn't fit this case! You're a prime suspect in a murder case. There's no way you're going to be able to stonewall the cops when they come calling –"

Simon interrupted, "Prime suspect? Yes ... but maybe not the first one the police will suspect."

That stopped Cooper cold. "Your fingerprints on the weapon, along with your engraved name, for god's sake! You're rumored to be a love interest! And you don't think you're the first choice?"

"I wish I were. But I think Robert will be favored."

"Robert? Why?"

They were back at the front door by now. Simon stepped to the elevator with Cooper, saying, "Well. You're the ex-cop. All I know is what I read in the police procedural novels. But wouldn't you be curious about someone who's had two young attractive wives die 'accidently' ... at the same location, but seven years apart?"

Cooper stood stock-still. "*Two* wives die?"

Simon held the elevator door open. As he entered the elevator, Cooper saw Maria, standing halfway down the hallway, in the arched entry to the darkened living room. Something about her overall posture and stillness told Cooper that she'd been listening. He wondered how much of what Simon had told him had been edited for Maria's benefit.

Simon saw her too. He nudged Cooper outside and pulled the door shut behind them. Only then did he respond.

"Yes. Two wives. You need to know about Rachel."

A Tragic Incident

It was twelve years ago. The "hundred year storm" was still seven years in the future.

The McKay home would never make the cover of Architectural Digest. It was a sprawling reflection of its owner's legacy and lack of taste. Amos McKay was an uneducated Easterner who became rich in the late nineteenth-century American West through sheer rapacity. He built a personal monument disguised as a house, driven far more by ego than architecture or aesthetics. The estate sat on a bend of the river, overlooking modest rapids running through a narrow gorge. Eighty years after its construction, it was still the biggest house in Stanton. It featured a vast ballroom with a thirty-foot ceiling, an interior gallery circling all four sides of the ballroom, and a grand staircase copied from a French chateau that provided access to the family's living quarters. There were twenty other rooms, but only Edith and her father James McKay lived there.

Tonight, the estate was being used to its fullest extent. James McKay was hosting a barbeque to celebrate the Stanton Panthers' first-ever state high school basketball championship. A blanket invitation had been extended to the extended school community and it seemed as though most of them had accepted, along with a contingent of the larger community for whom "civic pride" was part of their job description. All of the Radners were there, partly because Nathaniel was a star player on the team. It was the first time in six months that Simon and Robert had been together as a foursome with their wives, Maria and Rachel.

The only scheduled event was a semi-organized ceremony in the ballroom to honor the kids on the team. Simon's son Nathaniel had been voted (along with his best friend Marcus) as "co-most-valuable-player." There were a few clichéd speeches and a lot of spontaneous yelling by kids who – despite the not-very-determined efforts of a few adults – had gotten into the tubs of beer. It was a warm cloudless evening and the party spilled over onto the immense lawn that overlooked the river gorge. The setting sun cast long shadows that intermingled on the bright green grass.

Simon stood with James McKay on the terrace that extended the outside length of the house, overlooking the river and the many clusters of adults and high-school kids that dotted the lawn and moved in and out of the house. A lot of the kids had paired up and were sitting head-to-head on the lawn that sloped down to the river, each pair apparently oblivious to the goings-on.

Seeing these couples, Simon had three thoughts in quick succession: *I'm old*; followed by *I remember when Maria and I were like that*; and finally, *I wonder if Nathaniel has a girl friend?* For some reason he did not pursue, each of these thoughts made him sad.

"Have you seen our newly-famous son recently?" he asked Maria when James was distracted by one of the caterers.

"Not for awhile. But let him celebrate. How often do you get to be MVP?" And then, after a pause, "I think he said something about meeting Marcus near the stables. My translation is that they're going to filch some more beer."

Simon had Nathaniel's MVP plaque in one hand and a bottle of beer in the other. James and another couple in their small group held wine glasses, but were spilling more than they were drinking, making excited gestures to emphasize the points they were urging. The discussion had started when Rachel had teased James, "What's it like living in a palace?" Simon had winced, knowing that James was sensitive on this point. He had witnessed him in numerous settings where he was clearly embarrassed by his late father's ostentatious life style.

James protested, "It's not a palace … just a very large and tasteless house."

He went on to say that he and Edith felt at home in the old house and wanted to stay there. He suggested that Rachel should wander around to see for herself. "Feel free to poke around. I think you'll see it's just a home, not a palace." Robert and his wife Rachel had just left for their self-guided tour of the McKay home, with Maria tagging along.

James and a woman with a loud voice were trying to outdo the other in telling exaggerated stories about the difficulty of raising teenagers. Simon didn't participate outright, but he was amused by the conversation. *Some contest! Either of their kids could be poster children for a Teenager of the Year award!* He was glad that Robert wasn't around for the discussion, and he wondered yet again if Rachel's inability to have children and their subsequent childlessness was painful, especially at times like this, when confronted so vividly by the casual joy that others take in their children.

James broke into his musings, "OK, Simon, you're father of the MVP. Tell us: Are today's kids going to hell in a hand basket?"

For some time afterward, Simon wondered how he would have responded if given a chance, if the world had not changed just then. An amused chuckle? Some inanity? "Boys will be boys, after all." Faint disapproval? A sense of pride?

The noise from the ballroom behind them abruptly changed from the loud drone of many people talking at once to a sharply pitched collective gasp, quickly becoming discrete cries of surprise and alarm. The most ominous sound, however, was the near-silence that quickly settled on the ballroom, with that undertone of hushed voices that is unique to accident scenes and public scandals.

They turned to enter the ballroom, but found themselves at the back of a dense crowd, all pressing forward toward the staircase at the far end of the room, the source of the silence. James pushed through the crush, followed closely by Simon. The resistance was passive but stubborn, offered by people whose attention is directed elsewhere. Then they were through and found themselves at the foot of the grand staircase.

Rachel was sprawled facedown across the bottom steps, at the end of a cascade of flowers and shards of colorful clay pots trailing down the staircase. She lay with her head turned at an impossible angle, as though admiring the train of color she had left behind her. The only movement was a slow trickle of blood from a gash behind her ear.

She was dead.

A week later, the shock was still palpable. For a long time, Simon's first thought on waking, in the few seconds before consciousness was fully restored, was of Rachel's absolute stillness and that strange angle of her neck.

All of the institutions designed to enable the living to deal with unexpected and unearned death were fully functioning. Rachel was interred and mourned. Robert was comforted and counseled. Distant family members had come and gone, memorials written and held.

But the usual formalities failed – as they always do -- to satisfy the forlorn and unanswerable questions *"Why?"* and *"How could this happen?"* It was safer to ask, *"How did this happen?"* But in the case of Rachel's death, even this question lacked a satisfactory answer.

Several members of the Stanton police force were there as guests, including the Chief of Police, and they restored some order after about ten minutes of mass confusion. Dmitri was there, but spent most of his time looking for Nathaniel to inform him as gently as possible what had happened to his aunt.

No one saw her fall. The few hundred individuals actually in the ballroom were unaware until those closest to the stair heard a cry and looked up to see her tumbling down the last few steps amid the broken pottery. *"All loose! Like a straw manikin..."* was one of the more vivid descriptions. The ballroom itself was brightly lit, but the interior gallery at the head of the staircase was in semi-darkness. No one other than Rachel had been on the second level, as James had asked the guests to stay on the ground floor or outside and to please not wander around the second floor – the personal rooms for him and Edith. The caterers had arranged dozens of flower pots on the entire length of the staircase as a colorful deterrent to any such ascent.

Robert said that he had headed for the bar and stayed in the ballroom rather than tour the house. And Maria said that she had gone outside on the veranda to look for Nathaniel, leaving Rachel alone on her tour. The stairs themselves did not reveal loose boards or any other hidden dangers that would cause a fall.

The ruling was quick and straightforward, that the cause of death was "a broken neck resulting from an accidental fall."

Rachel's death seemed a watershed. The high school basketball team lost most of their games in the following season. Nathaniel graduated and went away to the upstate university, the beginning of a drifting, ambitionless existence that continued through today. Shortly after Rachel died, Dmitri and Cooper were suspended from the Stanton police force and confronted with new and stark choices. Simon and Maria spent less and less time in Stanton, preferring their luxury apartment in the upriver city. Robert seemed caught in some post-mourning time warp that precluded romance. He and Simon drifted apart, became awkward with one another, and rarely called one another.

The McKay's seemed most affected by the tragedy. Edith dropped out of the local state university, left town, and was not heard from again until she returned five years later, just before her father's death. A year or so after Rachel's death, James was diagnosed with a highly aggressive lung cancer. He seemed disinterested throughout the surgery, chemo and radiation therapy that preceded his death a few years later. The McKay house sat unused.

It was as though Rachel's fall had set latent forces loose, something less than a curse, more like permission to stop caring quite so much, to recognize the flimsiness of some of the facades, to stop trying quite so hard to maintain old civilities.

An Unexpected Encounter

Cooper was jarred by his meeting with Ellen Pastore. He felt less sure of himself, vaguely threatened by his strong reactions to her. Somehow, without any apparent effort or intent, she caused him to question his carefully constructed self-image; his view of himself as satisfied with what he had and who he was. He wondered if the *I don't need anybody* defense shield that he had erected was as pathetic to others as it now seemed to him, making him simultaneously smug and lonely.

He did not understand why she had this effect on him. Some of it surely must stem from their prior roles as adversaries. Did he have a need to demonstrate that he was different, somehow "better" than she remembered? And she seemed to be as self-conscious about what she had been as he was.

At an objective level, he knew that part of his attraction to her was that she seemed to share his tolerance for ambiguity when questions of guilt and innocence were involved. That caused him to wonder in turn about Simon and why he gathered such people around him.

What he had come to think of as "the Pastore effect" was tangled up with emotions brought about by being back in Stanton, the scene of so many personal failures. As if he really did want to remember, Cooper spent most of a day wandering aimlessly around Stanton. He quickly realized that he had forgotten – more precisely, suppressed -- a great deal over the last few years. And the city had changed as well, transforming itself from a sleeping self-contained enclave – the kind of place where people came to raise their children and those children stayed once into adulthood -- into the classic American exurb, a bolted-on dormitory for the big city upriver. The stores had become chains, the houses McMansions, the local real estate agents had rescaled themselves as "developers." Even the river was different, seemingly more subdued as it flowed between parquet bike paths lined with non-native trees. He recalled that

Dmitri had been wearing a tie the last time he saw him, indicating that even the police force was succumbing to gentrification.

But people are still occasionally killing their neighbors and spouses, Cooper wondered why that idea pleased him so inordinately. *Probably because I'm getting old and need to have some constants to hold on to.*

He followed the riverfront road out of town until he came to McKay's Riverbend property about five miles from the city center. An ambivalent sign indicated that it was in the process of being preserved as a "historic Stanton estate," but a large red "X" had been crudely painted over the lettering. A very elaborate and tasteless ornate gate stood open, framing the house standing about two hundred yards away at the end of a tree-lined drive, with several ranch-like outbuildings closer to the river. Several heavy-duty construction vehicles were parked at one side of the main house, but there was no sign of activity. Cooper drove to the side of the house, parked and walked around the house toward the river. There was a fifty=yard-wide strip of lawn sloping steeply down to the river. At its nearest point to the house, the riverbank was scarred by a narrow strip of excavation, accented by yellow crime-scene tape.

He stood quietly for about three minutes at the approximate spot where he thought Edith might have stood when she was attacked, trying to imagine an intense rainstorm and a killer armed with a hammer. He did not sense any of the mystical auras and emanations that his ex-wife insisted must remain present at a murder scene, awaiting discovery by a properly receptive investigator. Cooper's view was that any such auras and emanations sprang entirely from the observer's imagination, that a graveyard was just a graveyard.

Maybe if I come back when it's raining? He turned back to the house to see a van and a pickup truck park alongside his car. The lettering on the truck said 'City of Stanton'. Five men and a woman exited the van and joined two men in hard hats from the pickup. All eight of them looked at Cooper standing in the middle of the lawn. The men from the pickup were dressed in work clothes and were carrying what looked like rolls of blueprints. The other men were all in suits and three of them were looking at their cell phones even as they exited the van. The only one that Cooper recognized was Robert Radner, who somehow managed to convey the impression that he was the leader of the group.

The lone woman left the cluster and walked purposefully toward Cooper. She wore a tailored suit, with a skirt short enough to highlight very nice legs. But the high heels didn't work well on Riverbend's rain-softened lawn, so she switched to walking on her toes, making her look like she was hurrying to get to Cooper. She was familiar to him, but he couldn't quite place her. *Someone from my past life in Stanton, I suppose.*

She teetered unsteadily the last few feet. He reached out and she stopped herself by putting her hand on his forearm. Once steadied, she looked up at him and said, "Damn shoes! Hello Cooper."

The husky voice and the unforgettable brown eyes did it for Cooper. They had always been his favorite features.

"Hello Natalie. Divorce has been good to you. You look great." *Should one apologize for failing to recognize an ex-wife? Or is that a good sign? Maybe it signifies the "moving on" that everybody says is so important?*

"Just like you left me, other than the dyed hair, thirty fewer pounds, facelift and designer wardrobe. And the years, of course, but we won't mention those. And don't pretend you recognized me until the last half-second. I could see you thinking 'who is this woman' from the second I got out of the van."

He smiled ruefully. "It has been a long time. And you do look different. In a good way." *I wonder what I look like to her. Nature run its course, I imagine.*

Then he realized that what he was feeling was relief. *She's done well without me. No long term damage.* The emotion surprised him and he wondered if he'd been carrying a subconscious load of guilt around with him since their divorce.

He asked, "How are you, Natalie?" in a way that made it clear it was something more than just a polite question.

She answered in the same manner. "I'm fine. I really am. I've got everything a modern middle-aged woman could hope for. Except a man."

Cooper winced and started to reply, "Natalie, I – "

She tightened her grip on his forearm and said, "Cooper, that last bit – 'except a man' -- is neither a criticism of you nor an implied hint that we should start over. I like the way my life is now."

"I'm glad. But it's funny. I was just thinking of you. About your belief in auras and emanations at crime scenes."

Her eyes twinkled. "Did it work?"

"I'm a bad subject. Too much imbedded cynicism. And five years is a long time."

She went strangely silent, and he waited.

"I was here that night," she said. "When Edith ..."

What she didn't say was that she was upstairs in a bedroom when the lights went out, waiting for Robert. Nor did she say anything about how the blackout made the sex so much more intense, as though groping for one another in the pitch black with the noise of the rain made it permissible to regress to pre-civilized behaviors. Robert wouldn't report Edith missing for several hours because he and Natalie stayed in that bedroom until the lights came back on, making further sexual play ordinary and uninteresting.

Cooper went on before she could continue, pointing at the group of men approaching them across the lawn. "Who are these guys?"

"You're looking at the RDC, standing for the Riverbend Development Committee. We're out here to kick the dirt, as we like to say in the real estate business."

By then, the men had come up to them, forming a half circle around Natalie and him, with Robert in the middle. He noted that Natalie moved next to Robert, standing just close enough to make him wonder about her exact status.

Robert said, "Hello Cooper. I hear you're working for Simon." He did not offer to introduce any of the others, and none of them seemed offended by the omission.

Cooper nodded to Robert. "Technically, I'm employed by his attorney – Ellen Pastore."

The name 'Pastore' caused a quite visible ripple in the line of people facing him; a sudden stillness of posture and sharp glances at him, as if he had suddenly become interesting. Natalie started chewing on her lower lip and would not look at him.

Robert, on the other hand, seemed amused. He said, "Not our favorite person. But I hope she does a good job for Simon. He needs all the help he can get."

Robert turned away and walked toward the river. Everybody except Natalie moved with him, starting to talk among themselves.

Natalie stood and looked at him, seeming to be searching for words. Then, finally, she sighed and hurried after the others.

Cooper watched her go. *Unexpected encounters with ex-wives! Surely, that should come with auras and emanations!*

Natalie

Natalie trailed the group of men around the Riverbend property.. The two in hard hats led the excursion, talking about sightlines, frontage, density and all of the arcane aspects whereby land and space are converted into money. But Natalie was mostly lost in her own thoughts, set off by the encounter with Cooper.

Marcus is just like him. Except he doesn't have the ambivalence. They'll probably find a gene for that one of these days. Then they can say, "It's not my fault." But that's not fair: he never did blame anybody except himself, even when I was a raging bitch. And it wasn't just the liquor; he's predisposed to forgiveness... for others. Maybe that's a gene too. And God knows, there was enough blame to go around.

I told him, 'I like the way my life is now'. But that's an exaggeration.

When they divorced, she just kept doing what she was already doing, just without Cooper in the house. Marcus went off to college and she devoted time and attention to becoming the most successful real estate agent in Stanton. Her renewed interest coincided with Stanton's growth spurt and she did well for herself, finding that she liked her new professional image. She was also honest enough to acknowledge that being mistress to Robert Radner helped her advancement enormously.

At first, she looked on it as occasional sex with some career-enhancing benefits for her; an age-old *quid pro quo* between a powerful man and a realistic woman on her own. But then the infamous "slippery slope" came into play ... the process with the deceptively simple first step that – once taken – precipitates a long and involuntary downward slide.

One could argue that her first step onto that slope was that very affair with Robert Radner. But that had been going on for so long now with so much inertia built into it that she did not view it as anything so dramatic. They had been occasional lovers for over fifteen years, spanning the last few years of her marriage to Cooper and both of Robert's ill-starred marriages. It had been entirely clandestine, which suited both of them. Even after Edith died, neither of them sought to go beyond their longstanding arrangement.

The real first step – her last and best chance to retain her sense of being in control -- was her silence about Charles Hicks. Through her closeness to Robert, she became aware that Hicks – a city official -- was taking bribes from Robert to facilitate real estate deals. She found it easy to overlook such banal corruption, especially when her own commissions were involved. And once she was on the slope, it made it easier – not easy, but easier – to not question Robert about bothersome details when Hicks conveniently committed suicide.

But the really difficult act of remaining silent and the confirmation of how far she had slid was her never-ending internal dialogue about that night in the rainstorm five years ago. It was a conversation with herself that never went anywhere.

Robert said, "Wait for me, no matter what." And I did, in that upstairs bedroom with the ugly four-poster bed, even when the lights went out. And when he finally came, carrying a flashlight whose batteries promptly expired, he said, "Don't worry about Edith. I'm quite sure that she won't bother us."

When he asked her to witness Edith's signature on the Conservancy document with the revised language, she did so without a qualm. She had reached the bottom of the slope.

Coffee Shop Advice

Cooper sat in his car looking at the McKay house, but thinking about Natalie and their early days together. After five minutes, he literally shook himself and called Dmitri. They agreed to meet at a local coffee shop, one that had so far survived the Starbucks invasion. Cooper got there first and was standing in line when Dmitri arrived.

"Hi. Can I buy you a donut? All cops eat donuts, don't they?"

Dimitri didn't even smile. "That's really lame. You need to brush up on cop humor. You've been a civilian too long; things have changed. Maybe catch some of the new TV crime shows if you want to know how real cops talk. But you can buy me a large black coffee with extra cream if you want to."

Cooper wondered if the "real cops" that Dmitri referred to would have picked up any auras and emanations from the McKay estate. He decided not to ask Dmitri.

They sat outside at a tiny table on the sidewalk. They were silent long enough that it became uncomfortable, and it made Dmitri's opening comment seem particularly important.

"I'm glad you called. It's really good to see you again."

Cooper did not understand either the psychology or the physiology involved, but he was suddenly quite aware that he had a lump in his throat.

Damn! He thought. *I'm becoming pathetic!*

He didn't change the tone, however, but said, "Me too. I've missed you."

Both men realized that something significant had just occurred and both knew that it was not for further discussion. To cover the pause, each played with his coffee cup, sliding it around in little circles on the tabletop while avoiding eye contact. The table was small enough that each was quickly aware of the other's discomfort.

Cooper cleared his throat. "You probably already know that I'm working for Simon Radner. I don't know exactly what I'll be doing for him, but it means you and I may have some conflicting interests from time to time."

Dmitri grinned broadly. "I already heard about your new job. And if we have – how did you put it, 'conflicting interests' – I think I can deal with them OK, being an officer of the law and all that stuff that you're not. And if those interests get too conflicted, I'll even send you some good books to read in jail. Have you read the new history of the German Army's experience at Stalingrad? It's particularly instructive about the perils of arrogance."

Cooper flashed back to his early times with Dmitri, to the constant surprises as a seriously disenchanted ex-Soviet cop slowly revealed himself layer-by-layer. He surprised himself with how easily he responded in the old way, "Funny how your literary recommendations always have the Russians as the good guys! I'm surprised that you left Russia!"

"It's easy to be the good guy if the villain is Hitler. And I didn't leave Russia; Russia left me."

Both men smiled. Cooper sighed audibly and changed the subject. "Actually, my reading has been about local history. I've been going through the archives on the McKay drowning five years ago."

Dmitri grimaced. "Instructive, no? Particularly if you're interested in police procedurals. And it wasn't a drowning."

"The cops did everything that was called for," Cooper commented. "I don't see anything else that you could have done … other than to reroute the river and excavate the river banks."

Dmitri was instantly dismissive. "Thanks. Tell that to the killer who's had five years to walk around free."

"Not your fault," said Cooper. "In any case, you have a truly fascinating cast of characters and overlapping motives."

"If you've read through the public stuff, then I'm not telling you anything that you don't know." Dmitri then recited, in his press conference voice, "Simon Radner is a person of interest, but not the only one. We're awaiting lab reports and some other investigative outcomes that will give us more to go on."

Cooper smiled to let him know that he appreciated his unhelpful response and quickly asked, "Some really ancient history: What about the death of Rachel Radner seven years before Edith? Same husband, same location, same 'accidental' conclusion ... That's an awful lot of sameness. Kinda pushes the envelope as to coincidences!"

Dmitri was shaking his head even before Cooper finished talking. "That's not even a starter. The newspapers love the angle, but there's no motive and no evidence to suggest Rachel's death was anything but a slip and fall. Sometimes an accident is just an accident, even for homicide cops."

He continued, but in a different tone, as though faintly depressed, "Between us, and absolutely off-the-record, I think Simon Radner is guilty as hell. If I were him, I'd be worried."

Cooper said, "One of the puzzles is that he doesn't seem all that worried. He's got himself a lawyer, but that's about it."

He paused, and then went on in a carefully neutral voice, "I did meet with her – Pastore – and I agree with you; she's not the same person that put you and me through the departmental grinder."

Dmitri smiled and winked, and Cooper remembered how good Dmitri was at picking up nuances and finding the hidden meanings when they were interviewing witnesses or suspects. Dmitri said, "Methinks I detect an extra-legal interest?"

Cooper said, "I'll assume that's a rhetorical question. But she does make an impact."

"Yes, she does. And, by the way, she's been through a grinder of her own for the last few years. Cosmic justice for what she did to us, maybe?"

"I don't think so. We had it coming. And, in any case, cosmic justice is beyond my pay grade. I'm still struggling with the terrestrial kind."

They talked for about twenty minutes, until their coffee was cold. Cooper filled Dmitri in on what he'd been doing, soon realizing – as he listened to himself – that he had little of interest to offer the police. And he knew that Dmitri wouldn't share key details of his investigation. They agreed to keep in touch and Dmitri left, taking his cup of cold coffee with him.

Cooper sat, watching the pedestrians pass by and feeling like a tourist in town for the first time, steadily more depressed. *All these people, but no one I know. Even though I lived in this town for twenty years. One big alcohol-soaked blank spot!* He looked at his watch and thought about his options for the rest of the day.

Quit kidding yourself! You know what you're going to do. He finished his coffee and walked the four blocks to Ellen Pastore's office. He was amused to discover that he was nervous about seeing her again.

A Roving Interview

Pastore's office was in a downtown office building, not the usual location for a profession that preferred proximity to the courthouse and its spawn –the bail bondsmen, pawn shops and check-cashing storefronts that sold their services to customers with little time or flexibility. Her office was one of several on the third floor, between a CPA firm and an insurance agent. The door was open, so Cooper walked in and found himself in a small anteroom with an unattended receptionist's desk. There were two other offices, each visible through the glass wall running the length of the corridor. One office was vacant, but was clearly a working office, showing a large desk piled high with papers and a wall full of weighty-looking legal books. The other was a conference room, holding a table with eight chairs and whiteboards on the facing walls. Ellen was at the head of the table, talking to two men and a woman seated around the table. She saw him, pointed to her watch and held up five fingers.

The meeting ended within the next few minutes and everyone except Ellen left. She waved Cooper into the conference room, staying in her seat. He took the chair directly opposite her, across the table. There was some kind of complex multicolored diagram sketched on the whiteboard behind her. It looked like an elaborate decision tree with forked branches going off in different directions. At the end of one of the branches, in red ink, underlined for emphasis, was the word "Acquittal!" Cooper wondered what was at the end of the other unlabeled branches.

She saw him looking at the board, and said, "Clients don't like hearing about outcomes, options and probabilities. A picture keeps them focused on what matters. Helps them appreciate the difference between hopes and forecasts."

Cooper thought about that difference, and decided that what she had said pretty well described his own ambiguous reasons for sitting there. He wondered if he could even begin to diagram his motivations for being there and what words or phrases would be at the end points of the various branches.

He asked, "Do you suppose the DA is drawing pictures too?"

She smiled, but quickly became grim. "I hope so. It would get rid of a lot of the posturing and bluster ... and the plea bargaining would work a lot better than the present crap shoot!"

Cooper again glimpsed a strong sense of right and wrong just beneath the surface, and something in her tone reminded him of Dmitri's hint that she had been through some serious personal troubles.

Pastore said, "Look, I've only got a few minutes. There's a hearing I have to get to."

"I understand. And I have no claim on your time. I should have called for an appointment. But I was downtown anyway so --"

She interrupted. "No problem. What can I do?"

Cooper paused, and then went on, "Two things, I hope. One easy, one not so easy."

"Make my day. What's the easy one? Maybe I'll actually be able to point to some one tangible achievement today."

Cooper said, "It's pretty simple. Hire me as your official assistant for the McKay case. If I'm on your payroll, we can use 'attorney-client privilege' in the event I learn something harmful to Simon's defense."

She nodded, "That is easy. In fact, it's already been done. I drew it up as a temporary project assignment as soon as Simon told me he was going to talk to you. I'm not sure how well it will stand up if the cops really want to get at you, but it's worth a try. What's the not-so-easy one?"

Cooper hesitated, suddenly realizing that he had no idea what he was going to say next. *Great planning, genius!* But she bailed him out. As he ran through some possible lines, she stood up and said, "Look. I can't be late for this hearing. It shouldn't take long. Why don't you ride over to the courthouse with me and we can probably finish this on the way?"

She took a briefcase from her office and they went down to the garage. It was late afternoon and the elevator was half filled with suburban types on their way home, so they didn't talk. Cooper spent the time in the elevator speculating about what kind of car she would drive. He had decided *foreign, sporty, and relatively expensive* without analyzing his rationale. They walked directly to the far corner of the garage and Cooper thought, *Zero out of three! My profound understanding of women is evident once more!* The vehicle was a seven-year-old Ford Bronco.

She drove aggressively through the heavy traffic. *No surprise there!* Cooper asked her about the obvious changes in the downtown area since he had lived and worked there, and they spent the travel time lamenting the gentrification of the old neighborhoods. They seemed to share nostalgic feelings for brownstones and corner grocery stores.

She borrowed four quarters from Cooper for the parking meter at the courthouse. Looking at her watch and doing some inner calculation that might have been about either her schedule or Cooper, she said, "I still haven't heard the 'not-so-easy' thing that you wanted to talk about. This thing I've got should be quick... maybe 30 minutes or so. There's a coffee shop where you can hang out, and we could continue this if you like." Her voice rose on the last phrase, making it a question and leaving the decision up to Cooper.

Cooper looked at his watch as if he had complex scheduling issues to be worked out before deciding. He couldn't help laughing at himself inwardly, at how badly he wanted to impress this woman!

He said, furrowing his brow and pursing his lips for added credibility, "I think that can work. I'll wait for you in the coffee shop."

She turned and took the steps into the courthouse two at a time. He took a minute to try an impromptu call to Dmitri, but hung up without leaving a message when routed to the answering service. He thought briefly about paying a visit; he was only three floors up. *Marcus is up there too. Maybe drop in… say hello?*

It didn't take long for him to recognize what a bad idea that was. Instead, he headed across the cavernous lobby of the courthouse toward the coffee shop, but was stopped by the electronic board that displayed the different courtrooms and their cases. He wondered which one was hers.

That turned out to be easy – Courtroom 110 was hosting *Pastore v. Pastore* at four o'clock. Ellen's hearing was going to feature her as principal, not as an attorney!

He stood looking at the board for a full two minutes, weighing the risks … the coffee shop or the courtroom?

Cooper looked through the small porthole in the doorway to see a mostly empty courtroom, perhaps seven or eight people at the front of the courtroom, all seated in front of a judge in street clothes. A dozen or so spectators were scattered around the large room, but none of them seemed particularly interested in what was going on. As unobtrusively as he could, he slid into a seat at the very rear of the room near a pillar. He felt guilty. This was clearly a breach of the casual contract that they had struck. *I told her, "I'll wait for you in the coffee shop."* Worse, he wondered what he might be forfeiting for the sake of his curiosity, reminding him once more about that hypothetical decision tree and the missing labels on the endpoints.

For the next thirty minutes, he witnessed the dispassionate legal process being used with devastating effect against Ellen Pastore.

The other Pastore was her ex-husband. *Even from a distance, they don't look like a compatible couple. They just don't go together.* Perhaps it was the adversarial courtroom setting or his own ambiguous feelings about her, but Cooper could not imagine the two of them together in a domestic setting. *I wonder what that means about me?*

The hearing was apparently one of several scheduled to deal with a series of motions the ex-husband had filed alleging professional misconduct on Ellen's part in her role as an advisor in some real estate joint venture or other. He was also seeking a million dollars for alleged damages. The discussion was highly legalistic, but as far as he could tell, each of the rulings was going against her, despite the arguments of Ellen's attorney.

Neither Pastore participated in the verbal arguments, but each was talking almost continuously with their respective attorneys. Cooper imagined that he could detect the cumulative weight of the unfavorable rulings by Ellen Pastore's body language. By the time the judge was checking his calendar to set the date for a continuation of the hearing, Ellen was sitting slumped in her chair, silent.

Cooper quickly left his seat and the courtroom. He did not think that Ellen had seen him in the courtroom. The coffee shop was across the lobby, with only a few scattered customers at the tables. *I still have the option ... take the easy way out.* But then he realized that he didn't have a choice, that his initial decision to go to her office was an implicit contract with himself; a contract with vague terms but still one with a strict mandate for honesty.

He waited for her just outside the courtroom door. She came out within a couple of minutes, walking fast with her head down. When he stepped out in front of her, she stopped, glanced at the coffee shop, and then looked accusingly at him. The first thing she said was, "You saw that?"

"Yes. It was pretty brutal." He paused, and then added, "I feel like a voyeur. I wouldn't have gone in there if I had known what was going on. I'm sorry."

She looked directly at him with a hard stare that had the barest hint of curiosity. "You could have gone into the coffee shop and pretended that you had been there the whole time."

"I already feel crummy for watching. That would have made me feel a lot worse."

"Join the crowd," she said, and then, "That bastard!" with a vehemence that surprised Cooper. And again, "That goddam bastard!" Cooper saw the glint of tears and the white-knuckled clenched fists gripping her briefcase.

He touched her arm, feeling the rigid muscles. "I can't fix it, but I know some emotional first aid. How about a drink?"

He drove her Bronco while she sat wordless. He took her to his favorite bar. It was close, a half-mile from the courthouse; a place with a lot of oak, greenery and dark corners. She ordered a glass of Chardonnay and he got his usual coffee. After the first sip, she began talking and didn't stop for almost an hour.

Her story had sub-plots, gaps and digressions. And it circled around on itself a couple of times, so that Cooper knew that this was the first time she had told this story from start to finish. The story itself was an ancient one. It had villains, unreasonable hopes and poor judgment. It was about the disappearance of love, leaving a void for lesser emotions to fill. A bitter divorce featuring scorched earth tactics. A vengeful ex-husband using an excess of power and money to humiliate.

When she stopped, she seemed exhausted. Cooper wasn't sure that she knew he was even there at that particular moment.

After a moment, he spoke, very softly. "Once, in a high school English class, I remember being asked to use the word 'catharsis' in a sentence … but I didn't know what it meant then."

Ellen shook her head wonderingly. "You said emotional first aid. That was more like major surgery!"

Cooper shrugged. "Blame it on the Chardonnay. That's one of the reasons why I quit drinking."

And then he started talking. About himself. At first, he told himself that it was for her sake; so that her self-consciousness might be diminished and the therapy wouldn't seem so one-sided. After awhile, he knew that he was talking for himself, out of an enormous need that this woman had unloosed.

He talked about people and failures that he thought were long forgotten or at least off-limits for discussion. About his family, Dmitri and Marcus. About booze and a messed-up marriage. About Emily and Danielle and his fear of being alone.

About the horror of those falling dots on September 11. He talked about everything except why he had gone to her office this afternoon.

Somewhere during his monologue, the waiter came by and she ordered another glass of wine. And he resumed talking.

When he stopped, each of them sat unnaturally still, acutely aware that whatever was said next would be hugely important. The silence continued for what seemed a long time.

She started to speak, stopped and cleared her throat. Cooper knew that she had changed her mind about what to say. What she finally said was, "Well, what is this 'not-so-easy' request that we've been putting off for the last couple of hours?"

Cooper stared over Ellen's shoulder and thought about all of the possible responses he could make – the cowardly, the flip, the lies, the cautious requests, and still others. The silence lasted long enough that he realized that anything but the truth would sound like what it was – a lie – so he simply said, "There really isn't one. I thought I would just make up some excuse for dropping in on you. I just wanted to see you again." And he literally held his breath.

Ellen sat very quietly, slowly turning the stem of her wine glass, thinking. She was silent long enough that Cooper started breathing again and began imagining better phrasings for what he had just said, as if he could reset the clock and start over.

Then she leaned forward and said, "Catharsis? Wasn't that the name of a Greek general?"

He had no idea how to respond. Then she stood up, looking directly at Cooper. "Drive me home, will you? We'll find you a cab tomorrow morning."

Revised Possibilities

Days later, Cooper could recall only fragments of the twenty minutes between the bar and her condo. He drove slowly and deliberately, a self-inflicted discipline that reflected his need to make what was happening real, not just a continuation of a barroom therapy session.

Ellen sat on the passenger side, as far away as she could get from Cooper. They did not touch. She sat upright and still, with her hands in her lap. Other than giving directions, she said nothing and did not look at him. Cooper was nervous, afraid of the silence but even more afraid to risk a gesture or phrase that would alter whatever strange decision was driving her, somehow knowing that the silence was necessary to the transition that she had committed herself to.

But is it just an extended form of catharsis? Or something else? He decided that he could not possibly make that distinction. More importantly, he decided that he didn't care.

Once her front door closed behind them, Ellen took his hand and led him to her bedroom, stopping only to kick off her shoes.

They talked very little in the next several hours, as though they had exhausted their stock of words and stories. A new vocabulary came into play, involving sighs, moans, whispers. Other and more primitive senses drove out mere speech... touch, smell, vision. These hours were about sensation. They were about wants and needs, discovery, hunger, mutual pleasure, reciprocity, laughter, play, warmth and wetness, shadows and crevices, softness and pliability, the conforming of opposing surfaces ... the alternating of attack and retreat, of slowness and incredible haste.

Somewhere during the night, Cooper remembers thinking, *I was wrong. I don't want to be alone.*

Negotiations

Cooper slept, but not well; the kind of sleep where one's conscious worries are woven into what passes for dreams. Somewhere in the predawn darkness, he began to analyze what had happened since he walked into Ellen's office late yesterday afternoon. His first and strongest instincts were skeptical, downplaying what he really wanted to believe.

You know better than to think this is about any kind of real biochemistry. At best, it's a temporary and purely coincidental convergence of two people's needs. Maybe excusable as harmless escapism practiced by consenting adults.

And at worst? She wouldn't have looked twice at you if her self-esteem hadn't been shredded in that courtroom! And that barroom therapy session? Face it. You wanted to get her into bed, and that was the quickest way!

But then there was the other voice, the one that articulated what he hoped for, not what he feared. *This is special. It doesn't matter what caused it. Accept it. See where it goes.*

Sometime shortly after it was light, Ellen's phone began to ring at about ten minute intervals. She answered none of the calls. And there was no mention of a cab to take Cooper home. Somewhere around nine in the morning, they showered together, still reluctant to talk much, as though ordinary conversation would jeopardize something as valuable as it was fragile.

They dressed. Ellen made coffee and they sat facing one another over her granite kitchen counter. She looked at Cooper, smiled and said "Wow!"

He grinned. "I've been trying to think of something really eloquent to say, something that would do partial justice to what just happened to me."

"And ...?"

"'Wow!' is as close as I can get. But you say it so much better than I can."

She wrinkled her brow and said, "Well, I guess 'Wow' could be termed 'eloquent' ... if you're writing for comic strips!"

Cooper thought about his warring voices in the darkness of the bedroom and cursed himself for his introspection. He reached for her hand and put on his most serious expression. *Why can't I leave it alone? Good things can happen to people like us, can't they?*

"Ellen. I want ... I need to -- "

She interrupted. "No. You're wrong about that. You neither want nor do you need to say what you're about to say."

"Am I that transparent?"

"I used to be a prosecutor, remember? I can recognize guilt from a mile away in all of its forms, and you're a lot closer than a mile."

"I feel like a looter in a flood zone. I lied to you, spied on you, --"

"And then you listened to me ... really listened. And let me ravage you ... twice, as I recall."

"It seemed fairly collaborative to me."

"And that's the takeaway for this conversation. Whatever happened was unequivocally mutual. And, whatever it was ... or is ... I want to see where it goes."

She put her hand on top of his and said in her most businesslike tone, "Now. Let's talk about ordinary things, like any other perfectly ordinary couple who just had mind-numbing sex on their first date."

Cooper felt like he'd been exonerated from a crime that only he knew he had committed. He said the first thing that came into his mind.

"Tell me about that courtroom scene. Your ex-husband seemed determined to humiliate you."

"His name's Anthony and he has a hard time dealing with rejection. This is his way of recovering his manhood."

"Can he hurt you?"

She paused, clearly thinking about his question. "There's a chance that he could make me look a little bit unprofessional. And cost my insurance company a couple of hundred thousand dollars."

"Why? What's he got to work with?"

She began talking, sounding like someone who has told an unpleasant story too many times. "It goes back a few years. I was active on two not-for-profit agencies. One was the family foundation that Edith McKay set up to preserve the Riverbend property. The other was as an advisory member of the Planning Commission for the city. I gave a lot of legal advice to both groups. Tony is part of a syndicate of Stanton VIP's that want to develop the Riverbend property. They thought they had a deal with her father, but she changed his mind.

"They fought with Edith since the day she showed up back in town. Then when she died, I sort of became the spokesperson for what Edith was trying to do with Riverbend. That made Tony and me business enemies as well as just hating each other. He's asserting – by filing a lawsuit – that I had a conflict of interest because of being involved in both boards… that my failure to disclose it and recuse myself from decision-making was a violation of professional standards."

"Sounds flimsy to me."

"It is. But he can drag it out in court – and in the newspapers – for several months. What you saw yesterday was the third preliminary hearing. It's war by attrition, much more about doing damage than winning."

Cooper half-registered what she was saying. The other part of his brain was alternating between two puzzles. One – the obvious one – was how she could have been married to such an apparent loser. It was easy to stay silent on that one because he recognized that this was the wrong time and place – and he was probably the wrong person – to ask such a question. The other nagging puzzle was that he knew he had come across the name "Anthony Pastore" somewhere in his past life. It was a coincidence that he was determined to pursue, but he didn't think that asking Ellen was the best way.

His problem was solved when the phone rang again. She glanced at the caller ID, then at Cooper and said, "Time to earn my keep. That's Dmitri calling."

She answered "Pastore," listened without interrupting for two minutes, and then hung up after a simple "Yes. I understand." She looked at Cooper and said, "We've run out of time. I wonder why Dmitri waited so long?"

She called Simon at his office, using the speakerphone so that Cooper could listen.

"Simon? It's Ellen. The Stanton police want to interview you. With the DA sitting in. They won't tell me what they want, but I suspect that their intent is to cover some of the same old ground – your relationship to Edith, what she said to you that night, your handling of the hammer, etc. I also think there's about an 80/20 chance that they'll arrest you at the end of the interview and immediately present a search warrant for your home, office, computer, car, etc."

Simon said, "Not much of a surprise, is it?"

"I'm surprised only that it's taken them this long." Ellen responded. "You're still their best bet, and they're getting some heat from the politicians and the press to show some progress."

She paused and then said in a different tone, "I have some inside sources in the DA's office and they tell me that she is especially eager to get you in court. You sure you don't want to tell me what's going on with her?"

There was a long silence, then Simon said, "Yes, I'm sure. That I don't want to tell you. But I will tell you that she's only damaging her own case."

Ellen was abrupt. "That's great, but I'm the one that has to deal with her in court. And not just in your case."

"I promise you that the hostility is for me only. You're just the momentary surrogate."

Before she could say anything, he asked, "If they want to 'interview' me, can we do it with Nathaniel and Maria present? And you should try to get Cooper to hang around as well."

"I can ask, but Martine and Dmitri can and will dictate who they're going to talk to and in what order. And I can promise you that whatever they decide, it will be one-on-one sessions. But, even if they agree to having all of you in the vicinity, are you sure you want the whole bunch around?"

Simon said, "Ellen, you know that we're not exactly the All-American family. We've got pathologies oozing out in every direction. This may be the only way we'll be able to talk about certain things that need to be talked about. And frankly, I'd rather be there to hear what they have to say to Dmitri."

Ellen pushed the "mute" button and said to Cooper, "Simon's playing games with us again. He needs a Marriage & Family Counselor at least as much as he needs an attorney!"

She released the mute button and said to Simon, "You're the boss, but I think you need to pay more attention to your own interests. You do know the sentencing guidelines for premeditated murder in this state, don't you?"

Simon simply said, "I'll see you at the so-called interview. Let me know when and where."

The phone call changed the atmosphere in Ellen's kitchen. When she hung up, he reached across the counter and took her hand. She smiled; sadly, he thought. Then she brightened, and said, "OK. I'm not sure exactly what happened during the last twelve hours. But why don't you work on articulating the word 'Wow', and we can check your work later this evening? I've got to work on prepping the various Radner's for a hostile interview. Should be an interesting task."

Cooper merely said "OK," but was already planning his next project. *I have my own interesting task to work on. Let's think of it as "The Tony Project."*

Cops Reminiscing

Cooper, like most cops, had an inbred and deep-seated distrust of coincidence, especially when asserted by those with a vested interest in a particular outcome. Whether it was a stockbroker accused of insider trading or a killer seeking to get a first-degree murder charge reduced to manslaughter, the invocation of "chance" as a mitigating circumstance invariably repelled him.

The stockbroker's, "I was just unlucky. The stocks always went down after I bought them." Or the killer's, "He hit his head on the curb. I didn't mean to kill him." These were invocations of superstition; appeals to the jury's belief in luck, or fate, or coincidence. They were an easy way to get to the defense attorney's holy grail – a "reasonable doubt."

The coincidence that was presently troubling him was the name "Pastore," as in Ellen's ex. It had been important to him at some point in his past life, for reasons he could not recall.

He called Dmitri. *It's interesting how I always think of him when some question comes up about my personal history.*

"Dmitri. I've come across a name from our common past, but I'm fuzzy on the details."

"Cognitively speaking, you were in a fuzzy state for most of that past life. The only proper names you could be trusted to recall were Stolichnaya and Absolut."

Cooper was surprised by the sudden onset of wistfulness that Dmitri triggered. He said, "My best and truest friends, for a long time." And then he surprised himself by asking, "Tell me, do you miss them?"

There was a long silence with only a very faint hum from the phone line, long enough that Cooper regretted asking the question. When Dmitri spoke, it was in a very tentative voice, as though reassembling an obscure memory out of hard-to-find bits and pieces.

"Do you know that an ordinary glass of water looks exactly the same as a glass of vodka? The same clarity and impression of perfect coldness ... And do you know that I do not drink water today? Only those liquids with distinctive colors ... lemonade, tea, Coke..."

It was as if Dmitri's words had activated some dormant video in his brain. Suddenly, he was seeing the two of them sitting side-by-side in a bar. The video was in full color, apparently taken from their left, showing them in profile. They were both slouched – as much as you could on a barstool -- each staring into the half-full glass of clear liquid in front of them. He recognized the time and place. They had just finished a systematic beating of the insurance agent who had tried to bribe them. *We were drunk that day, long before we went into that bar.*

The video stopped abruptly when Dmitri loudly cleared his throat and then went on in a very different and brusque tone. "You said something about a name from the past?"

"Pastore. Not Ellen, but Anthony. Didn't we come across him in the line of business?"

"Yep. We surely did. He went by 'Tony' then. Somewhere in the latter 1990's, when we were impersonating sober police officers and investigating a series of arson incidents at the homes of members of the construction workers union. Somebody's grandmother died in one of the fires."

"What did that have to do with Tony?"

"He ran a so-called 'security company' that had mob connections. They had a lock on the commercial construction market in Stanton. Among other things, Tony kept their large corporate customers secure from union organizers. Some of his tactics were a little harsh. Baseball bats instead of injunctions, the occasional fire, that sort of thing."

"I vaguely remember. Did we do any good?"

"He laughed at us. So I guess you could say we helped him develop a sense of humor. He had more and better lawyers than we did. Another lost cause for the forces of justice."

Dmitri's tone changed again, featuring a definite note of suspicion. "And you care about Tony – now know as Anthony - - because …?"

"I watched him assault his ex-wife – verbally and quite legally, without leaving any visible marks – in court the other day. It made me mad."

"This is the same ex-wife that recently hired you, I presume? Our mutual friend Ellen?"

When Cooper didn't respond, Dmitri continued talking to himself. "But she didn't hire you to carry on some quixotic quest on her behalf. As I recall, the job had to do with Simon Radner. So it must be that you have decided to become personally involved, probably without her knowing about – or approving of -- your view of her as damsel-in-distress -- "

Cooper interrupted, with more heat than he had intended. "Y'know, Dmitri. I'm not one of your AA sponsorees. I can manage my own inner life."

Dmitri's silence was profound, and spoke volumes about what he thought about Cooper's belief in his own powers.

He sighed. "Cooper, give me some credit. What's going on between you and Ellen is quite apparent to anyone with eyes and ears, let alone to a highly trained police investigator such as me. And, speaking both as your friend and as an admirer of Ms. Pastore, I'm all for it. I even envy you. But I'm not going to aid and abet a vendetta against ex-husbands."

Cooper smiled as he listened. *It must be tough for Dmitri – a hopeless romantic saddled with a policeman's rulebook! Let's make it real easy for him.*

He said, "As a famous TV detective used to say, 'Just the facts, ma'am'. What can you tell me about the present-day Tony, aka Anthony?"

A very audible sigh came from Dmitri. "He's quite rich and therefore respectable. Runs something called the Riverfront Development Company. Rumor has it that he gets what he wants, Ellen being a notable exception to that rule. Definitely not someone you want to have mad at you."

"Is he legitimate these days? No more mob connections?"

"Officially, all I can tell you is that the police department has no official interest in either Mr. Pastore or his company."

"How about 'unofficially'?"

"That's a different – and confidential, as in 'you didn't hear it from me' – story. He cuts a lot of corners.... Almost always involved in contract disputes and civil litigation. Uses lawyers like the mob uses hit men. But its all been civil stuff. No criminal allegations."

"It's interesting that his name came up in the context of the Edith McKay estate."

"Not if you were up on your Stanton history. Riverbend – the McKay property – has been Tony's fixation for the last decade. Along with a lot of other people who wear three-piece suits to work, he wants to develop it. Edith's father James was negotiating with some of our city fathers about the sale when she came home again and promptly squelched the deal. Some of our citizens who have watched too much TV think that Tony wanted to marry Ellen because she was Edith's friend and would give him an inside track."

"Did it work?"

"Ask Ellen. But rather the opposite, I think. I'm a hopeless romantic – as you know – so I choose to believe that she divorced him because of his bad hair and undesirable character traits."

Cooper was pleased that Dmitri shared his views of Anthony Pastore's compatibility with Ellen. He said, "Both you and Simon told me that the DA considered the possibility that the Stanton business interests would have liked to have Edith taken out of the picture. Was Tony considered a suspect five years ago?"

"We're still talking unofficially, remember? *Unofficially*, I can tell you that we looked at Tony. Very closely. He had the right connections to arrange such things and had a strong financial incentive. Nothing came of it at the time. No evidence, just speculation. And nothing in the last few weeks has changed that view."

"Was he at the party? The night that McKay was killed?"

"Yes, but so was everybody else that mattered in Stanton. That's our problem. We've got a whole gaggle of equally likely suspects."

"Thanks Dmitri. And I take back what I said about my ability to manage my inner life. I need some good advice."

"OK, then here's two starter pieces of good advice. Don't mess around with Tony Pastore or he'll make your life miserable. Maybe even shorten it. And hang on to Ellen. She's the real goods."

Cooper thought, *I don't think I can do the latter without the former,* but didn't say anything.

Dmitri hung up, leaving Cooper with a dial tone and a growing determination to ignore the first part of his advice. He was going to make Tony a special project.

Encounter With a Citizen

Cooper spent most of the next day either online or in the Civil Records Office.   Armed with that research, he spent another day talking to people who had crossed paths with Pastore during his time in Stanton.   At the end of that time, he knew a great deal more about Tony Pastore.   He began to think of the public narrative as a morality play, as if Horatio Alger had been commissioned to write a biography of Al Capone.

Tony seemed to exist at three distinct levels.   There was Tony the upstanding citizen, as made visible in the public record.   In this role, he gave lavish amounts of money to civic projects – the theatre company, hospitals, churches, the policeman's ball, homeless shelters.   It was always a highly publicized gift.   He appeared in a lot of society page photos wearing a tuxedo and a fixed grin.   He was being touted as "Man of the Year" by local shills.

The next and overlapping layer was Tony the businessman/developer.   He began with strip malls and freestanding office buildings, buying up distressed properties at fire sale prices, then rehabbing them and selling them back into the market at marked-up prices. Some of the disgruntled sellers hinted that he fomented the distress in the first place and then profited from it.   Then he began developing or redeveloping riverfront property, usually by quietly arranging for rezoning decisions that permitted higher densities and commercial uses. The projects were always joint ventures and his partners were always prominent business figures in Stanton, including Robert Radner.

There were whispers about bribes and corruption, but nothing stuck.   Some city commissioners retired early and a member of the Planning Commission committed suicide when served with a subpoena, but Tony waltzed through it all.

Then, like the classic robber barons of the nineteenth century, Tony moved beyond strong-arm tactics and outright bribes to "respectable" methods, using an army of lawyers and covert lobbyists to get what he wanted. These days, Tony was spending most of his entrepreneurial energy on getting and developing the Riverbend property.

Despite himself, Cooper was impressed with both the speed of Tony's ascent and his uncanny knowledge of where and when to take advantage of Stanton's rapidly changing sub-markets. He seemed to know who was vulnerable, which properties were up for rezoning, where the new highways were going to go. Briefly, Cooper began to think of Tony as some kind of criminal genius, but finally decided he was just lucky. That judgment was helped by his need to believe that Tony was not all that smart.

Then there was the third level, the least visible and most interesting one – Tony the real person. Cooper assembled a composite profile from the society pages, gossip columns and legal depositions that were in the public record. And then filled in that profile from his conversations with the spectrum of ordinary people willing to talk about Tony, ranging from an ex-partner to caddies, waitresses and his lawn service crew.

It was not a flattering picture. In person, Anthony Pastore was a volatile combination of insecurity and power. He abused those who had no recourse but to smile and take it – the caddies, waitresses, and parking attendants. He was charming to his social peers, but was quick to imagine condescension and would fly into monumental rages that – so far – were passed off as quirks, forgivable due to his social position and our hard-to-understand tolerance for others who have more money than we do.

In short, Cooper's impression was that Tony was a highly insecure sociopath with great connections.

Cooper's research was complicated by his commitment to keep Ellen unaware of his interest. It would have been much easier to just ask her, the ex-wife. She could have filled in some of the glaring gaps in his research; for example, his life prior to

Stanton. Cooper found it particularly interesting that the narrative began when Tony showed up in Stanton fifteen years ago. There was virtually nothing known about the first twenty-five years of his life.

He dialed Dmitri once more, getting a very terse response. "No more about Pastore. You're on your own."

"Just one question. When you and I leaned on him about those arson incidents, he was new in town. Where did he come from? How did he get started here?"

"That's two questions. San Francisco. Uncle Vinnie. Now leave me alone!" And he hung up.

Uncle Vinnie? Cooper sat looking at the phone, remembering fragments from an arson investigation in the late 1990's. Then he began dialing, arranging for a flight to San Francisco that afternoon.

It took two days in San Francisco, most of it spent tracking down and talking to old men with too much time on their hands and with nothing to lose by talking about a past that – for most of them – seemed more attractive than the present. For some of them, he was a journalist doing a feature on Tony Pastore. For others, he played a lawyer untangling a complex inheritance. And for some, he was himself -- a man on a quest, in defense of a woman that he cared for. He was surprised at first by the candor and willingness to talk, but soon recognized that Pastore's hometown legacy was built around broken promises and bitterness. The term *son-of-a-bitch* was used frequently.

The few that would not talk to him about Tony mentioned "Uncle Vinnie" as the reason for their reluctance. A couple of hours on the internet reading through old editions of the San Francisco Chronicle provided ample information about Uncle Vinnie. The most recent item was an obituary that ran for half a page. It told him that the late Vincent Capricio had been a second-tier mafia figure, one of the more vicious ones. The obit also informed him that Vinnie had a large and sprawling family, including a nephew named Anthony Pastore.

At the end of the two days, Cooper felt like an archeologist at the end of a long dig, and thought he finally understood Tony Pastore. He went home to put that knowledge to good use.

He called Tony at his office on a Monday morning, using the direct number that he found in Ellen's rolodex. It was a very brief conversation.

"This is Anthony Pastore."

"My name is Cooper. I'd like to meet and talk with you about some things."

"Cooper? You're the one who's screwing my wife. Why should I talk with you?"

That's interesting. He knows about me and Ellen. Is he having her watched? OK, that simplifies things.

"She's not your wife. And you should talk to me because it's in your best interest to do so."

"Fuck you!" And he hung up.

Cooper pictured him slamming the phone down, but knew that he was envisioning what he wanted to happen rather than any reality.

From his research, he knew that Tony played golf every Monday afternoon, so he went to his country club, driving up the long tree-lined drive to a gatehouse. When he said, "I'm a guest of Mr. Pastore's," he noted with interest that the gatekeeper's expression changed from a professional disinterest to wariness. Once inside, he waited in the bar where he could see the entrance to the men's locker room.

When he saw Pastore go in, he followed him to his locker and sat down at the far end of the plain wooden bench in the alcove, boxing Pastore in as he began to change clothes. They were alone and Pastore paid no attention to him until Cooper's stare became so obvious that it couldn't be ignored.

"Hey man! You lost?"

"My name is Cooper. I called you earlier. I'd still like to talk with you about some things."

Cooper watched closely and was disappointed when Tony's only reaction was to drop the false smile and replace it with a sneer so stereotyped that he must have practiced in front of a mirror.

"How's my wife? Does she still wear those black silk panties?"

"She's not your wife. You seem to have a hard time accepting that notion."

"No, what she is is a first-class bitch. Most women are interchangeable second-class bitches ... they all look alike when they take off their clothes and stand on their head. But Ellen, she's special ... and I'll treat her like she's special... so special that she'll wish she'd never thought of divorce."

Pastore turned away, like someone who really believed that he'd had the last word.

"Kind of like Lisa Capetta?"

That stopped Pastore. He looked closely at Cooper and the sneer slipped away, replaced by a calculating look, perhaps tinged by uncertainty. His eyes slid to the side of Cooper, looking for a way out, but he was standing in a cul-de-sac in his boxer shorts and Cooper was blocking the only exit. He reached into his locker for a pair of plaid Bermuda shorts.

Cooper continued in a conversational tone, as though the two of them were arranging the bets for the first tee. "Her acid burns are still there, even with all the facial surgery that Uncle Vinnie paid for. And she almost talks normally now. But she still isn't talking, especially about ex-husbands ... if you know what I mean. Oh! And that pink shirt doesn't go with that plaid. You OK? You seem distracted."

"Fuck you, asshole! Who let you in here? They'll regret it!"

"Regret it? Kind of like Alfredo?"

Tony's expression changed again, for the first time exhibiting a slight fearfulness. He sat down on the bench, still in his shorts.

"Let's see. Alfredo ... Wasn't he your youngest brother? Oh, yeah. He was the fifteen-year-old kid who told Lisa – your wife at the time – that he'd seen you in bed with her sister. The sister was fifteen too, as I recall. I saw Alfredo a couple of days ago. He still walks with a severe limp. Not surprising when you consider what a baseball bat can do to a kneecap. That surgery set Uncle Vinnie back a good bit too. Three operations, I think."

"Fuck you!"

But the expletive had no force behind it, becoming just a verbal placeholder while Tony was thinking of ways out of a conversation about his past. Cooper watched the rage build in Tony, starting somewhere behind his eyes and then radiating outward, forcing him to his feet in his incongruous white boxer shorts with little red cupid figures, his fists clenched, shouting at Cooper.

"Fuck you! I buy and sell little people like you every day. Fucking asshole! You'll learn! Just like they did! You can't fuck with me!"

Cooper watched the disintegration, thinking of ways to hasten and enlarge it. He wondered if there were others in the locker room, probably entranced by what they were hearing.

"Oh, but I can. I know things. Things that you don't want others to know about."

"Cocksucker! You and that cunt!" Now almost a full-throated scream, working himself into attack mode. He slammed his forearm repeatedly into his locker door, a resounding metallic crash that drowned out his ranting briefly.

Cooper wondered if the rage would trigger an attack. He thought not. Everything he knew about Tony pointed to an insecure little man who would operate in the dark.

Cooper played one more card. "Then there's Uncle Vinnie. I'm thinking of the headlines. 'Local tycoon funded by mobster' maybe. Something along those lines. Probably some sepia press photos of the checks he wrote to set you up here in Stanton. Stuff like that. The local papers will love it."

The rage subsided as quickly as it came, its place taken by a sly look. "Uncle Vinnie, huh? He'll kill you – very slowly -- if you bring him into it. You'll wish you were Lisa or Alfredo. They got off easy. In fact, I think I might place a call to Uncle Vinnie --"

"You'll need some special equipment. He died last month. I guess you didn't get the word, being somewhat estranged from the family ... Apparently, you weren't mentioned in the will."

Tony slumped back down on the bench, drained. Cooper stood up and turned to leave. Just one more nail to put in place. He held up the iPhone that had been in his hand throughout the encounter. He pressed a button and Tony's voice said, 'Hey man! You lost?'

Tony looked at the small black device with growing horror. "You taped this?! That's illegal! You can't use it!"

"It's not tape. Everything's digital these days. Amazing what high quality video and audio you get. And, yes, it is illegal. And, no, I can't use it in a court of law. But I can arrange for it to be posted on the internet. I met some people in San Francisco who would enjoy it, I think. Do you know the phrase 'go viral'?"

He watched Tony, thinking of evil and how it exists in such mundane forms. He felt dirty.

Tony stood, his mouth opening and closing, still holding the plaid Bermuda shorts in one hand.

Cooper took three steps forward, closing the distance between them. He put his hands on Tony's shoulders and spoke to him from a distance of about eight inches, speaking slowly, as though to someone unfamiliar with English.

"I expect you to drop your various lawsuits against Ellen. Take your time, but be sure to call your attorney anytime within the next hour."

Cooper turned to leave, but stopped and faced Tony. "If I find out that you've talked to her or done anything counter to her best interests, I will share this" – He showed Tony the phone – "with the world. I will also call upon you and express my displeasure in a more direct fashion."

And he left.

A Shooting

Ellen called the next day. When he saw the caller ID, he had a flash. *She's going to tell me – very surprised -- that Tony has dropped all of the legal actions against her.* But he was wrong.

"Dmitri called. He 'requested' an interview with Simon later today. He's agreed to meet him at his home and has agreed that Maria and Nathaniel can be somewhere nearby. He'll almost certainly talk to them as well, but separately."

"Shouldn't they have a lawyer as well as Simon?"

"Absolutely. But they don't. The whole family is nuts, in my opinion. Including Simon."

"When?"

"Four this afternoon. You can be there but strictly in the background. I don't think Dmitri liked the idea very much."

Ellen arrived at Simon's early. She wanted to try to prepare Nathaniel and Maria for what was likely to be a confrontational interview; maybe even talk them hiring their own lawyer. When she walked into the living room, Nathaniel was sitting in a soft upholstered chair near the window. Maria was in the other corner of the room, a relatively dark recess. She was wearing dark clothing and said nothing when Ellen entered. Ellen thought, *She's like something out of a Victorian novel ... a brooding presence.*

Ellen went to Nathaniel and said, without any preamble, "I'm not your attorney, but I wanted to caution you to be careful what you say with the cops in the room. It could work against your father."

Nathaniel just looked at her without any expression. Then he muttered quite audibly, "That would be a first ... me being able to actually have an impact on my father!"

Ellen stepped close to Nathaniel, leaned over him, and said very emphatically and distinctly, "Get over yourself! It's time to stop blaming him for what you've done to yourself, all by yourself and for yourself!"

Nathaniel shouted, "Fuck you!" and pushed Ellen away violently.

Ellen's response was instantaneous. She took Nathaniel's head between her two hands and spoke to him from inches away, fiercely, "I don't know what or who you care about. But don't you mess up other people's lives just so you can feel good about being a loser!"

She pulled back from him, swinging her arms as though trying to throw his head apart from his body. He was slung sideways in his chair, and stayed in that position. Ellen left the room, with only a glance at Maria, who was utterly still throughout this brief exchange, sitting motionless in the corner, her eyes intent on the other two.

Nathaniel, who is this woman? And why is she so close to you? What is she telling you? Why are you listening? What kind of trouble have you gotten into this time? I've told you about women. You need to be careful; never trust them. Why is she holding you like that? Why don't you make her go away? Make her stop!

Simon and Dmitri were in Simon's home office when Cooper came in, seated at a small conference table in the corner. The table surface was bare except for a black folio in front of Dmitri. Joan Martine was standing just outside the door of the study talking on her cell phone.

Cooper asked, "Where's Marcus? I thought he was coming too?"

Dmitri replied, "He's here … went off looking for the bathroom."

Simon stood and said, "I'll go get Ellen – my attorney – she's in talking with Nathaniel and Maria."

As Simon left, Cooper saw Ellen beckoning to him from the other doorway. When he approached her, she grabbed his sleeve, looked meaningfully at Dmitri still sitting at the table, whispered urgently – so softly he didn't understand what she said -- and pulled him into the darkened hallway, all the way to the entrance door.

Cooper remembered how close Ellen was, and how long the hallway seemed, dark at either end but with stripes of light from the several open and lighted rooms on either side of the hall. He remembered seeing the flash of light from the other end of the hall, and he could remember the incredibly loud simultaneous sound. But he could not – no matter how hard he tried – remember the impact of the bullet or falling.

Reconstruction of a Crime

The next day, Cooper remembered even less. One of the nurses told him that such memory loss is normal for trauma victims, even if the only damage is a cracked rib and some blood loss. Dmitri confirmed it by noting that he'd been shot twice during his Soviet career and couldn't remember any details at all.

The doctor had just left, a Chinese woman that – to Cooper – appeared to be about sixteen years old. However, that first impression was more than offset by her bedside manner, brusque in the extreme. She pulled the bandage off with one grand swipe and probed the edges of the ugly six-inch long groove in his side, not very gently.

"You're very lucky." She sounded disapproving, as though it was Cooper's fault that he had survived a gunshot wound. She put on a new and smaller bandage, scowling throughout the brief procedure.

"The bullet glanced off your rib. If it had continued on its original trajectory, several of your internal organs would be damaged. You can go home this afternoon. Try not to get shot again."

With that, she disconnected the IV, glared at him and flounced out of the room as though walking out on an abusive husband. She passed Ellen on her way into the room.

Ellen watched her go. "What did you do to that poor young thing?" She asked in an accusing tone.

Cooper thought about it. *It can't be anything I said, since I didn't say anything. And how come Ellen blames me for the woman's snit? It must be some kind of subliminal female bonding thing. No way I'm going there!*

He shrugged. "I think she was hoping for more of a medical challenge than I seem to offer her."

The coldness and austerity of the hospital room was lessened considerably by having Ellen sitting on the end of his bed. She was his second visitor of the day but his only source of information since being shot and tethered to an IV stand. Dmitri had stopped by earlier, but had been less than forthcoming. Not an unwarranted reticence, given that he had just arrested Cooper's employer for murder – one accomplished (Edith) and one attempted (Cooper).

Cooper sat cross-legged at the head of the bed, finally free from IV lines and facing Ellen in a matching posture at the foot of the bed. They looked as though they were about to play a chess match.

Cooper said, "OK. How about the old game of Twenty Questions?"

"Fair enough. But you may need more. A lot has happened."

"I'll try to stay focused. First question: I'm not dead?"

Ellen slapped at his foot. "You've just wasted one of your twenty questions!"

Cooper shook his head. "I remember so little about what happened yesterday that I feel like I'm in some other world. It was yesterday, wasn't it?"

"You're definitely not dead. And I'm glad. What's your next question?"

"OK. An even more personal one: Who shot me?"

"Dmitri says it was Simon. But I'm not so sure. And I don't think he can prove it."

Cooper looked puzzled. "Why not? The place was swarming with people, including two perfectly competent cops."

Ellen almost giggled. "It's like one of those Agatha Christie mysteries, with the Chief Inspector from Scotland Yard and all of the aristocratic tuxedo-clad suspects gathered in the drawing room – drinking sherry, of course -- when the lights fail and a shot rings out in the dark. A few seconds later, the lights come on to reveal Lord Throckbottom lying dead on the billiards table and the pistol on the floor nearby. No one knows who fired the shot!"

Cooper started to interrupt, but she said, "Just listen for a bit. It's not as absurd as it seems. Based on self-report and without any dissenting witnesses: Marcus was just coming out of the bathroom. Dmitri was sitting alone at the conference table in the den. Simon was looking for Maria, who actually was sitting alone in the living room. Nathaniel had just stormed into the kitchen. The DA -- Martine – was standing outside on the balcony to finish her cell phone call. You and I were in the hallway at one end. So, we've got lots of people moving around, but everybody happens to be on their own at the precise moment that you get shot."

"The shot is fired from the other end of the hallway, where the shooter has multiple choices of entry or exit. No one saw the shot fired except you, and all you saw was a muzzle flash. Everybody heard the shot and rushed into the hallway. Except Maria who just kept sitting in the dark. The whole crowd was hovering around you for thirty seconds before someone – Marcus, I think – said that the shooter might still be out there. That started a small stampede."

"What about the gun?"

"A Beretta, 38 caliber. It was dropped at the end of the hallway, one shot fired. It was legal, registered to Nathaniel. He kept it in a desk drawer in the kitchen, near the back door. Not very smart. And any one of the lot of us could have picked it up out of the drawer and shot you!"

"So why does Dmitri like Simon as the shooter?"

"Three reasons, I think." Ellen said, and proceeded to tick them off on her fingers.

"First, he thinks Simon is the one who killed Edith and this is somehow a continuation of that."

"Second, when we all ran into the hallway after hearing the shot, Simon came from that end of the hall."

Cooper started to break in, but she stopped him. "Yes, yes! I know that's flimsy. But then Simon did a really stupid thing!" She folded down her still-extended third finger. "He was the one who first saw the gun lying on the carpet at the other end of the hall. He picked it up ... with a proper grip, as though he was about to pull the trigger. He's lucky that Dmitri and/or Marcus didn't put him down. It was quite tense for about ten seconds!"

Cooper thought for a minute, and then said as if to himself, "So Simon has his fingerprints all over another weapon..."

"He does. But he denies shooting you. And, as far as I know, he hasn't even tried to explain why he would pick up the gun. But he doesn't seem worried about it."

Cooper said, "OK. Those are the facts ... easy questions to answer. Now some hard ones. How many questions do I have left?"

"You get to keep going until you ask what I think is a dumb question," Ellen said.

"OK. Why would any of them want to shoot me? I'm no threat to any of them. I know less than anybody involved, don't have any hot leads, nor any particular animosities toward them ...."

"Good question. And Dmitri wants to spend some time with you backtracking what you've been doing. He thinks – and I agree – that you must have stirred up something that you're not even aware of."

But Cooper didn't hear the last bit. Even before he finished asking his question, he was visualizing Tony Pastore in the locker room, standing in his boxer shorts looking confused and afraid.

That was then, with me in his face. I thought I had him pegged ... too much to lose to revert to his old gangster ways. Maybe I was wrong.

Cooper's left leg was asleep, but he feared to stretch it out because it might cause Ellen to move to the visitor's chair. He winced, and said, "Another fact question: Can anybody be ruled out as the shooter?"

Ellen grinned. "Well, me, of course. The shot came from the other end of the hall. I was standing about eight inches away from you, trying to tell you something."

She ran through the possibilities in her mind. "Other than me, everyone else is theoretically eligible. However, I think we can rule out Dmitri – If he didn't shoot you when you were his drinking buddy, he's hardly likely to do it now. On the same grounds, Marcus doesn't seem likely – unless you've read the Oedipus materials. Anyway, neither of them – or Martine -- would have known where to find the Beretta."

"And one more thing. Marcus says that he saw Simon near the bathroom only a few seconds before he heard the shot. If so, then Simon couldn't have been the shooter."

Cooper said thoughtfully, "Leaving only Martine, Nathaniel and Maria unaccounted for …"

"We can probably leave out Martine. She didn't know where the gun was and DA's usually don't shoot members of the defense team. They prefer to humiliate them in court."

"What do they say about what they saw or heard?"

"Each of them except Maria says exactly the same thing. They were alone when they heard the shot. They rushed into the hallway – the natural place to go –saw you, and went to the end of the hallway where you were lying."

Cooper paused. "Just one more question for now, a really scary one, I think."

"OK. "

"Are you sure that it was me they were shooting at?"

Tony

Cooper could not know it, but his instinctive suspicions about Tony Pastore's intentions were well-placed. Even while Cooper and Ellen were crossing off possible assassins from the list of suspects, Tony was trying very hard to think of ways to put Cooper underground. His problem was that he didn't have enough imagination to work out how to balance two conflicting desires: his need to *personally* cause Cooper real pain and his need to be able to walk away.

His thinking was complicated by the way his mind kept revisiting his humiliation at the country club. He could not help seeing himself standing in his underwear screaming curses at a man who simply stood there and looked at him like he was a piece of dog shit that he'd stepped in.

And when he forced that image into remission and tried to visualize the specific revenge he would inflict on Cooper, memories of Lisa and Alfredo popped up instead; the way they cringed and begged before he threw the acid or swung the baseball bat. He would not admit it and probably did not even realize it, but those two acts of vengeance were the high points of his personal history, the times when he felt most alive and powerful.

"Anthony, are you with us on this?"

The question jarred him back to the present, which was a late afternoon meeting in a conference room in Stanton's Civic Club. The oak-paneled walls were lined with photographs of the Club's Citizen-of-the-Year Award. All of the photos except one were serious-looking old white men. The lone exception was Edith McKay. The photographs were the sort where the eyes seemed to follow the observer and Tony was particularly bothered by McKay's unblinking gaze.

The six other individuals in the room – five men and a woman -- were all looking at him curiously.

He sat up and tried to remember what they'd been talking about before he'd slipped into his reverie about ways to kill Cooper. It didn't help that he viewed five of his six companions as self-important nobodies that had to be humored.

He gave up, shrugged. "Sorry. What was the question again?"

Saunders, the president of the local bank and the nominal head of their task force, said, "The Teamsters' local. They say they want the non-union construction crews off of the Riverbend work ... that they will stretech it into a ten-year project if we –"

Tony waved dismissively, cutting him off. "What they want and what they get are different. I'll take care of it. Tell me again where we are with the goddamned environmentalist shitheads."

He could not stop himself from looking up at the Edith McKay photo. She still was looking directly at him.

Saunders winced and two of the other men looked around nervously as if suspecting hidden listeners, confirming Tony's low opinion of them. *Bunch of hypocritical wimps. OK for me to cut every corner in sight to get the job going, but profanity in public? That's a little too much!*

A Saunders lookalike except for his bow tie – his name was Fitzhugh, head of a local law firm – spoke up. "The final package is at the Planning Commission office. They'll issue the final go-ahead within a day or so. All they're waiting for is for some low-level hydrology guy to sign off. Riverbend is ready to go. We've won."

Saunders said what they all were thinking. "It's been a long five years. Time and money down the drain!"

What he didn't say but everyone in the room was thinking about was that Tony's ex-wife was the single biggest reason for the five-year delay that had been jammed down their throats and made most of their monthly meetings an exercise in frustration. She was the unofficial leader and spokesperson for the loosely-knit coalition of environmentalists and preservation diehards that fought them at every turn and had almost prevailed. Ellen Pastore had become the avatar of Edith McKay's ambitions.

Tony had many obsessions, most of them stemming from his own insecurities. But the one at the forefront of his brain was Ellen. *The bitch! Not enough of a woman to live with me. And she couldn't just walk away ... had to take everything she could get from me and then spend her time blocking the one thing that I really wanted! And then sends her new boy toy to blackmail me! I'll fix both of them ...*

One of the men in the room – the only one in their meeting that Tony respected – got up to leave, signaling the end of their meeting. But he stood aside to let the others leave the room before him. Once they were out, he closed the door and sat down again opposite Tony, who was still immersed in his internal fantasies.

Then the man said an unexpected thing. "It took a while, but this would never have happened if Edith hadn't died that night. In that storm."

The phrases hung in the air between them. Robert Radner and Tony looked at each other with wary expressions, in the manner of two conspirators sharing a secret, one that would ruin both of them if discovered. This was the first time since Edith's death five years ago that the topic had been mentioned between the two of them.

The two men were dissimilar in every way except one. Robert was contained, as buttoned up as an actuary at his first job interview. Tony was expressive, obscene, prone to physicality. Robert was respectable; Tony was colorful. Although they both wore expensive suits, they still managed to portray different social classes.

The trait that they shared was avarice, honed by a profound absence of conscience. And they had complementary strengths. Robert knew the territory – the complex web of power brokers, financing arrangements, and politics that make up a growing city with all of its financial possibilities for someone with the will to fully exploit that understanding, especially if they are not constrained by the scruples and laws that limit ordinary businessmen. For his part, Tony offered Robert the hands-on kind of criminality that is not taught in Ivy-League business schools; the kind where on-the-job training is essential and where "winning" is as much about inflicting suffering as it is about making ungodly amounts of money.

They made an ideal team: an amoral entrepreneur with inside information and a sadist who wanted to be rich. Between them, they covered the crime spectrum – from the genteel white-collar felonies to the more violent sort. The synergistic effects were far larger than Robert had expected. An offer to buy out a competitor at a low-ball price was much more likely to be accepted if Tony was on the negotiating team.

Normally, it would not be a sustainable relationship, but it endured; at first because of a grudging respect for the other's skills and finally because of their shared recognition of their dependence on one another. They were like ice climbers roped together: a slip by either one would be disastrous for both.

That dependence became absolute early in their relationship when Harold Hicks got cold feet. Hicks was a City Inspector who worked as a staffer for the Stanton Planning Commission. He had accepted modest bribes from Robert Radner for several years to accelerate and/or approve commercial real estate projects that were important to Robert, or to slow down others. Then he got careless and was subpoenaed to appear before a grand jury.

Robert called on Tony.

"This Hicks guy is a serious threat to us, I think. Can you talk to him? Maybe make clear to him what the alternatives are? Express our concern about his continued cooperation?"

Tony was amused. *Alternatives? Express our concern!? I'm supposed to hold hands with some moron that will cave in as soon as some mean-looking cop reads him his Miranda rights?*

He looked hard at Robert. "I think we need to do more than talk."

Robert was at first alarmed and then angry at himself for his naivete. *What did you think? That everything ends happily for everybody in the game? That you wouldn't need somebody like Tony?*

That people like Hicks wouldn't come along as surely as night follows day?

Even then, he tried to leave enough ambiguity that – whatever happened – he could say, "I never intended *that*."

"Do what you have to do, but don't go too far."

Tony smiled. "Sure."

He picked Hicks up when he was leaving a neighborhood bar at closing time. The man was drunk, moaning about his life being ruined. How he had to tell about what he'd done, get right with God. A babbling semi-coherent stream of self-pity fueled by booze, fear and conscience.

Tony got him to write a note saying, "I'm sorry for what I've done. Please forgive me." He didn't need much convincing, confusing Tony with some kind of God-given counselor sent to him in his moment of drunken contrition. Tony poured another half a quart of vodka into him, to the point where Hicks was barely conscious. He used Hicks' city-owned official car to drive them to the Stanton reservoir, a narrow hundred-acre artificial lake a few miles from the city center. It was off-limits to the public, surrounded by a high fence with a locked gate. But part of Hicks' job was a weekly inspection of the facility and he had the key in the car that he drove. Once inside the gate, Tony stuffed some loose bricks into Hicks' pockets, got him into the small boat kept there for inspections, rowed him into the center of the lake, and manhandled him out of the boat.

Hicks splashed about feebly for about ten seconds and then sank.

Tony rowed back to shore and then pushed the boat back out into the lake, aimed approximately at the spot where Hicks had disappeared beneath the surface. He left the "I'm sorry" note on the middle seat of the rowboat, weighted down by the empty vodka bottle. He then walked out of the gate, leaving the lock hanging.

It took an hour for Tony to walk back to his own car. It went quickly as he replayed and enjoyed over-and-over the images of Hicks – his surprise when he rolled him into the water, the stark fear just before he went under for the last time, the way his white face finally faded out of sight.

A week later, Tony met Robert at a city council meeting. He watched Robert closely, saying, "Too bad about Hicks. Guy with a wife and two kids choosing to go out like that ..."

Robert looked back, perfectly bland. "Yeah, a real tragedy. But maybe it's simpler that way for everybody."

The topic of "Hicks" only came up only once more between them, but it was always there, lurking like the elephant in the living room. They were alone, the last pair of diners in a downtown restaurant. When he looked back on it, Tony realized that it was just a week before Edith died.

Robert had drunk quite a bit, but he showed little sign of it other than an increased precision in his speech. They had been talking about Riverbend; how it was going to be off-limits to development; how Edith was about to sign it over to the state Conservancy. Robert changed the subject abruptly.

"Remember Hicks?"

He went on before a startled Tony could reply. "Of course you do. You were intimately involved with his confession." And Robert smiled in a lopsided way and actually winked at him.

"Robert. This is not –"

"I know. I know." Robert waved both hands in front of his face in the classic "never mind" gesture. "But I was thinking of some parallels with our present situation."

"Parallels?"

"You know. With Riverbend."

"No, I don't know. Hicks was a problem ...one guy who needed to get out of the way ... the kind of problem that comes with an obvious solution. What's that got to do with Riverbend? Every goddam treehugger within a hundred miles is in our way."

Robert leaned forward over the table and stared hard at Tony. The shift in posture and the sudden intensity of Robert's gaze made Tony wonder whether Robert was as drunk as he thought.

"There are similarities," Robert said. "In both cases, we've got a single person who's blocking us ... a threat. Hicks ... and now Edith. She's the owner. The treehuggers can't do a thing if she's signed off on the deal."

Christ! Is he asking me to off his wife?

Then it got even stranger. Robert leaned back, but his eyes remained locked on Tony. "What's it like to kill a person? Is it easy? Can anyone do it or does it take something special ... something most people don't have within them?"

"Robert. What exactly are you saying?"

"Nothing. Absolutely nothing. But what if Edith was not around ....?"

That was five years ago. Now they sat in the oak-paneled conference room and Robert had just said, "This would never have happened if Edith hadn't died that night. In that storm."

Robert's startling statement instantly took Tony back to their meeting five years ago, when Robert asked him, "Is it easy to kill a person? " And, "What if Edith was not around?"

This is crazy! Not ... definitely not ... something to be talked about!

But then he remembered his present concerns – the man Cooper and his bitch ex-wife Ellen. The surge of anger overrode his instincts.

"It's too bad that Ellen didn't go with her. Would have saved us the last five years of aggravation."

Robert knew him well, and proved it with his next question.

"It's not just Ellen. I heard about your very loud country club encounter with the man Cooper. What are you going to do about that?"

Once again, Tony was startled, especially when he realized that Robert was looking intently at him, clearly waiting for his answer. *What does he want me to say? Or do? How in the hell did we get here from Hicks?*

Finally he shrugged, accepting – even grateful for -- the complicity. He began talking.

"I have this problem. I know what I want to do. I can visualize it down to the last detail, but I don't know how to …"

The two men talked until the room became dark and the cleaning lady knocked on the door.

Assisting With Inquiries

Simon was under arrest, held without bail for the moment.

While Ellen & Cooper were sitting on the hospital bed reconstructing events at the shooting scene, Dmitri and Marcus were interviewing the three Radners – Simon, Nathaniel and Maria – about their parts in that same event.

The interviews were uneasy ones. Part of the uneasiness stemmed from the near-certainty that one of the three was the shooter, so the Q&A oscillated between the polite form that police use with a distraught witness, and the more hostile, in-your-face style reserved for suspects. And there is no way to soften a Miranda warning, so the interviews began on an adversarial note. Interestingly to Dmitri, both Nathaniel and Maria Radner waived their right to have an attorney present.

And, although neither spoke of it, some of the edginess in the interviews was because both Dmitri and Marcus were faintly embarrassed by an unsolved murder attempt that took place within twenty feet of them.

Dmitri remembered his Soviet experience with interrogations. It was a much simpler system if you were a policeman. The notion of the suspect's "rights" was – quite literally – a foreign concept. The notion of the suspect even having rights was laughable. "Interviews" were designed to extract confessions, not to ascertain facts for an informed judgment. *Guilty* or *innocent* were labels applied early and arbitrarily, often based on the individual's standing within the Party. Dmitri was a misfit within the system, but sometimes – especially on days like this one – he remembered with fondness how easy it was to administer a crude and instant justice.

He thought the American expression "a can of worms" was particularly apt for this case. The two of them had just finished their first interview with Maria Radner. It was quite strange.

She needs a healthy dose of Xanax! was Dmitri's first and lasting impression. She was quite nervous, unable to sit still; and her thoughts seemed to jump around even more erratically. She thought that they wanted to interview her about the confrontation between Ellen Pastore and Nathaniel in the living room, and she became indignant when they insisted on asking about her own movements during the few minutes before the shooting. She kept returning to how Ellen had been "disrespectful to my son" and how she was a dangerous woman. When they finally got her to focus a bit, she admitted knowing about the gun in the kitchen drawer, but said she had never touched it and had never fired a gun during her lifetime. She also said that she was alone in the living room when she heard the shot fired and she had seen no one in the hallway before that.

She claimed that she did not even know Cooper and did not recall meeting him.

The interview ended abruptly when Dmitri asked what he thought was a straightforward question about when Nathaniel had left the living room. Maria became enraged, standing and screaming that she wanted a lawyer. Dmitri called for a policewoman to take her to a neutral spot and try to calm her down. He also cautioned her not to question Maria until a lawyer was on hand.

When she left, Dmitri looked at Marcus and said, "I feel sorry for Nathaniel. That must be tough to live with! How'd you like to bring your girl friend home to meet her?"

Marcus was silent. *Dmitri doesn't know it, but his question is a brilliant one. Nathaniel's girl friends – real or imagined – don't go over well with Maria.*

When Marcus said nothing, Dmitri went on, "Let's get Nathaniel out of the way. I don't think we'll learn anything new. But I'd like to try leaning on him a bit. It's his gun and he's had some minor scrapes with the law. Let's split up for a bit. Why don't you track down Pastore and find out what you can about her yelling at Nathaniel? I'll start on Nathaniel with the 'bad cop' routine and then – when you come back – you can be 'good cop,' his best friend. You're his age and have a little bit of history together."

Dmitri noted that Marcus was decidedly uneasy. He asked in a neutral tone, "Something wrong? Got a better idea?"

Marcus was clearly picking his words carefully. "OK. But I'd recommend going easy on the mother/son stuff. I don't think that's got much to do with our shooting. And I think you'll shut him down if you push too hard on that topic."

Dmitri said, "Sure. I'll be careful. Be back in half-an-hour, if you can."

Nathaniel and Marcus crossed paths in the door to the interview room, exchanging looks – defiant on Nathaniel's part and calculating on Marcus's part. Marcus stared hard and long at Nathaniel, and Dmitri had the distinct impression that Marcus was trying to send some message. Nathaniel looked away with a shrug and came into the interview room and sat down.

Marcus stood outside the closed door, trying to analyze his retained image of Nathaniel as they faced one another in the doorway. *Scared? Of course. That's become a life style for him by now. Is he scared enough to say something stupid? Probably. We need to have our little talk again. Remind him about what's important.*

He looked at the closed door, thinking about going back in. Then he shrugged and headed down the hall for his office, walking like a man with places to go and things to do.

Dmitri could have catalogued the emotions that Nathaniel was experiencing, so transparent they might as well have been printed on the T-shirt that he was wearing. Defiance, anxiety, slyness, anger ... exactly the muddled mindset one would expect from a person trying to appear less guilty than he felt.

Dmitri tried an oblique opening. "So, your father's arrested for one murder and the probable shooting of Marcus's father, using your gun. How do you feel about that?"

When Nathaniel just looked at him, he went on, "And your mother's a mess. Apparently she views you as a punching bag for various women --"

Nathaniel rose halfway from his chair, and Dmitri thought he might come across the table at him. But he slowly sat back down with a stony expression and stared at the wall behind Dmitri.

Then he said something that stunned Dmitri into his own silence.

"I think I know why Edith McKay was killed."

It was Dmitri's turn to stare. *What I want to know is who, not why. But that's a good start usually.*

He asked simply "Why?"

And Nathaniel surprised him once more. "It starts with Rachel."

Revisionist History

The word "Rachel" hung in the air.

Dmitri tilted as far back as he could, crossed his arms on his chest, and looked down his nose at Nathaniel. He started to speak, but Nathaniel broke in immediately.

"Look. If you want to hear this, you've got to let me tell it my way. We're going back twelve years, to that day Rachel died. You were there, so you know what I'm talking about. And you're not going to like what you're hearing, but don't interrupt."

Dmitri said, "I already don't like it. But I promise that you've got my full attention." He knew very well that there was a time to be quiet when a suspect feels a need to talk without interruption.

Just a quick CYA maneuver. He made sure the voice recorder was running and asked, "You've waived your right to have an attorney present for this interview. Do you want to reconsider that choice?"

Nathaniel sat stock still, looking inward. Slowly, he shook his head and said "No."

"There's a back story. But it's so ordinary that we can get it out of the way real quick. Call it, say, 'the generation gap'. The fact is that ... back then, none of you – Robert, Simon, McKay, any of you ... or probably anybody over forty in the whole damn town – knew anything about what was going on with their kids those days. Not your fault, just normal role separation. And it isn't that we were wild, sex-crazed, hard drinking potheads ... just your everyday walking bundles of hormones thinking that they're immortal and omniscient."

Dmitri couldn't help the thoughts that flooded in. He almost voiced them aloud. *I'm exempt from responsibility. No kids. And I was either drunk or gone ... hard to tell the difference ... most of the time ... And so was Cooper.*

Instead, he said as mildly as he could, "Pop sociology, I think! Is any of that relevant?"

Nathaniel waved him off impatiently.

"That discussion is for you and Cooper ... and another time and place. But it explains some of what you're going to hear."

He went on, "Anyway, I don't want to talk about the merits or demerits of teenage behavior, or the sociology of parenting in Stanton in the late twentieth century. But you need to understand that day ... the day Rachel fell down those damn stairs ... there was a lot of stuff going on ... not just the rah rah good feelings and hand-in-hand strolls on the lawn along the river..."

He paused, clearly arranging his thoughts. Dmitri wondered how much editing was going on in Nathaniel's mind, scripting the emerging narrative to reflect what he wanted Dmitri to see. *I remember that night. I was there. Brand new homicide cop, mostly hanging out at the bar for the free drinks.*

Nathaniel turned sideways in his chair, not quite looking at Dmitri and talking in a low voice. "Marcus and I knew Edith pretty well, even though she was older and in college. Stanton was still a small town in a lot of ways and she was probably the most visible non-adult around. But it was 'Hi, how are ya?' kind of stuff for the most part. She was light years ahead of us, being older and a McKay.

"Right after all the ballroom speeches and stuff, she grabbed Marcus and me and dragged us off to the old stables. She said we were going to do a 'proper celebration for the co-MVP's.' We'd already had a few beers each, but Edith said that she had something better. That turned out to be a couple bottles of scotch that she had stashed in the stable, apparently some fifty-year-old single malt from the liquor cabinet. She'd already drunk part of one bottle."

Dmitri said, "I think I know where this is going ..., but it wasn't Edith that fell down the stairs."

"Quit interrupting. And you have no idea where this is going!

"After awhile, maybe half-an-hour or so, all three of us were pretty well out of it.... A lot of giggling and grabass clowning around. Edith was hung up on the co-MVP award. She kept coming back to it: 'What's this 'co' stuff? There can only be one MVP! Let's vote again!' So we came up with this so-called playoff to see who was the 'real' MVP. We were in a big empty room with a lot of ancient ranch stuff in it. We took some kind of old horse collar and wedged it into a window about eight feet off the floor as a kind of basket. Marcus and I started a kind of drunken one-on-one, using an old shoe for the ball. It was pretty stupid, but Edith was watching and keeping score. We were kids, but it began to feel a lot like two men and a beautiful woman stranded on a desert island. Marcus and I were trying pretty hard to be alpha dog."

Dmitri muttered, "Tennessee Williams should have been there."

"He was. In spirit. But it gets worse ... or better, depending on your perspective. After awhile, Edith wants to play too. So we invent some half-assed two-on-one game, and it gets more physical ... bumping into each other, falling down. Then Edith says 'Hey! Too hard to tell who's on what team! We need shirts vs. skins!' And she pulls her T-shirt off over her head ... and, believe me, there's nothing but skin beneath it.

"That stops the so-called game. And I think it sobered Marcus and me up just a bit. We were kids, but I was eighteen, and Edith ... Well, she had this great body and was standing there breathing heavily, with straw in her hair and her shirt in her hand. I don't know about Marcus, but I couldn't have moved if the place was on fire.

"The three of us stood there looking at each other, nobody knowing what comes next. Then Edith said, 'I still think this co-MVP stuff is shit ... and I know a way to settle it once and for all. C'mon. We'll see who's most valuable ....' She put her shirt back on and headed for the door. She stood in the doorway ... I remember the sun was just setting behind her ... and said, 'Well, are you coming or not?'

"We went up some back stairs in the main house, to her bedroom on the second floor. All of us were breathing pretty heavily ... and not from climbing the stairs ... but no one said a word until we were in her room – right at the head of that damned staircase -- and she'd closed the door. I remember a lot of noise from the ballroom downstairs. The only thing that I can remember being said from then on is Edith saying, 'So. I get to decide who's most valuable. The test is really simple.'

"About then, it gets pretty blurry. All three of us are naked and Marcus and I are looking at each other a lot, like one of us could tell the other what to do. It didn't matter. Edith was running the show, doing exactly what she wanted."

Dmitri couldn't help himself. He asked Nathaniel, "Do I really need to know this stuff? Considering that Edith is dead and Marcus works with me and has communication difficulties with his father already --"

"You're the detective. Aren't you supposed to wallow around in all this steamy human stuff ... sort of an occupational hazard? But hang in there; the story's almost over.

"I really have no idea how much time had passed before the door opens, very tentative at first and then pushed back all the way. My aunt – Rachel - is standing there, with another vague shape behind her. 'Transfixed' is overly fancy, but it's appropriate in this case. I'm standing a few feet away from her, but she doesn't even see me. She's looking at the bed. Marcus and Edith are writhing around, trying to untangle themselves from the sheets and cover themselves all at the same time, pulling the sheets off of the other in doing so.

"Everything else happens all at once. Except for me, I don't ... I can't ... move. Rachel said something, 'Oh!' I think, and then turned away and started to pull the door closed. Marcus said, 'Wait!'

"I know, I know ... what's he going to do? Say 'It's not what you think!' But none of us were thinking at that particular moment.

"Marcus moves first. He lunges off the bed to close the door. But his foot is still tangled in the sheets, and he ends up half falling into the door. It slams into Rachel's back and knocks her forward ... toward the staircase ... and slams shut. The three of us ... Marcus on the floor, Edith still on the bed in a tangle of sheets, and me standing in the middle of the room ... for maybe ten seconds, look at one another stupidly and then start scrambling for clothes. It sinks into us that the noise level from the ballroom has changed and I think we were all thinking the same thing ... that Rachel was standing on the staircase telling everyone in the ballroom about what she'd come across.

"We cracked open the door to listen. It didn't take long to realize that she'd fallen down the stairs!

"No. That's wrong ... I should have said 'that we knocked her down the stairs'.

"We were out of there, down the back stairs, and out on the lawn in about thirty seconds. Everyone else had packed into the ballroom to see what the confusion was about, so we had time to calm down and then join the rest."

Nathaniel stopped, staring blankly. A faint look of surprise came over him, and Dmitri knew that he was wondering what had come over him.

"That's the last time the three of us were together. Edith just stayed away from us, and then she left town. And none of us ever talked about what happened."

Dmitri sat absolutely still in a welter of feelings – anger, sadness, remorse – each emotion coming in waves and then receding. He thought of an eighteen-year-old Marcus and how little he knew of him, of the randomness of consequence, of the unfairness to Rachel, of Robert's losses, of the gulf between Nathaniel and Simon. He thought ... he wondered .... if time does actually heal, or whether suppressed wrongs must, at some point, imaginary or real, be released back into the world in a magnified form. Whether twelve years was long enough. He was deeply sad.

Nathaniel said, "It was a stupid, stupid accident! And I think about it ... relive it ... every goddam day! And it always ends the same way ..."

"And it always will." Dmitri adds.

Then he asked, against his cop instincts, but with genuine curiosity, "But why are you telling me all this ancient history now? Why not let it be?" *Especially when your story makes you a look really bad. You've just provided yourself with a medium strong motive for murder.*

Nathaniel's voice hardens. "Because Edith – the night she died ... about ten minutes before the lights went out ... she grabbed Marcus and me... She was all amped up. Not scared, just really excited. She said that something had happened that changed everything... that she had to tell what happened that day ... the whole story ... and that some people might not like it!"

Internal Debates

Five years ago, the night of Edith's death

Simon sat in his car in the rain swept drive, staring at the lighted McKay house, but unseeing. He said it again, aloud: "You are a pathetic cliché ... married man in clandestine love with much younger companion."

He ticked off the symptoms. He'd renewed his lapsed gym membership and started a diet. He'd purchased a second cell phone for cash, and only his lover had the number. He told everyone he was starting to play golf again, so that he could explain those four to five hour gaps in his schedule. He experienced intense bouts of elation, guilt, remorse, giddiness, anguish; each emotion coming in random bursts and being succeeded by its antonym.

How strange that this should be. Each of us with so much to lose; and so little reason ... or excuse ... to seek more than we already have. Each of us fearful of causing so much hurt to others that we care about but remaining absolutely selfish in our actions, totally unable to not want the other. Are you as ambivalent as I am? Or – maybe because you're from another generation – can you rationalize your mid-afternoon nakedness with me as justified by our needs? Or worse -- much worse – by Maria's increasing dementia? Do you feel as I do: that this must end badly?

More and more in the last few weeks, Simon found himself locked into this same trance-like dialogue with himself. The last time had been two days ago, sitting among the debris of his wedding anniversary party; streamers, half-empty champagne glasses, paper plates – the standard litter. Almost-but-not-quite drunk, he was halfheartedly trying to perfect a metaphor, one in which the colorful clutter symbolized the faded ambitions and euphoric expectations that are discarded as two people navigate through uncharted emotional territory.

Can I leave Maria?

So many emotions! Each of them favoring a solution in conflict with the others. Pity, of course. For a woman who will be truly alone if I leave, made far worse because she's been dumped. Guilt, because it is desertion, with all of the associated baggage. Anger – or its close cousin, resentment – because he so badly wants to be with his lover but feels obligated to Maria. Nostalgia, for decades of closeness and shared growth, for what she was to him.

Is lust an emotion? It surely exists. Perhaps even more intensely than how it was with Maria.

When did it change? Fairness, with all of its overtones of morality and ethics, has little to do with obligation. When ... no, not "when," "why" ... why does obligation become a tiresome burden rather than an expression of love? How should we calculate "enough?" How do you trade off one person's needs against another's?

He did not allow the other thought into his consciousness. *Why should I stay with a crazy woman?*

When Simon mentioned to a friend that "Maria is acting a little strange these days," his friend's response summed it up neatly: "How can you tell?" For Maria, unpredictability was a life style, eccentricity as natural as breathing. Nathaniel once captured it nicely when he described his mother as "lovably perverse."

Maria was always different. Some of it stemmed from her Central European upbringing, but even more resulted from some need to be seen and admired for her mind and wit, something more than her spectacular looks. In conversation, she would act the contrarian. And, more often than not, her comment would close out the topic and launch the conversation into a completely new direction. Maria loved aphorisms and epigrams – all kinds of one-liners -- and Simon knew that she had read and re-read authors like Oscar Wilde, Ambrose Bierce and Dorothy Parker; carefully jotting down the memorable bits.

Simon thought now that what some saw as eccentricity was the forerunner of the mental disorder that was so obvious to Nathaniel and him today. His very first attraction to Maria was the air of suppressed wildness she traveled with, the sense that whatever she was about to say or do would be extraordinary in some way. It made her mysterious, sensuous. Now, he recalled episodes over the past decades where Maria's behavior signaled something far more serious.

When Nathaniel was born, Maria was convinced that he would die if out of her presence. She stayed with him virtually every hour of his first year of life, sleeping in his room, refusing to leave him with a babysitter. Several years ago, she spent a week in New York for what she called a "girl's vacation," but Simon learned was really for daily consultation with a psychiatrist. In the recent past, Simon would often find Maria sitting alone at different places in their home, simply staring at nothing for long intervals. When startled into awareness, there was a brief second when her eyes betrayed a panic, one that she would not admit to.

Symptoms grew into the syndrome of today. With a single exception, she slowly and surely ended all personal relationships, with both friends and family. She would not answer the phone, and rarely left the house. She no longer slept with Simon. Their conversations were stilted and would end abruptly. She spent most of her time reading or watching television, but apparently without any comprehension of what she was reading or seeing.

The only breaks in her self-imposed isolation came if Nathaniel called or visited. Then she would be animated and appropriately 'normal', but always with a brittleness that both he and Nathaniel mistrusted. Simon strongly suspected that Nathaniel's aversion to women was his way of protecting Maria from herself. To his credit, he blamed himself as well; his half-dozen extra-marital affairs during their long marriage almost certainly contributed to Nathaniel's apparent sexual isolation and to Maria's emotional deterioration.

Simon had hoped that their anniversary party would be one small step toward normalization; that it would reset Maria, both to herself and their marriage. It had been a disaster. She began the evening with a fragile cheerfulness, her voice too high, with a fixed smile and a manic unfocused energy. She talked with many guests, leaving them faintly uneasy about the evening ahead. Halfway through, when the unscripted toasts were beginning, she left abruptly but came back fifteen minutes later, in a set of mismatched flannel pajamas, standing on the fringes of the group, completely silent.

People left as quickly as they could, in embarrassment, still extending congratulations. *For what?* Simon asked himself savagely.

The rain increased in intensity; dimming the light from the house looming in front of him. It was time to go in. And he knew that all of his careful and dispassionate weighing of alternatives, all the wrestling with ethics, was irrelevant. He had chosen.

The hell with it! He had vowed "For better, and for worse," but that was motivational poetry, not a binding contract. Insanity is a special case!

And inside the house, his lover was waiting for him.

Thicker Than Water

I've come full circle! Cooper was back in the same Starbucks on a weekday morning, and had just ended a cell phone call from Simon. But beyond the sheer coincidence, he realized that a circle was the perfect symbol for his state of mind: he knew nothing more about Simon's guilt or innocence than he did when he started.

Almost wistfully, he recalled the simplicity – the linearity -- of murder cases as he had experienced them in his police career. Somebody is killed, usually for an obvious reason that seems petty to all but the killer. The killer is known or discovered almost instantly. Case closed. Most of the apparent melodrama is invented, cobbled together by newspapers with a need for circulation.

In the case of Edith McKay, nothing is simple. Everyone is connected to everyone else. It's more about families than it is about individuals – the McKays, both sets of Radners, Pastores, even himself and Marcus. Simon's pathologies, and his crimes, are understandable only in the context of the social group called "the Radner family."

What was it that Tolstoy had written? "*Every unhappy family is unhappy in its own way.*" Cooper was beginning to understand that Edith's murder would be "solved" only when he understood in what particular way the Radner's were unhappy.

Cooper thought about the concept of "family." He thought he understood the nucleus -- "the man and a woman" part of it, the binding power of lust and the primitive need for companionship that was so impressive when seen in others or experienced within oneself. He had felt the passion, the bone-deep comfort of belonging, as hard to sustain as it is to forget.

Clearly, it was not something to be trifled with. He knew what all cops knew; that the most dangerous call is the domestic violence incident, the one where the cop winds up in the middle of a man and a woman, galvanizing an "us vs. them" tribalism that begets violence against outsiders, even the well-meaning ones.

He recalled the rookie cop they'd called Bosco, a black grad of the academy with dreams of a "new policing model," fond of words like "underclass" and "community." They paired him up with Ruskin, a sixteen-year veteran who probably couldn't even spell "underclass," but was the most streetwise cop on the force. They made a strange pair, but the sergeant figured it was the fastest way to get the kid up to speed.

Their third call together was a 273D, the code for a domestic dispute. Ruskin briefed the kid on procedure during the ten minutes en-route, and they did it by the book all the way. Ruskin used some considerable force to restrain the husband on one side of the kitchen – a fat drunk who'd been beating his wife with a heavy coiled extension cord and didn't want to stop even when they showed up, yelling "You fat bitch!" even as Ruskin wrestled him away from her. Bosco got the woman on the other side of the kitchen to calm her down and get enough of the blood cleared away to see how badly she was hurt. He turned to see how Ruskin was doing and she stabbed him in the back of the neck with a steak knife that she grabbed off the counter.

Bosco is now and forever a quadriplegic. When arrested for attempted murder, all the woman could say was that she didn't want to press any charges against her husband... that she loved him.

But, for Cooper, the even greater puzzle involved those parts of the family that radiated out and away from that man/woman nucleus, where lust and primal passions were attenuated by time and distance; the brothers and sisters, mothers and children, the generations before and after; all the human tributaries that made up the tribe called a "family."

He'd asked Dmitri once, in a bar, when they were still drinking together and too much, "Do you miss your family ... the ones that are still in Russia?"

Dmitri turned his whole body toward Cooper, as drunks do, and stared for a long moment with a hard-to-read expression. His tone was angry, "They're reason number one why I left. They're a bunch of misfits and bastards!" And he turned away from Cooper.

Cooper tried only once more. "Hey! I read somewhere that genetics is destiny. Where did you come from? What's –"

Dmitri spun and grabbed Cooper's arm, hard, spilling the drink he was holding. "Stop right now! I don't ... I repeat, I don't ... want to talk about family! Yours, mine, or anybody else's!"

This is not the usual Dmitri. The booze usually makes him quiet ... introspective and sentimental. I think we should stay away from this topic!

A month or so later, Cooper was in Dmitri's apartment, waiting for him to finish a phone call. The apartment was stark, decorated professionally in a minimalist style featuring few but expensive items of furniture and a vast expanse of white walls. Cooper was drawn to what he thought was a very large brightly-hued painting of geometric shapes. Looking closer, he realized that it was an arrangement of elaborate Russian iconographics and that it was an impressive piece of art. It was also Dmitri's family tree; his name was one of many at the bottom of a pyramid. Above him stretched – by a quick count – seven generations of Russians. The topmost layer apparently had been a branch of the Tsarist nobility and had something to do with the building of the Trans-Siberian railway. It also indicated that Dmitri seemed to have three brothers, that his parents might still be alive, and that he had probably twenty aunts and uncles and at least as many nephews and nieces.

The family tree dominated the room and was the only personal item visible in the entire apartment. *I wonder what the shrinks would say about a man that purports to intensely dislike his family and keeps this massive reminder on his wall?*

Cooper thought about his own family tree. He could draw what he knew about it on a cocktail party napkin. Two layers – him, his siblings, his parents. He knew nothing – facts, stories, names – about anybody before that. He had two brothers that he had seen twice in thirty years – at their parents' funerals, a pair of vague figures in his memory who died drunk and young. He talked to his brother and sister perhaps half-a-dozen times during those decades. They seemed to have nothing in common. Even their recollections about growing up together were so different that they wondered if they were talking about the same historical events. As he stood considering Dmitri's artwork, he wondered how much difference there was between him and Dmitri, and whether alcoholism narrowed or widened the gaps between people in the social groups we call "families?"

James McKay systematically broke apart everything his father had built while raising a headstrong daughter. Edith McKay, an only child of a caring father, left him for five years, effectively disappearing from his life. But she came back when he was dying, buried him and then committed the rest of her life to finishing what he started.

Robert and Simon? Another case study for the psychiatric social work crowd. Fraternal twins in a solidly middle class family. Apparently inseparable until something – what? -- wedged them apart. Robert was stiff and cold when Simon was near; whereas Simon seemed to have a massive case of approach-avoidance conflict in talking about Robert. And Robert's decision to hand over the hammer that would convict his brother of murder!

And then there are the children! Understanding our relationship to our ancestors and siblings is a piece of cake compared to figuring how to talk to our kids.

Marcus.

I wonder how you are ... what you're really like ... whether the twice-a-year phone calls and occasional 'safe' emails have made me a more sympathetic villain ... whether the memories of the first few years – the good ones -- are ever invoked ... or whether the drinking, abuse and absences will always be the first-and-only memories. I would undo them if I could.

People tell me that forgiveness is hard. How would I know? I'm usually the object of forgiveness, the forgivee rather than the forgiver, so I have little direct experience. Maybe it's an occupational hazard? Or might it work the other way? Does your proximity to felonies and all of their lousy aftermath make you more ... or less ...

aware of the way grudges and regrets can fester, even with the lesser crimes that we commit against one another?

Cooper knew that part of the reason he was drawn to Simon was the feeling that Simon and he shared this inability to connect to their sons. Last week, while reviewing the status of the police search for evidence, Simon said, "Your son ... Marcus, isn't it? He seems quite competent."

"He is, no thanks to me. He did it all on his own."

"I doubt that. We know too much about genetics. It's more than getting the blue eyes and Aunt Ida's bad skin. We also pass on intellect, personality, skills ... maybe even values."

"Yes ... and schizophrenia, alcoholism, and probably some chromosomes that are predisposed to homicide."

"Yes, those too." And Simon visibly checked out of the conversation, into some internal space.

Cooper sat quietly. He was ignorant of the content, but he easily imagined the kinds of thoughts going through Simon's mind, probably heavy on guilt. *Funny how we still feel as though we're responsible for our adult children.*

He tried a question, "What about Nathaniel? Do the two of you talk – really talk – to each other?"

Simon winced, quite obviously. "Yeah. With all the intimacy of two strangers in an elevator." He paused, smiled, and said, "I'm a hotshot lawyer, words are what I do ... really well, apparently... and I can't even carry on a conversation with my son!"

"Don't be so hard on yourself. Half of the so-called great books of the Western world are about the inarticulateness – or worse -- between father and son. Remember Oedipus?"

Simon said, "Wow! A detective who reads, with a strong psychoanalytical bent as well."

Cooper ignored the sarcasm, seeing it as an attempt to deflect the conversation into safer waters. He pressed him, "You know, for an outsider looking at Nathaniel, it looks like a simple case of a kid intimidated by his father's success, and then recasting it – for his own ego reasons -- as a public rejection of the father's values."

"Still working the Greek mythologies, aren't you?" Simon said, not as a question.

Cooper admitted, "I agree. It's pretty hokey. But I often wonder why Marcus became a cop. Was it because I was a role model of sorts? Or because I had failed at it?"

Simon was clearly thinking about the question. After a few seconds, he said, "You know, when Nathaniel first starting 'acting out' – he was maybe sixteen or so – I tried to deliberately undercut the 'father as hero figure' role. Nathaniel was a great athlete in high school, good at everything he tried. He was on the basketball, football and golf teams, usually the best player on whatever team it was. So I took up golf. Partly to spend time with him, but – more importantly – to reverse our usual teacher/student roles... give him the chance to be the dominant male in our relationship."

Cooper asked, with real curiosity, "Did it work?"

"Who knows? I still play lousy golf and we still have trouble communicating. It certainly didn't stop him from dropping out of college or from dealing in illicit pharmaceuticals."

Cooper hesitated, then said, "I asked Marcus about him once. They were good friends at one time, did a lot of sports stuff together. Seemed to split up after Nathaniel finished high school. Marcus said something trite about Nathaniel 'needing to find his own space,' but he also said that he needed to get away from his mother."

Cooper thought he might have gone too far. But Simon seemed to think about it. He responded, "He's really close to Maria. They talk all the time ... I envy them. I worry more about her than him. She still sees him as a sixteen-year-old kid who needs to be shielded from harsher things."

"Not your usual over-protective maternal thing?"

Simon said, "Nothing harmful. I know she gives him money from time to time. And I know she's bailed him out of jail a couple of times ... pot possession, minor traffic stuff or some-such mischief. What really sets her off is if Nathaniel talks about his dates or girl friends. She says he's 'not ready'."

"That's a little weird. He's... what, almost 30 years old?"

Simon nodded. "It's a Maria thing. Nathaniel has just stopped talking about his love life ... if he has one."

There was a long silence. Then Simon went on, but as though Cooper was no longer there. "It's funny how inarticulate we are with those that we are closest to. You'd think it would be the other way around. We lie – either outright or by omission. We're cruel, petty ..."

And, after a pause, "We let each other get away with murder."

That's an interesting choice of words. I wonder if he's speaking literally or figuratively?

Robert

Robert Radner thought of himself as a professional beneficiary.

He understood that he enjoyed a special status because Rachel and Edith had died, each of them young, beautiful and married to him at the time they were so tragically killed. That he accepted tragedy as stoically as he did added to his image, although he knew – without regret – that what looked to the outside world as heroic acceptance was more like indifference. He simply had not cared that much. He said all the proper words, looked sad for an appropriate length of time, accepted the condolences, and banked all of the sympathy and goodwill that came his way, as a reservoir to be drawn on as needed.

He and his first wife Rachel met in college and continued on into a marriage that was sustained mostly by inertia. Each of them got what they wanted from the relationship – respectability and an absence of obligation. Robert himself was surprised by his detachment when Rachel died and only then did he come to fully appreciate the desolation of their marriage.

Perhaps that is why he and Edith were a natural fit. Although he did not know why – and he did not ask, those were the rules – they seemed to share a sad symmetry: an inability to need and an offsetting selfish unwillingness to share anything essential about themselves, to take on responsibility for others. That included their desire not to have children. Edith told him when they talked of marriage, "I do not want children. I am unwilling to give up that much of myself, for that long, for such an uncertain outcome!"

It was a marriage of convenience, like his first marriage except for the twenty-year age difference and Edith's drive to achieve. Robert quickly found both of those attributes burdensome. Unlike Robert, she was passionate, but about causes, things or ideas – not about people. The passion often took the form of wantonness, a consuming need for physical abandon that he could not match. When it appeared, Robert wondered about what her life was like during those five years she had been away from Stanton. And he understood Simon's attraction to his wife.

Robert's acceptance of Edith's infidelity was helped by his own violations of their marriage contract. He had been having an on-again, off-again affair with Natalie Benson for several years before his marriage to Edith; and it continued once he and Edith were married.

Robert was not curious about himself or his lack of emotion. He knew that some would label him a sociopath. A more kindly sort, say, a child development specialist, would say that his role as beneficiary was established early in his childhood. His twin brother Simon, was smarter, more ambitious. He took the lead in any situation where initiative was called for. Not for the rivalry, but rather to look out for his less assertive twin. With one exception, Robert rode his coattails – in athletics, classwork, dating, and – as they became adults – in their professional lives.

The major exception – unknown to Simon -- was Robert's diversion into criminality. It began simply, even innocently; doing favors for friends, always with a tacit *quid pro quo* attached. It was natural and probably inevitable that it would expand into bribery and the corruption of public institutions. Even those initiatives could be recast as "for the good of the community" for a person who needed such assurances; the sort of thing that overpaid corporate attorneys would dismiss as "victimless" crime, at most punishable with fines and community service. But his off-and-on partnership with Anthony Pastore was transparently illegal, a quantum leap into a much darker realm with very real victims.

At first, he used Tony's skills as a last resort and with a strong feeling of distaste, both for the man and his methods. Then, after what he thought of as "the Hicks affair," he found himself proactively looking for ways to use Tony. He realized that he was intrigued by Tony's world, trying to vicariously experience what it was like to frighten, physically intimidate – even to kill – a person. He knew it was a sick obsession, like a monk reading pornographic literature late at night in his austere cell.

Robert was also sufficiently self-aware to recognize that some part of the reason he married Edith was to prove something to Simon. No, maybe not to Simon; who would neither recognize nor acknowledge any competition between them. Rather to prove something to all those others who knew of Simon's role in Robert's successes.

The supreme irony, of course, was that Edith and Simon had been engaged in an affair for at least a few months before Edith died.

Robert's indifference – even relief – when he learned of the affair established forever in his mind that he was emotionally defective in some important way. He was unable to care very much about the conventional values that seemed to drive others. Despite Simon's dominance, Robert could not recall any instance where he had envied Simon, or any time where he felt any resentment of his own role as sidekick or, more recently, cuckold.

Until they found the hammer.

One of the laborers excavating the riverbank for the concrete piers brought it to him, still in its Lucite case which was in turn encased in its self-made depression in the lump of mud, as if it was a display in a Museum of Contemporary Art. The laborer was about to toss it in the dumpster with other construction debris, but Robert was nearby and he showed it to him as a curiosity. Robert took it from him and told him that he'd toss it.

He knew instantly what he had, even without reading the inscription. Five years ago, the police had conducted an intensive search of the riverbank for evidence pertaining to Edith's death. Their failure to find anything was a major reason why the coroner ruled "accidental death by drowning." Robert looked closely at the hammer. He thought that the claw part of the evil-looking head was nested in some strands of hair and some ivory-like chips that might be bone fragments. An image of Edith – as she was that night, vibrant and alive – came unbidden, and he shuddered.

I was so naïve. I asked Tony, "What's it like to kill a person? Is it easy? Can anyone do it or does it take something special?"

Two thoughts came rapid-fire. First, *if I turn this in, it all starts over again!* He was flooded with memories. Of suspicious police and friends of Edith. Of the innuendoes that dogged him for months. *Two wives in five years ... dying "accidentally" ... in the same place ....?*

The second thought was of Simon. *It's his hammer. It's got his name on it. He had it in his hand just before Edith was killed. If I turn it in ...*

Tony's Second Thoughts

Cooper could not recall a more satisfying day. It began early, about seven AM, with a very strange call.

"Cooper? This is Miko Andropov. We met last week in San Francisco."

"I'm sorry, I don't –"

"You were asking around about a mutual friend – Anthony Pastore."

I must have talked to fifty people, most of them mean-looking dudes with names from the old country. And some of them didn't like me asking around. Be careful about what you say to somebody named Miko from San Francisco.

"You must have me confused –"

"I don't think so. You probably know me better as Bluto."

It was if the renaming flipped an "on" switch, starting a video in his head. Miko – aka Bluto -- was easy to remember. He was completely bald, heavily tattooed, six and a half feet tall, weighing about 300 pounds distributed so as to make him look like an inverted pyramid. He would easily be confused with an aging NFL tackle except for a severe limp. And once one got past the visuals, Cooper found him to be even more memorable. In particular, Miko knew more about the early life and times of Tony Pastore than anyone else he met in San Francisco.

Cooper came across him in his last few hours in San Francisco. Several of the old men that he had talked to earlier mentioned "Bluto" as the single best source of information. Of these, the last old geezer that he talked to added, "He would have taken over when Uncle Vinnie passed ... except he's from the wrong part of Europe. We're not real committed to diversification."

Another white-haired old man told him, "Oh, and you should know that Bluto doesn't like people very much, particularly if they're from out-of-town and they ask a lot of questions and look like they might hang out with people with badges in their pocket. You should maybe think twice about finding him."

Everybody he asked knew who Bluto was, but no one was prepared to say where he was. Cooper was reconciled to doing without him. Then Bluto found him, about three hours before his flight home. At the time, he was sitting on a park bench in North Beach – "the Italian neighborhood" – talking to an overweight priest who was determined to say nothing bad about any San Francisco resident with an Italian surname, especially if they knew Uncle Vinnie.

The priest was just finishing a long story about how Uncle Vinnie had funded the installation of a wheelchair ramp for a home for retired priests. He stopped mid-sentence when a very large man sat down next to him.

The priest became instantly nervous. "Um. Hi Miko. This is Cooper. I was just telling him about –"

"Hello, father. And I know what Cooper's interested in. And it ain't about wheelchair ramps or stained glass windows or new pews or any of the other stuff that Uncle Vinnie spread around. Why don't you let me take it from here?"

The priest hopped up quite smartly, gave a little bow in Miko's general direction and walked off briskly, as though Cooper didn't exist.

Miko turned to Cooper. "Cooper, I hear you've been asking for me." Coming from him, the question transformed itself into a challenge.

Cooper edged as far down the bench as he could get and placed his feet in position for a fast start. He leaned forward and braced his hands on the edge of the bench. *He's big and strong. Could break me into little pieces. But he has to catch me first.*

"Uh, yeah I am, if you're somebody named Bluto. Several people suggested that you could help me."

"You're in luck then. I'm Bluto. It's 'Miko' only for my close friends, the Catholic Church and the IRS."

Cooper couldn't help himself. "That must be tough. The name, I mean. Popeye was one of my favorite cartoons when I was growing up. I hated Bluto."

To his relief, the man smiled and looked at him with renewed interest. "Honest of you. I don't hear that a whole lot. But in my line of work, the name's an advantage. Comes with an automatic fear factor."

"I can see that. Should I be afraid?"

Bluto didn't answer, seeming to be thinking about the question. When he did talk, it was to change the subject.

"You were a cop? Homicide, right?"

"A long time ago. In another world." As soon as he said it, he pictured the falling dots that had divided his life into distinct eras. *I wonder where Bluto was on September 11, 2001? Did it change him too?*

"And you're interested in Anthony Pastore, our home-town hero? Nobody else?"

"Nope, just Tony."

"Why?"

No way to sugarcoat this or dress it up. He already knows who I am and why I'm here.

He leaned a little more forward and prepared to push off the bench before he said, "I'd like to carve him into very small pieces and drop them into the sewer. For various reasons, that's impractical. So I'm trying to get some leverage on him, so that I can make him leave someone alone that I care about."

Bluto looked at him with real interest. "Leverage, huh?"

When Cooper nodded, Bluto stood up abruptly, saying, "C'mon. I'll drive you to SFO. You've got a flight in two-and-a-half hours and we need to talk."

That was last week. Between then and now, Cooper had used his research – including much of what he had learned from Bluto -- to confront Tony at his country club. He thought that it had worked; that Pastore would sulk but end up seeing it in his own best interests to leave Ellen and him alone. Somehow, he knew that the phone call from Bluto was proof that it hadn't worked. *You were wrong. Tony's self image won't let him leave us alone.*

"Cooper? Are you there?"

"Bluto. Of course I remember. The park bench in North Beach. I enjoyed our conversation. And you saved me forty bucks in cabfare to the airport."

"Well worth it for me. The video of Tony in the locker room is circulating among a carefully selected group of his friends even as we speak." After a pause, he went on in a different tone. "I only wish that I could do something more … physical … to Tony. But we have special rules for family members."

Cooper's premonition was getting stronger. "Why do I think you're going to tell me that our 'leverage' scheme didn't work? That Tony is going to try to wriggle out of his commitments?"

"He's an asshole. Even worse, he's a stupid asshole who's seen too many James Cagney movies. Doesn't know when to cut his losses."

"What's he up to?"

There was a long silence on the other end of the call. Finally, Bluto said, "Cooper, I like you. And I like what you're trying to do to Tony. But I need you to promise me that – from here on – this is strictly between us. No cops, no reporters, no local goons … just you and me."

Don't promise a guy like Bluto something that you can't deliver. "There's one other guy that probably has guessed what's going on. But we can trust him."

"If you say so. You know the rules, I think … And you know what happens if those rules get broken."

That was put very tactfully. "I get the message. So what's happened?"

"Tony went shopping. In San Francisco. For specialized talent. For a very delicate and hush-hush job in Stanton."

Cooper said only, "Job?"

"Can't be very specific on the phone. Let's just say he wants a contractor who can convince you to sit still while he shows you the error of your ways."

Cooper sighed. *I should have foreseen this. Now I have a whole new set of complications.*

He asked, "And you know this because…?"

A clear note of amusement was evident in Bluto's response. "Because I took the job. It's right down my alley. Nobody better than me to do what Tony wants done. And the money is good."

But you're calling me instead. I think I just got real lucky!

"What's the timeline?"

"I promised him he'd have what he wanted not later than this afternoon. I'm in Stanton. Actually, I'm about three blocks from your motel. Mind if I stop by?"

The Third Option

Bluto got there five minutes early. When Cooper opened the door, Bluto stooped to fit through the suddenly small opening. Once in, he stood just inside, looking around what he could see of the two-room suite. He particularly looked at Dmitri sitting in the chair at the desk. When Dmitri saw him, he slowly put both of his hands in full view, resting on the desktop.

"This is Dmitri Akov," Cooper said. "He's the one I told you about."

Bluto's expression did not change, but he did not shift his gaze away from Dmitri. And Dmitri had taken on a wariness that Cooper had never seen before. A watchfulness and tension settled on him that made Cooper think of a gunfighter facing off on a dusty Western street.

Bluto spoke very softly. "Akov, huh. Moscow? Not so long ago, I think?"

Dmitri nodded. "More like a suburb of Moscow. More than fifteen years now. And you?"

"Obninsk. Our 'Nuclear City'. An easy drive from Moscow."

Dmitri nodded. "With all those physicists who designed the Chernobyl reactors. Have we met?"

"No. But I know who you are. And who your family is." He paused and then added in a slightly raised voice, "I didn't like them very much."

"Neither did I. Anyway, my family – and Russia with it – are gone. This is my family now." And Dmitri held out his hand to indicate Cooper.

Dmitri's words and the inclusive gesture brought back the lump to Cooper's throat. When he spoke, his voice had changed.

"Bluto, Dmitri. We've got ten minutes before the show starts. Any questions?"

Bluto was first to speak. "The woman – there's always a woman in these matters – does she know anything about this?"

"No. And I don't want her to know."

They turned out the lights. With the blinds closed, it was semi-dark in the room. They each took their positions – Bluto standing by the door and Dmitri and Cooper out of sight in the adjacent room. Cooper turned on the camera and recording devices hidden in each of the two rooms.

Then they waited.

Tony Pastore stood in the doorway. He had on a jet-black rain suit with a very large Pebble Beach logo. The overall look was finished off with gloves and tennis shoes, also in black. He was carrying a black gym bag with some fancy gold logo. The bag looked heavy. The combination of all black with the high-class logos made him look like a ninja out on a date.

"We all set?" he asked Bluto, sounding nervous.

"Just like you drew it up."

"Any trouble?"

"Piece of cake. Come on in."

Tony came in very tentatively and Bluto shut the door behind him. "Where is he?"

"In the bathtub. Less mess that way once you get serious."

"What shape is he in? Is he conscious?"

"Of course. Wouldn't be any fun for you if he wasn't, would it? And I haven't damaged him much. A few bruises and lots of duct tape."

Bluto gestured at the bag that Tony was carrying. "What did you bring?"

Tony brightened at the question. "Whatever was handy. Knives, pliers, soldering iron … a big meat cleaver, a sock full of quarters …."

Bluto tried to look impressed. "I guess you've done this before, huh?"

"Not like I'm going to do him … start to finish … all the bells and whistles. And I'm going to enjoy every second of it."

"You need me from here on?"

"You can watch if you like. Just be somewhere handy so that you can help me get rid of the body ... or however many parts there are." Tony giggled.

Bluto turned away to hide his look of disgust.

"Tony. One more thing before you get started?"

Tony looked blank for a brief second. "Oh, yeah." He reached into the bag and brought out a packet of hundred-dollar bills. "Twenty-five thou, right?"

Bluto took the package of bills. "For you, Tony, I would have done it for a whole lot less."

Tony looked at him curiously, but Bluto just stared back at him with a blank look. Tony was fidgeting, unable to stand still. He was sweating profusely and beginning to breathe heavily. Bluto looked at his pinpoint pupils. *The man's juiced himself up with some pharmaceutical courage!* Then he thought of Lisa, Alfredo and the others that had irritated Tony and paid for it in Tony's special currency. *Time for this charade to be over with.*

He stood aside, gestured at the open arch into the next room, and said, "He's in there. I'm sure he's looking forward to seeing you."

Tony picked up his bag and moved into the next room. When he turned the corner, he came face to face with Cooper and Dmitri standing side-by-side squarely in the center of the space. He stifled a scream and froze in place for half-a-second. Then he flung the bag at them wildly and lunged backwards, turning to run. He traveled about eight inches before thudding into an immovable Bluto, who simply clutched his shoulders and turned him back around, holding him upright so that the toes of his black tennis shoes barely touched the floor. He looked like a salesman holding up a suit of clothes for a potential buyer.

Dmitri stepped forward and picked up the gym bag. He held it waist high, turned it over and let the contents clatter onto the carpet at Tony's feet. In addition to the items Tony had mentioned, the pile also had sandpaper, a rasp file, hacksaw, a kitchen implement that looked like a juice squeezer, and a vial of clear liquid wrapped in cotton.

Dmitri held up the vial and peeled the cotton away. "Acid, I think? If it's what you used on Lisa, it's probably past its expiration date. We should probably test it."

He uncapped the vial and held it, slightly tilted, in front of Tony's nose. Tony pulled his head as far as he could, but ran into Bluto's unyielding chest. His eyes almost crossed as they looked at the vial at the tip of his nose, adding to the image of stark terror that he was projecting. The smell of urine was suddenly very strong and Bluto held Tony another few inches away from him.

Dmitri looked directly at Tony. "I guess it's still OK to use, based on the subject's reaction." He recapped it and stepped back alongside Cooper.

Cooper stepped forward and looked closely at Tony. "Tony? Are you with us? I'm not sure you're tracking here." Tony was crying, blubbering "no, no, no..." without a pause. Cooper slapped him, hard. That opened his eyes and stopped his miserable chant.

"We don't need much from you. You don't even need to talk. Just nod." He took Tony's nose between his thumb and forefinger and moved his head up and down. "Yeah. Just like that."

"Now follow closely. You're going to have to choose one of three options when I'm done explaining. Do you understand?"

Tony was not processing, crying and twisting from side to side in Bluto's grasp, looking for a solution that wasn't there. Cooper gripped Tony's jaw in his right hand, pinning his head straight ahead so that all he could see was Cooper. He held him there until Tony's eyes focused on his.

"Are you listening? This is important."

Tony nodded frantically.

"Good. Remember: three options. And you get to pick. Here's option one. Dmitri here arrests you for various felonies ... 'conspiracy to commit murder', 'kidnapping', that sort of thing. A conviction is pretty much a slam dunk, as Bluto here will testify against you and we have both video and audio recordings of you in this motel room. If you choose this option, it's life imprisonment if the jury is in a good mood, or a few years on death row and then a lethal injection if they don't like you."

"Do you understand option one?"

Tony became almost coherent, mumbling a string of denials that – when he looked at Cooper and Dmitri simply staring at him, uncaring – trailed off into more sobbing.

"I'll take that to mean that you do understand option one."

"Option two: We decide that option one is too much trouble for us and the state judiciary system. So Dmitri and I walk out of here, leaving you alone with Bluto here. Now, I can't speak for him, but I don't think he'll be inclined to let you walk away. You see, he'd be at serious risk if some of his colleagues in San Francisco knew of this venture. And there's one more thing you should know about this option. Bluto likes Lisa and Alfredo. In fact, when Uncle Vinnie died, he set up trust funds for each of them. Covers college, medical, whatever they need. Wants to keep them out of the family business.

"Do you under—"

"Just a second, Cooper." Bluto interrupted. "There's no need to leave Tony in doubt, especially for such a serious choice. Let me be perfectly clear about my own view of this option."

He turned Tony around so that they faced one another. He lifted him straight up until their eyes were on the same level and held him out at arm's length. Urine dripped from the toes of Tony's dangling shoes.

Bluto spoke in the friendliest tones imaginable. "First, Tony, I hope that you select this option. I really do. And if you do, I want you to know that we'll have some quality time together before you check out. I promise to try every one of these tools that you brought along." And he poked the pile of hardware with his toe, causing a few brief metallic tones.

He turned Tony back around and lowered him to his tiptoes once more, then nodded at Cooper.

Cooper asked, "Do you understand option two?"

The man was sobbing uncontrollably, wracked by continuous shaking. Cooper slapped him, but gently, just to get his attention. Tony nodded, even stuttered out "Y...y...y...yes..."

"Good. Now listen to your third option. It's more complicated, so I need your full attention."

He waited for a full minute for Tony's sobbing to become a continuous sniffling. When he thought Tony could focus slightly better, he began.

"Option three: All four of us leave here and go our separate ways, back to our lives as if this had never happened... with a few exceptions. Unfortunately, most of those exceptions pertain to you, so listen closely."

"First, you drop all of your lawsuits against Ellen Pastore and you reimburse her for all of her legal costs incurred to date. If anyone asks, you're doing this based on very strong advice from your attorneys."

"Second, you set up trust funds for Lisa and Alfredo, similar in every respect to those already established by Bluto. They are to be fully funded and irrevocable. Bluto will advise you as to the exact language and the proper legal firms to use."

Cooper and Dmitri watched him closely. With each phrase, Tony seemed to become more aware of what he was hearing. The legalistic language was seeping in and creating a very thin veneer of normalcy in his overloaded senses. The sniffling subsided until it became an occasional hiccup and his eyes began to focus on Cooper as he was talking. The first slight signs of resistance were starting to appear – his head shaking from side-to-side instead of nodding, his hands coming up from his sides as though to protest.

"Third, you stay out of our lives, all of us, including Ellen. We do not see you, talk to you, or even think of you. You cross the street if you see one of us coming, leave the restaurant if any of us walk in the door, claim you do not know us if our names come up in conversation. You do nothing – nothing – that will make us aware of you."

"Do you understand option three?"

For the first time, Tony spoke, stammering only slightly. "But, that's –"

Dmitri broke in, "Tony, I know what you're going to say and you're absolutely right. It's illegal … blackmail, coercion, entrapment … all those things … it's illegal as all hell. Hard for me to condone … I'm a police officer, after all. Maybe we should just stick with the first two options."

Tony looked at the two of them in horror. Bluto shook him slightly, the way a parent might shake a child that was being inattentive, and spoke softly into his left ear. "Tony, we need to know if you understand the third option. It's important that you make an informed choice."

Tony nodded violently. "Yes, I understand."

It was Cooper's turn, speaking as to a child coming out of a temper tantrum. "Good. Now, which one of the three options do you choose?"

Finally, the absurdity of his situation overcame his cowardice and hopelessness. Tony almost yelled, "This is crazy! You can't make me choose!"

Still in the same reasonable tone, Cooper continued. "I understand your frustration. None of the options are very attractive. But you see, if you don't choose, then we'll have to do it for you. The problem is, each of us favors a different option. Dmitri likes the first one, Bluto the second one, and I prefer the third. But we've agreed that each of us will abide by your choice."

"I'll take number three." The words were mumbled, barely intelligible.

"What did you say? I'd hate to misunderstand such an important choice."

"Three. I want number three."

"OK. Three it is. You can go now."

"Go? Home?"

"Sure. That's what option three is. Remember? Back to your life, as though this had never happened."

Bluto let him down and released his grip on him. Tony staggered briefly, reaching out to steady himself. "You mean I can just leave? Walk out? Just like that?"

"Sure. We'll have Bluto hang around for a couple of days. He'll stop in to see you tomorrow. Make sure all of our agreements are followed up on."

Tony reached down for the bag, but Cooper stopped him. "Oh, leave all that stuff. We'll hang on to it for you. We may need it if we have to fall back on option two. Just in case option three isn't executed to our satisfaction. After all, you've already defaulted on our last agreement."

Tony turned slowly to look at each of them in turn. Finally, he shuffled head-down to the door and left, looking like a very old man wading through knee-deep water. They heard a car start a minute later.

Cooper was exhausted. He slumped down into the desk chair. "I hope it works. I can't do this again."

Dmitri slumped into a sitting position on the bed, his body language clearly conveying his massive ambivalence about what had just happened. He looked like a man who had just betrayed his best friend for the sake of an indifferent cause.

Bluto was seemingly unchanged. "I think this is hard for the two of you," he said sympathetically. "Not your everyday negotiating session."

He continued, "It'll work. Trust me. I deal with assholes like Tony every day. I'll see him tomorrow to make sure, but he's ours. And he knows it." He was talking to Cooper, but looking only at Dmitri as he was talking.

"I thought I was done with this," Dmitri said softly. "It's very Russian. We can arrest them or we can kill them, very slowly. At any time, for any reason. So they always take the third option."

Bluto said, "Politsiya rules." His tone was harsh, accusative.

Dmitri's eyes locked onto Bluto's. He sat up straighter. "But not my rules. Not there. Not here. Especially not here. Not now."

Bluto and Dmitri looked at each other, and Cooper knew that important judgments were being made about both past and present decisions, about character and family. *I envy them their history, that two such different men can call upon a common past to mediate current disputes.*

Very slowly, Dmitri nodded. In turn, Bluto stretched out his hand. Dmitri shook the extended hand, saying something very softly in Russian. Then he switched to English. "Thank you for helping my friend."

"It was nothing. Tony deserved everything he got done to him. And I made an easy twenty-five thousand bucks."

"And you got a new toolkit," said Cooper as he handed him the gym bag of improvised torture instruments.

Cooper said, "Thanks, Bluto."

The big man looked at each of them in turn, as though engaged in some internal debate. Then he said, "Call me Miko. Bluto's a stage name."

The Police at Work

Marcus called Dmitri. "I've got a couple of things that might interest you."

"You sound like my stockbroker. Come on up."

"Why don't you come down here in the trenches, where the real police work gets done? I've got a lot of paper spread out ... hard to move it all."

"On my way."

Marcus waved Dmitri into his work-space, one of many cubicles in the middle of a crowded floor. The fabric walls displayed a half-dozen glossy photographs, with yellow block arrows pasted on each. The table was covered with what Dmitri took to be thick legal documents, with multicolored tabs to mark places.

Marcus was in Levis and a polo shirt. If not for the holstered gun on his belt, Dmitri thought, he could be a college kid working on a term paper. The thought triggered a more sinister image – that of a teenage Marcus, naked on a rumpled bed with Edith McKay, while Nathaniel's aunt watched from an open doorway. *What the hell am I going to do with that little bit of knowledge?*

He realized that Marcus was looking at him with a curious expression. He forced the troubling image away and asked simply, "Whatcha got?"

"I got non-news, I got good news, and I got bad news. Which do you want first?"

"You and I may differ on what's good or bad. Why don't you start with the interviews? What do we have?"

"OK. That's the non-news part. There were fifteen citizens – including both Robert and Simon Radner – who reported significant conversational time with McKay in the ninety minutes or so of general mingling before it went dark. I reviewed their original testimony from five years ago with each of them, told them it was now a murder case, and asked them if they had anything else that occurred to them in light of that."

"Anything?"

"Nope. To a person, they expressed shock at the idea of murder ... and couldn't even recall what they had said originally five years ago."

"About what I expected. I can't remember conversations I had yesterday. Five years is a long time."

Marcus went on. "The bad news bit?"

Dmitri waited, eyebrows raised.

"I got a look at the fingerprint analysis. The DA – our Ms. Martine -- left out a couple of key facts when she said Simon Radner's prints were on the hammer."

"Weren't they?"

"Oh, yeah. They were there. Along with Edith McKay's. Perfectly consistent with Simon's story about the photo shoot before the cocktail hour. What she didn't mention was that both sets of prints were smudged in places. The lab guy thinks the last person to hold the hammer was someone with gloves on."

"That doesn't rule out Simon as the killer."

"No, it doesn't. But why do you suppose Ms. Martine – our super-detailed DA – left out that interesting fact?"

Dmitri paused long enough that Marcus could tell he was debating what to say.

He finally said, "She doesn't like Simon Radner. And there's more to it than the usual 'DA vs. suspect' hostilities. I think they have some history together."

Marcus leaned back and looked at Dmitri. "You're kidding me, right? I'd hate to do a lot of super-duper detective work and have it thrown out of court for prosecutorial bias."

"You just do the super-duper bit. I'll handle the politics in the DA's office.

"You said something about 'good news'...?

"The glossies." Marcus turned to the wall of photos and pointed to the first in line, a posed group of about eight individuals with Simon and Edith in the middle. There was a bright yellow neon arrow pasted on to the photo.

"We've got a ringer." He pointed to the arrow, which in turn was aimed at the figure second from the left, a smallish, middle-aged man in a not-very-well-fitting plaid sport coat.

"What about him? Other than that he doesn't look like he feels at home?"

"He isn't. At home, that is. Nobody knows who he is or why he's there."

Dmitri scanned the other photos. The same man appeared in each, once more in a posed photo of a small group and the rest of the time as one of the faces in the background, seeming always to be focused on Edith. In each case, Dmitri thought, he looked uncomfortable; "furtive" was the word that seemed to fit best. Most interesting of all, one photo showed him and Edith McKay talking together in the background, relatively isolated from those around them. She was turning away, and he had his hand on her arm, as though he was trying to keep her in place.

Dmitri turned to Marcus, who was watching him expectantly. "Stanton's not that big a city... and this is the in-crowd ... but nobody knows who he is?"

Marcus shook his head. "Nobody that I've talked to. But everybody assumes that somebody else knows him. So nobody thought anything of it. We've got a party crasher ... or worse!"

"A caterer? Household help? Delivery guy?"

"Nope. All accounted for. And look at these pictures -- how hard he's trying to fit in. But, just in case, I cross checked the invitation list and our interviews. Everybody matches and is known to somebody else at the party. This guy, whoever he is, wasn't on the list, wasn't invited and we didn't interview him. I think we've got ourselves a hot suspect, a party crasher with an obvious interest in McKay."

"OK. So now we have some old-fashioned police work ... the knock-on-doors unglamorous real world of detection. Find out who he is. We need to talk to him."

"Already underway. I've got a couple of uniforms showing the picture to everyone who was there that night. Someone must have talked to him ... taken away some piece of information ..."

Dmitri turned to leave, but Marcus said, "There's more."

Dmitri stood, simply staring at Marcus.

"You also suggested looking at the recent history of the disputed land use, remember? The fight about preserving Riverbend?"

"Yeah. That's a stretch, but ..."

"Pretty good hunch, as it turns out. There are about four thousand pages of legal documents over the last five years – thank God for digitalization. But the key document – the one that drives everything else – is the charter. It was drafted before McKay died and was scheduled to be approved the week after she died."

"Can you make this real simple for me, Marcus? Remember: I'm Russian. The government owned all the land, so there weren't any land use disputes."

"Until 1989. Then it was open house."

"OK. So you know Soviet history. What about Riverbend?"

"The file has two drafts of the charter. The first is dated three days before she died and has the phrase 'Riverbend shall be preserved in its present state in perpetuity'. The second draft is signed and dated on the day of her death. It is identical except that it adds the phrase, 'subject to the needs of the greater community'. It's in Robert's handwriting and it's inserted in the margin of the draft. That's the version that was delivered to the law firm for finalization by Robert Radner – then the owner of Riverbend because of McKay's death -- three months later. And that version has been the one that both parties have been citing during the last few years of scorched-earth litigation around what's going to happen to the Riverbend property."

Dmitri said, half to himself, "That 'subject to' phrase would be as good as a full-employment act for any developer with a law firm, wouldn't it?" Then, to Marcus, "So, couldn't the revision be McKay's? Maybe she changed her mind."

"Two problems with that theory. First, according to several people who talked to her the last few days she was alive, she didn't change her mind. She emphasized her commitment to the 'in perpetuity' language when she wrote the first draft.... To the entire Board of the Conservancy organization. She knew exactly what she wanted. She told the Chairman that she intended to announce that version of the charter at the award ceremony that night. Second, her fingerprints were all over the first draft, as you'd expect. The second draft has no new fingerprints of hers anywhere on its surface, just the ones of the prior draft!"

"That's not so unlikely, is it? If the document is just presented for her signature, she wouldn't necessarily handle it. Is her signature witnessed?"

"Not on the first draft."

Dmitri waited for him to continue. But when he looked over at him, Marcus was clearly unhappy, searching for words.

"Marcus?"

"There were two witnesses to her signature on the final draft. And each of them initialed the new language written in the margin. One was Robert Radner."

"And? Just tell me, Marcus!"

"The other was Natalie Benson." He added unnecessarily, "As you know, she's my mother."

Dmitri's first reaction was anger. *That tears it. My chief investigator's mother is a material witness in a murder case!*

Marcus watched Dmitri closely and knew what he was thinking. But he was ahead of him.

"Look, Dmitri, this is not that complicated. Both of them – Robert Radner and Natalie Benson – are legitimate witnesses for her signing. Each of them was and has continued to be heavily engaged in the negotiation of the Charter document. And I talked with them independently. Each of them says that Edith signed the document in her office at Riverbend just before the guests started arriving, with both of them in the room as witnesses."

Dmitri closed his eyes, as though he could visualize the possibilities more clearly. "So. The later draft supersedes the first one, and has greater legal force because of the witnesses' signature."

He paused, opened his eyes and looked questioningly at Marcus, who merely nodded.

Dmitri resumed. "But that later draft significantly changes the document, in ways that make it more susceptible to development. And the witnesses, although upstanding citizens, are two people with a strong bias toward such development."

Again, he looked at Marcus for confirmation, who again nodded.

"So," Dmitri continued, "a cynical and/or anti-development type might argue that it's possible that Edith McKay didn't sign the second version; that the later draft was just her original signed draft as amended by Robert Radner, unseen by McKay."

Marcus shook his head. "That would make it forgery ... which can succeed only if –"

Dmitri finished the sentence, "Only if Edith McKay was not around to challenge it."

An Exchange of Views

Cooper's cell phone rang. The area code was the one for Stanton, so Cooper answered, expecting Ellen. What he got was Dmitri; a very official Dmitri.

"Cooper. We need you down here right now. This is not a request."

Cooper said, "Always glad to help the forces of the law. What's it about?"

"I'll tell you when you get here. But you probably should review your notes on the Edith McKay case."

"Is tomorrow soon enough?"

If possible, Dmitri's voice became even more cop-like. "If you're not here by this afternoon, there will be a warrant out for your arrest."

Cooper watched his cell phone screen go blank, thinking, *If the cops are mad at me, I must be doing something right. But what?*

The county courthouse was an ancient building. Cooper had worked there for years and retained few positive memories from his time between those thick limestone walls. As he walked up to the third floor, he thought again about how it suited Dmitri – solid, unchanging, weathered … and merciless.

The office was a surprise: a solid walnut door with Dmitri's name & rank in gold lettering, a surprising reminder of his professional resurrection following his suspension. Cooper knocked, and heard an immediate *"come in."* When he did, he was face to face with Dmitri, seated at his desk facing the door. The office was quite small. *I guess the gold lettering must compensate for that.*

To his surprise, his son Marcus was seated immediately to his left.

He stopped cold, looking first at Dmitri and then at Marcus. The silence was profound, until Cooper said, "Well ..." and then could not think how to finish.

He had not seen Marcus face-to-face for a year and thought as he always did when they met, *You've changed. You're older.* Then, just as surely, came the unspoken thought, *Perhaps we can talk now ... as two people interested in one another, with some common history, or a possible future ....*

Then he remembered where he was. And said, "Well ... Reporting as ordered. Is this where you read me my rights? Or am I merely 'assisting police with their inquiries', as the English so quaintly phrase it?"

Dmitri grimaced. He pointed at the one unoccupied chair and said, "Sit down, Cooper."

Cooper sat. He looked directly at Marcus, but spoke to Dmitri, "I gather that I'm talking to the Edith McKay task force? I've read your press releases, so I know that you are making 'excellent progress'. How can I help?"

Dmitri and Marcus exchanged glances. Dmitri spoke again, "First, you can drop the helpful citizen comedy routine. This is unofficial. But we can make it official in a real hurry if you like. Do you know the meaning of 'obstruction of justice'?"

Cooper said, reciting in the most didactic tone he could muster: "I believe it refers to the crime of interfering with the work of police, investigators, regulatory agencies, prosecutors, or other government officials. The English refer to it as perverting the course of justice. It usually takes the form of lying to police."

Marcus sighed audibly, crossed his arms, let his chin sink to his chest, and slumped in his chair. Cooper recognized the characteristic posture from their many attempted discussions in the past. Dmitri just stared at Cooper, expressionless.

He went on, trying hard to sound sincere. "Let's see. I can't have lied, because I haven't even talked to any investigating officers. So it must be the 'interfering' clause –"

Dmitri said wearily, "Cooper. Stop."

"OK. But I really don't know what I've done to make you unhappy. Why don't you just tell me?"

To his surprise, Dmitri turned to Marcus and said, "You tell him."

Marcus was even more surprised than Cooper. He sat up in his chair and looked sharply at Dmitri, as though seeking further instruction. Dmitri, however, had swiveled in his chair and was gazing out the window. Cooper was inordinately pleased when Marcus recovered quickly and said quite briskly and without hesitation,

"One: You're running around town asking questions about the Land Conservancy deal. Two: We know you're trying to track down a witness to the McKay murder. Three: You're asking questions all over town, mostly about McKay's personal life. Four: we hear stories about you rousting Tony Pastore at his club."

Cooper said, "I have in fact done all four of those things, and probably more that would bother you if you knew about them. But where's the obstruction of justice? I'm working on behalf of Simon Radner, so it's legitimate behavior." *That's not quite true. The Tony venture – the one at the country club -- was quite independent of his work for Simon.*

Marcus went on as though Cooper hadn't spoken. "And how do you know about our so-called mystery guest, by the way? That's not exactly public information."

"C'mon, Marcus! You've been interviewing half the town, showing them pictures of the guy. We've got the same pictures you have."

Dmitri put a hand up to stop Marcus, leaned forward, and said to Cooper, "You're a private citizen, not even a licensed private investigator. No matter. You of all people know that these things are best left to the police. At best, you're confusing the citizenry about who's chasing whom. At worst, you might be – unwittingly – cuing legitimate suspects that they need to hide certain facts about their culpability."

"Ah, Dmitri. That's put very elegantly. What you left out is your fear that I know something you don't."

Dmitri asked mildly, "Do you?"

Cooper answered, "Based on Marcus's four-part indictment of me ... No. I seem to be pursuing the same avenues as you, with a similar lack of success."

But then he asked, "One thing really bothers me, though. That damn Lucite display case! Think about it. He – or she, to be politically correct -- bashes Edith with the hammer and then puts it back in its special-purpose display case before tossing it. Why would any sensible killer preserve the evidence like that? If he'd just tossed the hammer in the damn river, the elements would have eliminated all of the fingerprints and biochemical stuff and we'd be at Square One."

Marcus and Dmitri looked at each other, but neither spoke. Cooper went on, "It's like he –or she -- wanted to keep his or her options open ... to be able to start a murder investigation whenever he chose to, no matter how long into the future... maybe to blackmail Simon ...?"

Dmitri said, "Well, then. That's surely an interesting line of thought. You be sure to let us know if you ever find an answer to any of those many questions."

"I promise I shall," said Cooper.

Marcus raised his voice, "How do we know that?"

Cooper thought about all of the suppressed antagonism and unspoken accusations imbedded in that simple question and then about how much he would have liked to tell Marcus about himself. How he believed in justice, in restoring what he could to victims, in the law, about the impossibility of reparations, about the obligations he felt to those he loved.... Most of all, he would have liked to talk about the power of regret and how it sharpens as time passes.

Instead, he simply said, "You don't. But I promise that I will share any information with you if I think it would help your investigation."

Marcus glared and started to speak. But Dmitri sat up straight, and then leaned toward them and put his hands flat on the surface of his desk, as though reaching out to each of them. It was a gesture that Cooper chose to interpret as a confirmation of Dmitri's ambivalence, and his essential humanity. He wanted to reach out and place his hand on top of Dmitri's.

Instead, he stood, and said, "Thanks for sharing your concerns. I'll be in touch if I learn anything at all."

And he left.

Dawkins

Cooper got lucky. Usually, when it came to the nuts and bolts of finding someone who didn't want to be found, the police had all of the advantages – manpower, access to information, the ability to intimidate civilians. Occasionally however, chance intervened in favor of the underdog.

He knew that Marcus was focusing on the two hundred and thirty guests to see if they could recall seeing or talking with the mystery guest. Cooper couldn't compete with that. But he had another angle. He figured that Mr. X was from out-of-town, definitely not a local. Given the weather and road conditions both before and after the McKay party, he thought it likely that the man would have stayed in Stanton for at least one night. And based on his appearance, Cooper also thought it likely that he would be apt to frequent the lower end of Stanton's accommodations. That made for a list of seven motels that were plausible candidates.

It took a day and a half, twenty contacts and about three hundred dollars in bribes to track down motel desk clerks and to persuade them to dig out and let Cooper look at guest registers for the nights in question. Some of them just laughed when asked if they had records from five years ago. On the other hand, most of them remembered that particular night because of the massive storm and its impact on their business.

He was accumulating names and addresses -- about a dozen so far. Each of them was a man who had checked in on the day of the party and checked out the following morning. What they didn't have in common was geography; they came from different cities and in two cases from out-of-state.

No way that I can check out this many people in this many places. But I can hand the list to Dmitri. And until he clears them or finds this mystery guest on his own, they are legitimate suspects. Should take some of the immediate pressure off of Simon.

Cooper's luck was in finding Walter. Walter was a seventy-seven year-old black night clerk at the Riverside Motel, a run-down twenty-unit operation in one of Stanton's more questionable neighborhoods. Walter looked as ancient as the motel itself, but his memory belied his age. When Cooper showed him the picture, he identified the man immediately, even recalling that he had asked a lot of questions about the McKay family and Edith in particular. The register showed him checking in on the day of the party, and checking out very early on the following morning. His name was Frank Dawkins and he gave a street address in Mojave, California.

The next day, Cooper flew to LAX, rented a car and drove to Mohave. During the three-hour drive, he thought about calling Dmitri or Marcus to tell them about Dawkins. He could not think of any reasonable excuse he could offer for failing to disclose what he knew and where he was going. *Other than that I'm already so far into it that it can't get much worse.*

The first visuals of the small town of Mojave were startling -- dozens of shimmering tail fins towering in the desert air, painted in all the fluorescent colors of the world's major airlines. The Avis agent had told Cooper that the Mojave climate was ideal for the temporary storage of excess or obsolete planes, and that a mini-industry had grown up around that need. It transformed Mojave into an elephant's graveyard for airliners and a testimonial to the ironies of the globalized economy.

The phalanxes of idle aircraft provided a colorful backdrop to the main street, which fronted on and paralleled a set of railroad tracks that disappeared into the distance at either end of the town. The town had the characteristic look of a once-flourishing rural hub that had been bypassed by the interstate highway and was unable to adapt to the new and harsher reality. Cooper felt a distant kinship with that image.

He drove by the address. It was on a side street, one of a string of similar small and dreary ranch-style homes, all of them suffering from deferred maintenance. The street was only two blocks long, anchored at one end by a convenience store with two gas pumps and at the other end by the desert. The

Dawkins house was one of the few that did not have a pickup truck outside. It seemed to Cooper to be a sad house in a sad town.

Probably just my city-boy biases at work, he thought. He also thought that Mojave and Stanton were probably at opposite ends of any spectrum imaginable.

He asked the clerk at the convenience store if he knew Dawkins. The clerk spoke more Spanish than he did English, but Cooper worked out that Dawkins was a good customer and that Cooper would probably be able to find him at the Boxcar Café on the main street at this time of day.

The so-called café was more bar than café. The sign on the door read, *"Our customers are special,"* and the Dawkins – there were two of them, the only customers in the place -- certainly fitted that description.

Cooper stood just inside the doorway and studied Frank Dawkins. He did not seem a promising individual. Like the street he lived on, Dawkins seemed to carry with him – like his own little atmosphere – little pulsating eddies of hopelessness. But it was the white rat peering out of the pocket of his rumpled jacket and the equally rumpled small boy that was sitting chin-in-hand next to him that provided the final touches. The light was poor, but the rat seemed to have red eyes, never still. The boy, on the other hand, had dark brown eyes that were staring fixedly at the foam on Dawkins' beer glass, apparently gauging its unlikely stability. Neither the rat nor the boy seemed bothered about sitting in a dingy bar on a late afternoon with an old guy that paid more attention to his beer than to either of them.

The most startling fact about the boy was that he was somehow familiar. Cooper knew he had seen him somewhere before ... in a photo album ... on TV ... He couldn't make the connection, but he was certain he had seen the boy before today.

Cooper's next thought was of all the bad jokes that begin "These three guys walked into a bar ..." but he couldn't think of the punch line to fit this particular trio. That was followed immediately by Cooper thinking, *there's no way that this guy could kill somebody!*

The kid had a worn backpack under his chair and looked to be about ten years old, allowing for the dim light and a forgivable tendency to overestimate the age of kids in seedy neighborhood bars. Not nearly old enough to fit the circumstances. Cooper caught himself, and thought, *"Not my concern. I could probably help the rat though. What's a couple of lettuce leaves, after all?"*

Dawkins was of indeterminate age and prospects – somewhere between forty and fifty. He was unalterably drab. Part of it was the way he dressed – khaki pants, khaki shirt, scuffed brown work shoes and the jacket, some sort of puffy suede-like waist-length fashion that apparently made a passable rat habitat. But the drabness was intensified by a minimalist body language that deflected attention – small gestures, an inward look, a settling into himself that implied here was a person of little interest, short on prospects and without the means to find some. An image came to Cooper, of Dawkins morphing into the homeless guy with a crudely lettered cardboard sign, staked out on a traffic island at a major intersection, the kind that makes people run red lights rather than spend sixty seconds avoiding eye contact. The rat could probably help him … curb appeal and all that.

Cooper walked over and stood in front of Dawkins. The man looked up and adjusted his expression from depressed to quizzical.

"Mr. Dawkins?"

"That's me. Do I know you?"

"Nope, but I think we have some people in common." He paused and watched Dawkins closely. "I'm from Stanton."

The reaction was a rippling succession of tics and twitches, telegraphing indecipherable emotions. Dawkins cast a curiously furtive glance at the boy, whose expression hadn't altered in the slightest. Then, he lowered his eyes toward the tabletop and took on an increased rigidity in his posture, as though to withstand a blow.

Without looking at Cooper, he said, "This is my son, Darren. He's eleven." And then, to the boy, "Why don't you go back to the house and get started on that project we talked about? Your mother can help you. I need to talk to this gentleman."

He handed the rat to the boy. "Here. Take Minnie with you."

The boy stared at Cooper for a long ten seconds, but then simply took the rat, put him on his shoulder, picked up his backpack, and walked away. Cooper's lasting impression of him was *that's the oldest-looking eleven-year-old I've ever seen.*

Cooper sat down in the boy's chair, not speaking.

Dawkins said, "Look, mister. I don't know who you are or what you want, but I'm not interested. Funny how sure I was that we were done with all that."

"All what?"

"Stanton, the Radners … maybe even rain…. I've never seen rain like that."

So much for conversation starters. This guy wants to talk. So Cooper prompted … "Yeah. That was quite a night …"

"Never should have gone. It was a mistake all the way." Dawkins had a faraway stare, and Cooper suspected that he was seeing things that he did not want to see, revisiting old ghosts that Cooper had stirred up.

He prodded him again, "So why did you go?"

"Never should have gone," Dawkins said once more. "Everything fell apart."

"Mr. Dawkins…"

With that, Dawkins literally shook himself. And then he talked for ten minutes without an interruption. He reminded Cooper of a drunk, maybe ten days sober, telling his story at an AA meeting. The story was about him, his wife and their boy. They were happy, in a fairy tale sort of way. Then she – her name was Rosa – was diagnosed with cancer. It was still being treated but, according to Dawkins, she was dispirited and angry most of the time. Then he lost his job in the financial meltdown and the family of three began a long slow slide down the economic food chain. They moved from LA to Sacramento to Mojave, managing to stay above the subsistence level, but just barely.

When he paused, Cooper asked, "What did you want from Edith McKay?" And again, "Why did you go?"

"For money, of course. She had so much, and we had so little. I thought ... if I could explain what had happened ... how it wasn't our fault ... that she would help out."

Cooper had no idea what he was talking about. It sounded like emotional blackmail of some sort. He said, "And she turned you down?"

Dawkins laughed, more bemused than amused. "You really don't know anything at all, do you?"

"The last thing you said that I understood was that your name was Dawkins."

But Dawkins was still talking to himself, with that faraway look. "No. She didn't turn me down. Even worse. She wanted to fix everything. But it would have destroyed us!"

Cooper said, "I don't understand. What could she do to you?"

"She didn't even recognize me! Or even my name when I told her! She thought I was part of the crowd invited to the party. I got her attention, though,... She was trying to get rid of me ... So I grabbed her arm and just said 'LA, January, 2000'.

"You've heard the expression: 'She looked like she'd seen a ghost!'? Well, it damn well fit!

"I told her about Darren. How he always asked about her, how we took care of him and loved him, how things had gone bad for us ..."

"What did she say?" Cooper asked gently.

"I don't think she heard much of what I was telling her once she knew who I was. She interrupted me and just started talking non-stop about what she could do. She said that she could care for him much better than we could. That he needed a proper home, with a proper mother and a father. As though he didn't have them ... That Rosa and I could have as much money as we needed ... even move to Stanton to stay close..."

Cooper felt as though he had started one of those multi-generational Victorian novels in the middle rather than at the beginning. He remembered the society-page picture from the night of Edith's death, showing Dawkins holding her arm, inclined toward her, with an intense expression. He recalled Simon's feeling that Edith was experiencing some kind of emotional disorder just before the blackout.

He tried what he thought was a safe question: "So, what did you do then?"

"I just looked at her. And I wished that I had never come."

Cooper asked, "What did she do?"

"I watched her, hoping that maybe what I said to her would sink in. She was excited, fidgety. She looked around, like she was looking for somebody in particular ... even stood on a chair to get a better view. She clearly found them ... made a beeline right across the crowd."

"Who did she go to?"

"Two guys standing together, relatively young. And then to another guy standing in a group, older, kind of distinguished looking. She didn't spend more than twenty seconds with any of them, but she got their attention. That was easy to see. Then she headed for the door, as though to go outside.... in that rain ..."

Dawkins' voice seemed to be wearing out. Cooper thought he might be close to tears. He asked as gently as he could, "What did you do then?"

"I left. I came home. And we've kept to ourselves ever since. No more of that wishing for magic endings. They come with too high a price."

Cooper's sense of unreality was just about maxed out. The conversation with Dawkins – and Dawkins himself -- seemed to be stuck in some parallel universe, talking about people and events that only he could see.

There's only one way it makes any sense.

He asked, "Did you ever try to contact Edith McKay again?"

"No. I was … I am … afraid that she will find a way to get our boy away from us!"

"And she could do that because …?"

Dawkins looked at Cooper like he was a slow learner who had asked an obvious question one too many times. Finally, he just sighed and said in a voice that was a complex blend of anxiety and apathy, "She has lots of money…. And she's his mother."

Edith

Five years ago

Motherhood and all that went with it were not part of Edith McKay's world at the time of the hundred-year storm. The concept did not fit with the world that she had scripted, and all was going according to plan. Or so it seemed. At the moment, she was in the prime of her life; still young, quite beautiful, intelligent and wealthy. She was admired within all of the circles within which she moved and the inevitable stressors of her everyday life were ones that she enjoyed confronting; nothing that kept her awake or seemed insoluble.

Life was good. Even the once-in-a-lifetime storm did nothing except to provide her with an opportunity to demonstrate that she would prevail over it. It was if nature was also following a script, one that was written to center everyone's attention on the leading lady.

She was a woman that lived in the present moment. The past – to the slight extent that she thought about it – did not bother her, even though it harbored memories that she did not like; memories about the kind of person she had been and choices that she knew to be wrongheaded and selfish. And tonight, at this particular moment, it was particularly easy to not think about such things. She was the center of her universe – in a ballroom mostly filled with her admirers, there because she had asked them to come. Both the storm and her awareness that her several enemies were also there added a pleasurable thrill, a feeling that was sharpened by her acute awareness that her husband and two of her current lovers were within fifty feet of where she stood.

Then the man said, "LA, January, 2000," and her world shifted on its axis. Only then did the insistent little man come fully into focus, triggering a flashback to a tawdry negotiation; a deal hastily made but requiring six months of endless waiting to fulfill and requiring a shameful final act. For the first time in several years, she thought of waking up in a hospital room to see this man and his mouse of a wife standing over her, saying, "You have a son." She remembers them handing her the incredibly small bundle, but the only emotion she can recall is her surprise at how easy it was to finally identify who the father was.

She handed him back to the woman. "Here. He's your son, not mine. But I want you to name him Darren."

And until this moment, she had always thought of herself as childless, as though some memories must lie dormant until an outside agency reawakens them.

In the present, the little man was still talking, holding her arm while pouring out a stream of half-heard phrases about money, hardship and obligations. But his intensity and anxiety were lost on Edith; she was deep in her own fantasies about a possible new world.

A child! Someone that is mine, that is like me, that I can shape and teach to do all the things that I can't do alone. A person that will love me unconditionally. A boy who can grow up at Riverbend. In her mind, she visualized her own childhood – the only child of a loving father who modeled and taught her the values that drove her today. *A father who wanted, more than anything else, a grandson to continue the McKay line.*

Perhaps her thinking would have become more realistic and the future would turned out differently if she had taken some time – even a few minutes – to think through alternatives and their consequences; enough time to allow for her natural selfishness to reassert itself. But it was her style to make quick decisions, always favoring the risky and dramatic choice over the safe and conventional alternative. And, once made, that same style demanded swift implementation.

The man was still gripping her arm, looking at her, out of words and waiting, already knowing that his pleading had not taken, that all he had accomplished was to put himself at risk. She spoke briefly to him, empty reassurances intended only to make him go away.

She shook off the little man's grip on her arm and looked around the crowded ballroom. *Everyone who needs to know is here.* And she started her circuit of the ballroom, the one that would condemn her to a lonely death in the hundred-year storm raging outside.

One More Tragic Incident

Cooper spent the rest of the day and the following morning in Mohave and LA checking into the parts of Dawkins' story that he could. He called Ellen while he was waiting for his plane at LAX and told her everything he knew about Dawkins – how he found him, their conversation, and his conviction that Dawkins was not their murderer.

She listened quietly and then said, "That solves the mystery of why Edith left Stanton. And I think it moves Dawkins to the head of the suspect list, despite your impression."

Cooper said, "We have to share all of this with the police."

"Yes we do, and right now. But just the facts, none of your uncorroborated feelings about his innocence."

"I'll call Dmitri." He tried not to think about Dmitri's reaction about the twenty-four hour lag between his call and his discovery of Dawkins' identity.

Dmitri, however, was more reproachful than he was angry, as though unsurprised by the delay. "You should have let us handle it. I thought we'd established that."

"All we established was that I would share any relevant information with you. I'm doing that now. And, besides, it would have taken you three days to send an officer to Mojave to check out Dawkins. I figure I'm helping you manage your department on a limited budget."

Cooper heard the creak as Dmitri leaned back in his office chair. He also picked up on the skepticism in his voice. "And he had no idea that she's been dead since that night five years ago?"

"That's what he says, and I believe him. He's not that good an actor to fake the reaction that I saw. In ten seconds, he went from shock to relief to anger to – finally – worry, about how he's going to tell his boy about his mother."

Or if he even should tell him. That's a lot to dump on an eleven-year-old kid.

"We still have to talk to him. I'll give him a call to see if he's willing to come to Stanton without us sending an officer. And – despite your good feelings about him – I'll also ask the Mojave cops to keep an eye on him until he gets here."

By late the next afternoon, Cooper was waiting for Ellen, sitting in his parked car across from her office in Stanton. The late afternoon sun highlighted the red and orange hues of the trees lining the street. The fall colors and dappled sunlight had started Cooper thinking about the irony; how leaves are at their best just before expiring. He recalled lines from a poem he had been forced to memorize in high school: *And how death seems a comely thing, In Autumn at the fall of the leaf.*

Why do I remember such things? But he could not remember the poet. Maybe Keats? *Dmitri would know,* he thought.

His cell phone rang, showing "unknown caller" for the incoming call. He looked at his watch – still ten minutes before Ellen was due – pushed the "answer" button and said, "Yes?"

"You gave me your card and said to call you if I needed anything. That's what I'm doing. Is that OK?"

Cooper recognized Dawkins, as much from the insecurity in the tone as from the voice itself.

"Yes, it's fine. Is there anything wrong?"

As soon as Dawkins began to answer, Cooper recognized that he was hearing a rehearsed speech. He wondered if Dawkins was reading from a script.

"When you told me about Edith McKay – how she died, and what's going on now with the new evidence – I began to rethink what we – Darren, Rosa and I – should do to look out for ourselves. I remembered how she – McKay – wanted to help him, even though it would have been done all wrong. All wrong! She would have taken him away from us! But at least she had some maternal instincts intact, and I thought that she would still want to help Darren, that we might have worked something out if I hadn't rushed off and she hadn't died. So I did some research, and I think Darren has a legitimate right to some of her money. He's her only son, after all."

Dawkins' voice started out on an uncertain note, but the words tumbled out faster and faster and his voice became louder and more insistent as he continued until, by the time he paused, Cooper was holding the phone away from his ear. He remembered how beaten down Dawkins had seemed in Mojave just a short time ago, and wondered about what it took to create this kind of righteous indignation and what part he himself had played in Dawkins' reawakening. The cliche *"Let sleeping dogs lie"* came immediately to mind.

He sighed deeply, having learned long ago that murder investigations inevitably reactivate memories and animosities that have been stored away in the mind's attic; that violent death – an ending – paradoxically restarts so many things.

"I'm not a lawyer -- " Cooper began cautiously, but was immediately cut off.

"Lawyers be damned! This is about what's right! We have it coming to us!"

Cooper realized that Dawkins had made up his mind and was being driven by a sense of entitlement that – for the moment – was immune to reason. He also thought that Dawkins had a point that was both legally and morally defensible, no matter how it was arrived at or believed in.

"Look, Mr. Dawkins. You may be right. But there's a right way to go about this --"

Again Dawkins broke in. "I tried your 'right way' and he hung up on me."

"Who's the 'he' you're referring to?" asked Cooper, but he already knew the answer. And he also realized that he had triggered a series of events that was about to ripple through people's lives with unforeseeable consequences, people that had been too complacent about the last several years, about deaths that deserved more attention than they had been allotted. *Chaucer was right when he wrote, "Murder will out."*

He grimaced when he realized that he had just recited two classical literary segments to himself within the last three minutes. *And the poetry!*

Dawkins' voice reasserted itself. "Robert Radner. He got all of her money ... Darren's money, really ... He should be willing to share some of it. We don't want much."

"You called him?"

"Of course! Who else? And he laughed at me and hung up."

"Be reasonable, Mr. Dawkins. He may not know anything about Edith's history or even be aware of Darren's existence. Edith McKay kept secrets really well. He probably thinks you're a crank extortionist of some kind."

On the other hand, Robert may well know that Edith had a son and simply doesn't want to share any of the wealth with neer-do-well shirttail relatives from far-off places. Knowing what he did about Robert, Cooper thought this was at least an equally likely possibility.

Cooper immediately regretted his choice of words. Dawkins exploded, "Crank extortionist! I'll make him listen to me, by God! The rich bastard!"

"Look, Mr. Dawkins. Calm down. I do think you'll have a legitimate claim, but there's a lot of stuff going on around here at the moment. I'm going to meet with the police officer who's handling the murder investigation and tell him about our meeting and what you told me. He'll want to talk with you again, probably here in Stanton --"

Dawkins went on as though Cooper had not been talking, and Cooper suspected that his present mood was such that he was incapable of listening, let alone comprehending what Cooper was saying to him.

"I'm going to give him one more chance to do this the right way. If he still laughs at me ... Well, he won't be able to hang up this time."

Cooper was getting a bad feeling about the call, a growing sense that he was missing something important. He unconsciously gripped the phone tighter and asked, "Mr. Dawkins, where are you calling from?"

"I'm downtown ... in Stanton ... on my way to Radner's office. I thought you could help us but I was wrong. I'll do it myself."

And he hung up.

Cooper swore, then immediately speed-dialed Dmitri, but landed in his voice-mail. He hung up without leaving a message and tried Marcus, who answered on the first ring. Ellen got in the car just as Cooper started to speak.

"Marcus. This is urgent. Your missing man, the one in the glossies ... his name is Frank Dawkins, and he's in town and headed for Robert Radner's office. I think he intends to confront him about getting a piece of the McKay inheritance. It's a long and complicated story, but I think you and Dmitri should be there. I'm not sure that Dawkins is all that stable."

Marcus listened and then asked, "This Dawkins guy? He's our mysterious missing guest ... from the night McKay was killed?"

"Yes, but --"

"OK, I'm on the way. I'm only four or five minutes away from there now. I'll find Dmitri and bring him along if I can. You stay out of it!"

"Call Radner and --" Cooper began, but realized that Marcus was no longer on the line. He banged his fist on the dash and swore. Ellen put her hand on his shoulder and raised her eyebrows.

"You drive. Fast!" Cooper said, "To Robert's office. I've got to make some calls."

They switched places. Ellen made a highly aggressive U-turn and accelerated quickly, clearly picking up on Cooper's growing apprehension. Cooper tried Robert, Dmitri and – once more – Marcus. All three of the calls rolled over to voice mail.

Ellen was paying attention to her driving, a good thing as she was doing everything at high speeds except running the red lights. When he put down his phone, she asked, "Do you think he's dangerous?"

"Yesterday I would have laughed at the idea. But it sounds as though he's gone slightly wacko. I think he must have discovered how many millions of dollars are involved and has developed a very strong sense of entitlement."

Ellen said, "It happens. Lawyers make a very nice living off of that combination."

"I didn't get the feeling he was stopping off to hire any lawyers on his way to see Radner!"

Radner's office was midway down a tree-lined city block that fronted on the river, one of a row of stately red brick buildings that dated back to the founding of the city and now housed upscale law firms, architects, boutiques and "in" restaurants, many of them with sidewalk tables. On a blustery fall day, there were not a lot of people on the sidewalk, so it was easy to pick out Dawkins walking fast, looking at the numbers on the buildings. He was still about half-a-block from Radner's office when Ellen turned onto the street. Cooper saw the unmarked car in front of the office with a single occupant. As he watched, Marcus got out of the car, leaned against the curbside door and stood waiting for Dawkins. At Cooper's gesture, Ellen turned into the nearest open spot, on the opposite side about fifty yards away, where they had ringside seats to watch Marcus and Dawkins.

Cooper opened his door to get out, but stopped when Dmitri pulled alongside and yelled through his open window. "You stay put! This is a police matter!" Cooper stood leaning on his open door, watching Dmitri start across the street.

Things happened very quickly. Days later, after countless retellings, Ellen and Cooper were still amazed at the sequence of events, at how much happened in such a short space of time. Cooper fantasized about having a "slow motion replay", so that one could decompose a single fluid action lasting a micro-second into a series of frames to study at leisure, to see what really happened as opposed to asking your brain to impose a story on fast-moving, imperfectly understood real time images unfolding from a distance.

Marcus unsnapped the retaining strap on his holstered pistol and kept his right hand on it as he stepped away from the car. He called something to Dawkins as he approached the entrance to Radner's building. Dawkins stopped, obviously curious, and waited for Marcus to approach. Marcus showed him his ID, and they stood for twenty seconds with Marcus doing the talking. Whatever he said, Dawkins just shrugged and walked away, toward the entrance. Marcus called something after him, because Dawkins waved his hand dismissively without even looking back at Marcus. Cooper heard Marcus say something in a raised voice as he started to move after Dawkins, almost a shout, but could not make out the words. Dawkins stopped and turned around, clearly reacting sharply to whatever Marcus had said. As he turned, he reached into the inside pocket of his coat, coming out with a small black object.

Marcus shot twice, the bullets slamming Dawkins back against the building.

Cooper was there within ten seconds, dodging pedestrians running the other way. Ellen was right behind him. He almost cannoned into Dmitri, who was standing strangely still on the sidewalk, as though trying to absorb the entire scene, his gun held loosely in his hand. Marcus was kneeling alongside Dawkins, one hand resting on the sidewalk, still holding his gun, and the other alongside Dawkins' carotid artery, seeking a pulse that wasn't there. Marcus was expressionless, seeming unnaturally calm.

Much later, long after the witness interviews and departmental hearings, Cooper knew what seemed so wrong about the tableau formed by Marcus kneeling next to the man he had just shot. It was the almost-perfect symmetry. Cooper had seen people die. They sprawled, in impossibly contorted positions. But Dawkins sat on the sidewalk, his back against the building, legs straight out, his chin down on his chest, his arms hanging naturally alongside his body, both hands resting on the pavement, open and facing up. He could have been a sleeping panhandler on a sunny city street. Even the blood, oozing from the two holes in his chest, formed parallel vertical stripes down the center of his torso.

The most compelling piece of symmetry, however, was the small black pistol resting in the palm of his right hand, nicely balanced by the cell phone in the palm of his left hand.

Cooper could not help it. He thought again of the poem about fall colors: *And how death seems a comely thing, In Autumn at the fall of the leaf.* And only then remembered that the poet was Dante.

The "officer involved in shooting" hearing went as everyone expected. Marcus's actions were reviewed and deemed appropriate. Within the inner circle of police officers, he gained respect for his decisiveness in the face of a perceived deadly threat. He was helped by the reality that Dawkins was an outsider, without any natural constituency to argue his case. Marcus believed him to be a murder suspect and, thanks to Cooper's call, had reason to believe that he was harboring dangerous intent toward Radner. He had ignored Marcus's command to stop and instead brandished a weapon. A police officer believing himself to be threatened by a suspect with a weapon has a license to use deadly force. Dawkins' death was a tragic reminder that citizens need to obey police orders.

Cooper did not know what they told Darren about how his father died.

A Reasonable Doubt

Cooper and Dmitri met in a conference room at the downtown courthouse. A court stenographer was also on hand, but so far Dmitri had not given the signal to start recording their conversation.

Dmitri said, "Well, if he was telling you the truth, that's one less suspect ... not only because we've just shot him!"

"Oh, he told the truth all right," Cooper responded. "I already checked a lot of what he said with people in LA. And if you saw him, Dmitri, you'd put him at the absolute end of your suspect list. He's your perennial victim, passive to a fault."

Dmitri nodded absentmindedly. "And he's got something nobody else does in this affair ... an alibi."

In response to Cooper's questioning look, he went on. "Marcus interviewed the caterer for the McKay affair when we were going through our interviews. He had set up a shuttle service to take people from Riverbend to downtown on the night of the McKay party. The driver said he had only one passenger who got on the bus about two seconds before the lights went out. We showed him the glossies and he's 'pretty sure' it was Dawkins. A good defense attorney could challenge the ID, but I think Dawkins was gone before Edith went outside."

Both men were silent. Then Dmitri asked, "Was he left handed? Do you know?"

Where did that come from? Cooper thought about his meeting in Mojave with Dawkins, trying to recall movements and posture. Finally, he shrugged. "I don't know. Nothing stands out particularly."

Dmitri looked thoughtful, and Cooper recognized the telltale stroking of his already rumpled hair, an infallible indicator that Dmitri was unsure of what he was about to say.

"You do know, don't you, that Marcus was convinced that Dawkins was McKay's killer?"

Cooper zeroed in on what was really bothering Dmitri. "You think that maybe he wouldn't have had to shoot Dawkins if I'd shared this stuff sooner?"

As he said it, Cooper thought of the two men he had killed during his police career; how he still dreamed about them. Not nightmares, but elaborate, fantastical dreams centered around them. Years later, he could recall the tiniest detail in the seconds before he fired – sounds, colors, smells, the way the man looked the instant he pulled the trigger, and the way they folded up on themselves. Nothing about the aftermath, just the part up to them becoming dead. He wondered if Marcus would have the dreams. He thought not, and – without knowing why -- felt badly for him because of that.

Cooper's question was still out there, but Dmitri had fallen into the same kind of reflective silence as Cooper. *It's not just me that has dreams. Dmitri knows what it's like to kill people. And I'll bet he's blaming himself for putting Marcus in the situation.*

Cooper was wrong about Dmitri. The scene he was trying to bring into focus was today's shooting, not some long ago trauma. *I was fifty feet away and dodging cars in the street. Both Marcus and Dawkins were moving.* He closed his eyes, trying to recreate his fuzzy image of Dawkins turning, saying something, reaching out to Marcus. *With his left hand. Holding that object. Then the shots. But definitely his left hand.*

But the gun – a cheap revolver -- was in Dawkins right hand. Serial numbers filed off, untraceable. *A throwdown? Lots of street cops carried them. Much easier to justify a questionable shooting if there's a real weapon to point to. Much easier than trying to get a civilian review board to understand the potency of adrenalin and fear when you're chasing a bad guy who turns around and pulls a cell phone out of his pocket.*

I've done it myself, a long time ago.

Dmitri shook his head, dispelling the final image of Marcus kneeling alongside Dawkins, completely calm.

He looked at the stenographer, clearly deliberating whether to go on the record or to keep it unofficial for the moment. Cooper was reminded again that Dmitri was his friend, a friend who would risk professional censure to protect him. He felt sorry for him and started to say, "I was stupid, --," but was quickly interrupted.

"That goes without saying. You broke every rule. If you'd told us about Dawkins as soon as you found him, he might still be alive today, and Marcus wouldn't have him on his conscience."

He signaled to the stenographer to start taking notes, and switched on the recorder, stating the date and the participants.

Dmitri growled, "OK, so we have one less suspect. Dawkins had an alibi. But what's it do for the motives of the others? If we assume that Edith said something to either her husband or her – alleged -- lover about being the mother of a seven-year-old ....? That's your boy Simon and his brother, by the way."

Cooper said quietly, "I'm not so sure the number of suspects has changed. Lose one, gain one maybe?"

When Dmitri raised his eyebrows, Cooper went on, "We know that Edith McKay left here in early summer, twelve years ago. Given what I learned from Dawkins, we now know that she was pregnant when she left, went to LA, had the baby – Darren -- and immediately gave him up for adoption. The Dawkins – very middle class at the time – adopted him and raised him to the present point in time. When his wife got cancer and everything around him went to hell, Dawkins got the idea of asking Edith McKay – now married to Robert -- for some no-strings-attached financial support."

Dmitri objected, "But I thought that both sides – the birth mother and the adoptive parents – were kept in the dark about each other. How did Dawkins learn about McKay being the mother?"

Cooper waved him off. "The rules have really changed, Dmitri. It's much harder now to conceal the identities. But, in this case, it was even easier. Remember, I talked to Dawkins. Edith hired herself out as surrogate mother as soon as she got off the plane at LAX. The Dawkins paid her twenty-five thousand dollars to bear a child that they would raise. They knew each other quite well indeed."

Dmitri was clearly depressed by Cooper's recitation. He said, "Not exactly your maternal sort, was she?"

"You've got to remember that Edith McKay was very young, very ambitious and very headstrong. It's easy to see her doing the calculations and coming up with that kind of solution. I found her LA landlord and he said that she left for Europe right after the birth. As far as I can tell, she never went back to LA or contacted the Dawkins."

"So how does that add to our list of possible killers? We still have Simon and Robert with both opportunity and the motive? Who else?"

Cooper said, "Two things. First, think about the timing. Given the birth date, the child had to have been conceived while Edith was living here, in Stanton. She almost certainly left town to conceal the pregnancy. Second, remember what Simon told us. Edith came up to him just before the blackout -- and just after being accosted by Dawkins, who – we now know -- reminded her that she had a son. We know that she was obviously excited and that she needed to talk to him, urgently. And she also had some kind of intense encounter with Marcus and Nathaniel."

Those are the ones we know of! I wonder who else she talked to between the time Dawkins got to her and when she went outside? There were a lot of men in that ballroom!

Dmitri and Cooper looked at one another for a long moment. Then Dmitri said, "So. Enter stage left: A man who is either unaware that he is a father, or – even worse – a man who has willfully concealed his fatherhood for several years .... Suddenly confronted with a guilt-ridden mother who wants her rightful son back, and in the course of getting him back ... will disclose to the world who the father is.... And may even insist on him assuming his own paternal role ... for a six-year-old that he's never seen ... and probably doesn't want to see ..."

Cooper finished for him. "Voila! One more suspect! But we don't who he is."

Dmitri became unnaturally still. Then he said, "Maybe we do." His reluctance to continue was so obvious that Cooper sat quietly, saying nothing. *I've never seen him so nervous.*

Dmitri did not speak for what seemed to be a very long time. He quite obviously was planning whatever he was about to say with great care. When the silence continued, Cooper suddenly realized that he was about to hear something he didn't want to hear. It was confirmed when Dmitri turned off the recorder and dismissed the stenographer.

"Tell me Dmitri. I'm a big boy."

Dmitri straightened in his chair, smiled sadly, and said, "It concerns Marcus ... but a long time ago. He was a kid."

He then laid out the details of what Nathaniel had told him about the day of Rachel's death. How she walked into a bedroom, found Edith & Marcus tangled up in bed together, naked. How Marcus's frantic attempt to slam the door propelled Rachel headlong down the stairs. How the three of them had maintained a conspiracy of silence; a pact that Edith threatened to end on the night that she was murdered.

As he listened, waves of sadness washed over Cooper. Dmitri's words reinforced Cooper's enduring sense of guilt stemming from his massive failure as a father to a teenager. *Where was I then? Could I have prevented this?* He thought of Marcus and what he must have felt then and throughout the last twelve years, trying to put himself in Marcus' head. *I killed her! I'm a coward to keep this secret!* He thought of Dmitri, who had tried to shield both Marcus and Cooper from the pain of exposure, even though it contradicted both the law and his own innermost values.

"Does Marcus know that Nathaniel told you all this?" Cooper asked.

Dmitri shook his head. "I don't think so, but I can't be sure."

Cooper said as gently as he could, "You know that this means that both Marcus and Nathaniel had a motive for killing Edith McKay, to keep her from telling about that night? They have to be considered as suspects."

Dmitri spoke without looking at Cooper, "For a teenage sexcapade ... seven years in the past?"

"Among other things. There could be a possible manslaughter charge in the case of Rachel's death, for one thing. And I'm sure they've violated several laws about withholding information in a murder investigation – particularly Marcus, given that he wears a badge. But those are nothing compared to their possible involvement in the McKay case."

Dmitri remained silent. Cooper thought for a moment, and then went on. "Nathaniel said that Marcus was on the bed with Edith. He could be the father of her child, the one she was about to announce to the world!"

Dmitri objected loudly, "You can't know that! She could have – she probably did – cohabit with half of the Stanton male population! It could be Nathaniel, for god's sake! He was part of that lovely bedroom scene!"

"Yes, but –"

Dmitri cut him off. "And don't forget your boy Simon! Why did Edith go up to him at the party? Maybe to tell him he had a son?"

"Dmitri. Don't get ahead of yourself. DNA testing will confirm or disconfirm fatherhood. For the moment, it would seem that they did not know she had a child, let alone that it might be theirs, or that she was going to expose them as deadbeat fathers who had inadvertently killed their mother and aunt."

Cooper paused, thinking. "As I recall, all Edith told Nathaniel and Marcus before she went outside was that she had to 'tell the whole story' about that night. They didn't exactly know exactly what that meant, did they?"

He continued, thinking out loud. "What are the possibilities? What would frighten them so badly that they would – on the spur of the moment – try to kill her? What could she say?   'We had mad sex seven years ago? You are the father of my child? You accidentally killed Rachel Radner?' "

Cooper and Dmitri looked at one another, each now fully aware that their relationship to one another and to Marcus was unalterably changed, in ways that would have to be renegotiated in a highly ambiguous moral landscape.

A Day in Court

The court had been in session for over an hour, debating whether or not Simon Radner was entitled to bail while awaiting trial on murder charges.

Cooper watched Simon and was struck by the disinterest he radiated, as though he was watching a tennis match without caring very much about the outcome. His eyes roamed over the courtroom and followed the various speakers, but his expression never changed . Cooper also paid particular attention to Simon's family. His wife, brother and son were sitting in the same section, but the three of them clearly were not speaking to one another, each of them inward looking. *Not exactly the warm and supportive family unit. I wonder what they think of each other?*

Simon was watching the selective shafts of afternoon sunlight that penetrated the courtroom through a series of small circular windows high on the wall behind the judge. The effect was as though spotlights were being used to pick out players of interest on an overcrowded stage, leaving others in gloom. He was amused to observe that these random beams of sunlight really did affect those whom they fell on. They sat up straighter, became visibly self-conscious, only seeming to relax as the light inched away from them.

It added to the sense of unreality that had settled upon Simon since his arrest and that he now accepted as permanent, marked by a swirling internal dialogue that made it hard to pay attention to the court. What had started so melodramatically – "*Did he kill, with malice aforethought,*" as put by the DA – had morphed into a procedural drone that he could not associate with himself.

How does one deal with being accused of murder? Especially if wrongly accused?   The initial absurdity of such a charge is overwhelming; especially for someone whose self-image simply does not allow for the degree of impersonal hostility that goes with the proceedings. He recalled with amusement that he had actually asked the cop "Don't you know who I am?" when told that he was a suspect in Edith's death. To his shame, thoughts of Edith came later: the overwhelming sense of unfairness; the outrage that a life should end for cause, that some outsider should decide who should die or live. An accident is impersonal, or if you're truly devout -- which Simon was not — according to some great and unknowable purpose. But murder is willful and unforgiveable callousness.

He wondered if others who knew Edith had the same reactions. He looked over at the spectator area to where his entire family – his brother Robert, wife Maria and son Nathaniel – sat side by side, each exhibiting an overly erect stiffness, a correctness of posture that repelled physical contact and expressed a strong distaste for being there. Simon was depressed by the irony: *So this is what it takes to get the four of us in the same room!* Nathaniel in particular seemed shrunken into himself, as though trying to increase the space between him and them. He had made eye contact with Simon only once since sitting down.

So Nathaniel, how in the world did we get to this point? With all this suppressed pain & guilt but none of the redemption that is supposed to go with it. It's so supremely fitting that you and I, with our shared disdain for therapy and group-think, should be so completely inarticulate with each other. We are a caricature of the modern male, perfect practitioners of the stoical male ethic. For me, the model was Gary Cooper; for you, I don't know – presumably some super-cool thirty-something. We've been locked into this goddamned stereotyped father/son Freudian dance for as long as I can remember. Maybe a murder trial will let us connect.

Some particularly loud exchange brought Simon's attention back to the courtroom. *They're like the rival gangs in 'West Side Story',"* he thought as he watched Ellen and the DA – Joan Martine -- argue at the bench. *It's like a gang fight, but with elaborate choreography and strict rules. One side attacks, the other retreats... but never in a conclusive way. And then the action flows back the other way. Each side intent on its grace & form, not on the outcome... appreciative of the artistic abilities of the attacker rather than on the severity of the thrust.*

He was inordinately pleased by the simile, disproportionately so since the ultimate outcome at issue was whether or not he was guilty of killing a woman he once loved. The unreality of the whole scene was enhanced by the fact that – a long time ago -- he had slept with the woman who was accusing him so dramatically. Now she hated him, perhaps with cause. *I wonder if that makes this a more personal kind of combat? Poor Joan! She wants to convict me of murder to get even for my rejection of her. And she knows that if I were to tell the court about our past relationship, that she would be disqualified. We'd have an automatic mistrial. What a strange alliance we have!*

His lawyer and defender, Ellen, did not know of Joan Martine's long-ago affair with Simon. She was puzzled by the hostility that was so apparent in her courtroom exchanges with Martine. *What have I done to this woman that she dislikes me so? It's like she blames me for what she's accusing Simon of doing!*

Robert studied Simon, but – as always -- learned nothing about Simon's thoughts or intentions. He saw his fraternal twin as he always had – imperturbable, curious about what was around him, and feeling in control of whatever or whoever that was.

Such conditions existed from Robert's earliest memories and had defined their relationship through the present day. Simon had always been bigger, stronger, more extroverted. He was always dominant, the one to make the decisions, to take the blame (and to get the credit, even when disclaimed). Simon was Robert's protector. Even when Simon left for Yale and his subsequent big-law-firm-in-the-city career, Robert felt that his choices remained subject to review and Simon's approval. Simon was continually supportive as Robert arguably became the major public figure in Stanton, but that very support undermined Robert's self confidence and relegated him in his own mind to being Simon's inferior!

What does it take to make you feel uncertain about yourself, anyway? Can you even be frightened or unsure? I know it can't come from money or any of those multimillion dollar deals with your name on them. And you can't be bothered with anyone threatening your ego; you don't have one of those to speak of. Do you worry about betrayal from an inner circle? How in all hell do you deal with your failures – your insane wife, your drifter son, the death of your sister-in-law and adulterous lover .... With being charged with her murder?

The thought of Nathaniel reminded Robert that his nephew was alongside him. They had not spoken since entering the courtroom over an hour ago. He wondered what it was like to sit and watch passively while your father's reputation was shredded.

Like his father, Nathaniel was also fascinated by the shafts of sunlight, but he characteristically was more interested in the geometric patterns, the idea of columns of light as metaphors for the quest for truth that supposedly energized a court of law, rather than in the way real people responded when spotlighted. The different perceptions were emblematic of their history together. Given any situation, his father would ask, "How will this affect the people around me?" Nathaniel would wonder, "How did this happen? What are the forces at work?"

Surely, I got that from you – this damned detachment that runs so counter to our own best interests? That's what the shrinks are always telling us – that genetics is everything. And, boy, did we practice detachment with each other! What's so pathetically ironic about the charade is that I carry on this perpetual monologue in my head. No, not a monologue, because I also play your part; although – to be fair – my invented part for you is as straight man to my generalized brilliance. You're Watson, I'm Holmes. Much of that is your fault, in that we fell into this pattern a long time ago as we acted out the textbook models of father/son relationships.

Nathaniel looked sideways at his mother. Maria, as she always did, drew attention. It happened on the street, in the supermarket, entering a room, and – now – sitting amid a hundred other spectators in a courtroom. She was – there is no other word for it – regal. Part of it was bearing, something passed on from the Central European royal ancestors she claimed. Some of it was clearly visual. She was beautiful – white skin, dark eyes, black hair, slender figure, classical features with a tantalizing asymmetry. She dressed simply, in very expensive tailored clothing. At first glance or on being introduced, the first impression was that of haughtiness, but that lasted only until she smiled or spoke. Nathaniel was amazed at her composure. *I wonder if she'll make it through today?*

Beneath the carefully constructed and controlled exterior, Maria was slowly losing her mind. *Why is Simon sitting at the front with those other men? And he's wearing that dark suit that makes him look so serious. Why do I have to sit here like this, listening to these dreary people arguing with one another about something that happened five years ago? Robert said it's about a murder. Cain killed Abel, didn't he? Or was it the other way around? I know I should remember. But that doctor with thick glasses said that I'm having trouble with reality and there's nothing they can do about it. I don't see why it matters what one remembers or forgets. Simon can do it for me. Or we can hire someone. Oh, I do wish they'd let me talk to Simon. He could explain all this to me and then we could both forget about it. Murder? That's very unpleasant. I don't want to think about it.*

"This isn't right!" Simon wasn't sure if he'd said the words out loud or if they were merely the imagined and emphatic end to the reverie he'd slipped into. He knew that time had passed only because the shafts of light were gone.

When the judge banged his gavel and said 'Bail granted, in the amount of one million dollars," Simon realized that he did not remember any single part of the last hour in court.

A Touch of Madness

The bell was answered immediately when Cooper pushed it. Nathaniel said nothing, just stood looking at him, his expression alternating between hostility and apprehension.

"My father's not here."

Cooper looked at Nathaniel with new interest, remembering Dmitri's description of the scene in Edith McKay's bedroom twelve years ago. *That's where it all started. I wonder how many other things he hasn't told us?*

"I need to talk with your mother," Cooper said.

Nathaniel stood quietly, saying nothing and not moving, clearly evaluating his choices. *Is he protecting himself or his mother?* In the end, he shrugged and stood aside.

"That may be hard to do. But come in."

Nathaniel let Cooper into the apartment, but then stood in front of him once more, blocking further progress into the room. "Is this necessary? She's kind of distraught, what with the courtroom and all the reporters."

"It is essential. To your father's defense."

"OK," Nathaniel said, "But she may not be all that helpful. Today is one of her bad days."

Bad day? Somehow, I don't think that means the usual stresses of domestic life.

Nathaniel showed Cooper into the living room near the end of the hall. Maria was sitting in the same chair as on the afternoon Cooper was shot. He took the matching chair opposite her. Nathaniel stood behind her for a moment, his hand on her shoulder as though seeking sensory information, each of them rigid in expression and posture. *They look as though they're posing for a formal family portrait in the late 1800's.*

Nathaniel left the room without speaking and Cooper immediately sensed a slackening in Maria's uneasiness. She sat less rigidly and for the first time seemed to pay attention to Cooper. She was wearing the same outfit, a severe black dress that blended into the semi-darkness where she sat. Given her black hair and the contrasting whiteness of her face, it gave Cooper the impression that he was talking to a disembodied head.

"Mrs. Radner – Maria – I believe you can help me. There are some things that I think you know that would help Simon."

There was a long silence. Maria gave no sign of having heard. Then she said, without inflection, "Simon has never needed or accepted my help. He's not about to start now."

"What about Nathaniel? Has he needed your help?"

The head without any apparent body turned abruptly toward Cooper. "Who are you? Why are you asking me about Nathaniel? Where is he? He's not with her again, is he?"

I guess this is what a bad day looks like! Let's see where this goes. He asked, "With who? What woman?"

"That woman! I saw her!" She raised her arm to point. "She was standing right there, across the room. Screaming at Nathaniel!"

Cooper realized that Maria was operating from some world that he was not a part of, accessing disconnected memories, like a person randomly flipping through pages of an old photo album. Her posture had changed. She was leaning forward, gripping the arms of her chair so tightly that the tendons on her hands stood out clearly. She was staring intently at him, waiting for his response to a question that was still lodged in her mind.

He guessed at the context she was visualizing, the scene from the day he was shot. "She wasn't hurting him. She's a lawyer working for Simon. She's on our side."

Maria began to sway from side to side in wide arcs, still sitting. "She would have. Hurt him. If he'd gone out into the rain that night. That awful rain!"

Cooper said, "It wasn't raining. And it was in the afternoon, not at night."

"Why are you confusing me? We saw them. They were doing horrible things … Nathaniel had no idea what would happen ... what people would say. And I was right, she came back and it started all over again!"

"Who saw them? Doing what?"

"Rachel. She opened the door and that woman was there ... with Nathaniel... and ..."

She stopped abruptly, peering closely at Cooper. Her expression took on a sly look and that, with the semi-darkness and the black dress, made Cooper feel like he'd been dropped into the middle of a gothic novel.

She said, "Where's Simon? I need Simon to tell me what to do! But he's with that woman!"

Cooper watched with reluctant fascination as Maria's hold on reality disintegrated in front of him. *Now Simon, with a woman?* She was staring at him, but not seeing him or anything else except the disjointed visions haunting her. He said, "Rachel?"

Maria folded her hands in her lap, smiled and looked away from Cooper with that same sly expression.

"She fell."

"Fell?" Cooper prompted.

Maria continued to smile, a horrible, twisted smile. "She fell. She fell down in the rain."

"Why did she fall?"

"Because she saw them. And for what she did to Nathaniel."

Cooper felt a sense of horror rising within him, a foreboding that something nightmarish would happen if he kept asking questions. This woman's unnatural co-mingling of time and people hinted at human possibilities that he did not want to consider.

He asked, very softly, careful not to look at Maria, "What did Rachel see?"

Maria did not answer, her fixed stare aimed at something behind him. He turned to see Nathaniel standing there, and Cooper realized that he had been listening to the entire exchange.

Nathaniel went to his mother, stood beside her, and once more put his hand on her shoulder. He said to Cooper, "That's enough. I can tell you what she saw."

Nathaniel

"I can tell you what she saw."

But I can't, of course. Only she can do that. I can talk about what was happening. Who was doing what to whom, when. Not the 'why' ... that's gone with Edith. But what Maria saw, whatever meaning she took away from that scene, has been filtered in ways that I can't possibly reproduce or even understand. "What she saw" was lost to interpretation a long time ago, no longer accessible after twelve years of brooding paranoia. Surely, some version once existed within Maria's memory, but it would be hopelessly distorted, no more an approximation of the reality than an underlit, doubly exposed photograph.

Nathaniel sat in the kitchen after Cooper left. They had gone there to be away from Maria, but for different reasons. Nathaniel wanted to escape her certain censure of what he was doing, of the secrets he was exposing. Cooper simply sought normalcy, or what passed for it in the Radner household. What they shared, however, was a common fear that their conversation would trigger something in Maria that they could not deal with, some yet unseen form of dementia that should not be experienced.

Nathaniel had been asking himself the same question for the last three days. *Why am I doing this ... telling everyone ... first Dmitri, now Cooper ... about that afternoon? It's crazy. I keep it secret for twelve years ... hating every second of it ... and then start blurting it out to everybody in sight.*

The shrinks would have fancy words for it, touching on the power of guilt. The priests – whom he no longer listened to -- would chime in on the same themes with some pap about repentance thrown in. He had helped to kill Rachel. It was an accident, but he had remained silent all these years. Then Edith died, because she was going to expose what they had done. But, most of all, his mother's descent into horror was his fault. He had exposed her to the scene in the bedroom and she could not recover from it.

He also was self-aware enough to know that some of his compulsion to tell the story was based on his encounter with Marcus after the interrogation. Marcus drove him home, telling Dmitri that he was concerned about Nathaniel. *Part of the most obvious good cop/bad cop routine one could imagine. But that was for Dmitri's benefit. What Marcus wanted was to keep me under control.*

He'd started as soon as they were in the car.

"So what did you tell Dmitri?"

Nathaniel thought about how to answer. It was tempting to lie. *Dmitri might not even tell Marcus about their talk. It was clear that it bothered him. And he's got a thing about Marcus. Anyway, I'm tired of Marcus and his secrets ... our secrets.*

"Nathaniel ...?" Marcus said pointedly.

He said, "Nothing. I didn't tell him anything. I couldn't. Didn't see anybody. Didn't know anything."

Marcus asked, seeming unconcerned, "Nothing about Edith ... or Rachel ... or us?"

"Why would he ask that? He wants to know who took a shot at Cooper?"

Marcus looked closely at Nathaniel, but to Nathaniel's relief, he seemed to accept his version.

Then he asked, "Who did? Shoot at Cooper?"

An easy question to answer. I can almost tell the truth. "I don't know. I know it wasn't me."

When Marcus dropped him off, Nathaniel was numb, already second-guessing his reasoning. Fearing that Dmitri would tell Marcus what he had done and that Marcus would find a way to get back into his head; find a way to reinstate the past.

The sense of fatalism was still with him when he told the story to Cooper. *I told him what I saw. No, more than that. I told him what happened. Surely something different from the version that Maria carries around in her head. No interpretation or analysis; no attempt to derive deeper meaning about cause or effect. Nothing subjective. Just the sequence of explicit actions. Like diagramming a football play or tracing a picture of a rat's passage through a maze.*

And Cooper just sat there. He didn't ask, "Are you sure," "Why did she do that," "How did you feel," "Why didn't you do something!" None of the questions that are so natural, and so unanswerable; questions designed to make sense out of what is senseless. He just sat there and listened, looking sad.

Then Nathaniel experienced a sudden wave of anger. It was a recurrent sensation, repeated whenever he thought about the last few weeks; the time after that damned hammer was found and "the past" – the part of his life that he thought of as safe from discovery – had been brought into the spotlight. The anger always had the same focus.

Why did Edith have to come back? None of this would have happened if she'd stayed away. She did it to herself!

Confessions of a Sort

Cooper went home and went to bed. He slept for ten hours, dreaming about Marcus and rainstorms. He woke up depressed and tired, as though he hadn't slept. The phone rang while he was trying to decide whether to get up or not. It was Ellen.

"I just finished a conference call with Dmitri and Martine. They didn't say it, but I think they're about to give up on Simon. They don't have enough to go to trial."

"That's going to be tough on Dmitri. He doesn't like unsolved cases." *And even harder for Martine. No vengeance for whatever it is that Simon did to her.*

"He'll have to make do with Dawkins. They won't need a trial. Public opinion will provide the verdict. And he's already been executed."

"I don't like it."

"Neither do I. And I'm quite sure that Dmitri doesn't like it any more than we do. But Simon's my client – for the moment – and I'm going to file for the case to be dismissed."

They set a time to meet that afternoon. Cooper lay back in bed and thought about starkly opposing options.

It's time for this to end. No more secrets.

Walk away. You don't have a client any more. All you can do is hurt people.

The same two contending thoughts were replaying an hour later, as he was ringing the Radner's doorbell one more time. Simon came to the door. He did not seem surprised to see Cooper.

"I have some questions you may not like," said Cooper.

Simon stood silent, reminding Cooper of Nathaniel just a short time ago, trying to decide whether to let him in or not.

"I think we're done, you and I. I just talked with Ellen. She thinks that the DA is going to give up on me as suspect. So you can stop asking questions."

"I thought about that... not asking any more questions. But I decided it's too late to stop. There are too many of them... questions, that is ... and they need answering. Here, if not in court. And it's not negotiable. You can answer them or I'll find someone else. It will take longer, but I'll do it."

Simon did not respond, but stood looking at him as though about to debate the point. *So, the knight errant is in there after all. He has a new client. One named Edith. Well, I can't say I wasn't warned.*

Finally, he turned his back and walked to his office with Cooper following. He closed the door behind them and took one of the two chairs near the fireplace. He sat back in his chair with his hands behind his head.

"Actually I've been expecting them ... your questions. Go ahead. I'll answer them if I can."

Let's start with the easy ones.

"You did something incredibly stupid. But you're not stupid. I can't help but wonder why you did it. Why did --"

Simon managed to smile and look sad at the same time. He wondered the same thing. And he knew that any attempt to answer Cooper's questions would be unsatisfactory to both of them.

He interrupted. "I think I know what you're going to ask. Tell me if I'm wrong."

Cooper made a slight "go ahead" gesture with one hand. Simon sat up straight, cleared his throat as though about to give a speech, and said in a stern stagey voice: "That day in your apartment, when I was shot ... Why did you pick up that gun ... the one lying at the end of the hall?"

Cooper said nothing, but spread his hands out and adopted a quizzical expression.

Simon sighed deeply. "I think Maria shot you." He said it in a normal tone, very matter of fact, as though commenting on the chance of rain.

He immediately added, "First, I have not shared nor will I share this view with the police; and, if *you* do, I will deny that I said it. I have no explicit evidence, so it's pure conjecture. I didn't see anything. I was walking toward the hallway when I heard the shot. But there's ... a kind of feeling ... almost an ESP thing ... that comes from living with another person for decades. There's nothing that a prosecuting attorney can use even if I agreed to testify... and I won't."

Cooper let that go for now. He just said, "You still haven't answered the question: Why did you pick up the gun?"

"I saw it lying on the carpet at the end of the hallway, and I figured that it was Nathaniel's, from the kitchen drawer. I also figured Maria's fingerprints would be all over it – that she just tossed it down after firing. So I picked it up and tried to wipe it clean. Then, to make sure that my prints would blot out any of hers that I'd missed, I held it as though I was going to fire it."

He smiled, reimagining the scene. "I thought Dmitri was going to shoot me!"

Cooper sighed. And then asked, without much real interest, "I know Maria is your wife and you're probably fond of her, but why would you take the risk of a long, long prison sentence by making yourself look like the shooter?"

Simon was sitting forward now, trying to convince Cooper with his body language as well as words. "Ah! But I can prove that I'm not. First, everyone there saw me pick up the gun; I didn't walk into the hall carrying it." He paused significantly, "And I have a great alibi. A policeman, no less. Marcus saw me a few seconds before the shot was fired ... nowhere near the spot."

"So. My official answer as to why I picked up the gun? I was stupid; I just didn't think."

Cooper nodded impatiently. "That'll probably work for the average juror. But your unofficial answer? Just between the two of us ..."

Simon looked hard at Cooper. Then he nodded. "I figured I could cover for Maria by wiping down the gun. And that, in the end, the police wouldn't be able to make the case against her or me."

Cooper nodded. "OK, so you're not stupid. Just incredibly protective of a wife who is making your life miserable!"

Simon sat quietly. Cooper thought of all that was unsaid. *The part about families and the pathologies disguised as loyalties that build up through time; the innocent kind that become part of divorce proceedings or our family histories, and then the more sinister ones, the kind that lead to axe murders, mercy killings and generations of tribal warfare.*

"Still off the record. Just between us. Why would Maria shoot me?"

Simon said, "Remember, I never said that she did."

Cooper waved his hand impatiently. "Right! This is an entirely hypothetical imaginary question that I never asked and you never answered. Why would she want to shoot me?"

Simon did not respond immediately. Cooper knew the answer, but still could not imagine the sorts of agonies that Simon must be experiencing. They did not show on his face, half hidden behind his steepled fingers. When he spoke, it was very softly.

"Maria is … let us say, unstable. She has rages. There are more scientific terms for the condition. The episodes are rare but extremely violent."

Cooper broke in, "And they're triggered by women that she sees as a threat to Nathaniel."

Simon was not surprised by Cooper's insight. He seemed relieved to have it out in the open. He said, "Yes. In this case, Ellen. Maria was shooting at her, not you."

The matter-of-fact way in which Simon recited these horrific phrases caused Cooper to wonder about Simon's own mental stability. He thought it likely that Simon welcomed this conversation, that it might be a sort of expiation for his sins of omission. He also knew that there was much more to be discussed, but he felt an immense weariness settle over him before he asked the next question.

"Did she kill Rachel and Edith as well?"

Simon answered immediately, in the manner of someone reciting uninteresting facts, without apparent emotion. "Rachel's death was a pure accident. And there's no evidence that Maria had anything to do with Edith's murder."

Cooper sat quietly, simply looking at Simon. *He knew I would ask him that question. He's rehearsed his answer.* He knew that they had already crossed some imaginary line; that what was being said – or not said -- was about much more than simple guilt or innocence. He also knew that Simon needed to tell him. He had learned that there is a very fine line between the confession to the police and the confession to the priest. The silence continued for a long time, broken finally by a deep sigh from Simon. Cooper thought again of the weight of guilt that he must be feeling.

"I think she did," Simon said softly. "Kill them ..."

Cooper prompted, "And you know why, don't you?"

"At first, I believed Rachel's death was an unfortunate accident. What else could it be?" Simon was talking mostly to himself now.

"But then I learned that something else happened that day... the day that she fell. Something involving Edith and Nathaniel that Maria walked in on ...."

I know this story, but let's let him tell it his way.

"Edith told me – just the week before she died -- told me about that day. It was kid stuff. She – Edith – was with Marcus and Nathaniel. They were half-drunk and half-naked, playing around. Rachel and Maria walked in on the three of them in Edith's bedroom."

Cooper broke in. "Why would Edith tell you about that, something that happened a long time in the past, a story that makes her look bad?"

"We were having a fight. She wanted me to leave Maria. She said Maria was crazy, that she was obsessed with Nathaniel and women."

He paused. "And I think she was even a little afraid of Maria. Maybe she even suspected that Maria had killed Rachel."

Cooper did nothing to disturb Simon's mostly inward monologue. Simon continued aloud, "It's funny. All I could think about when she was telling me the story was about Nathaniel – my son -- and Edith having sex so long ago, before I ever knew her. And how much I despised myself at that moment!"

"Maria and I have never talked about it," said Simon in a wondering tone. "Doesn't that seem strange?"

He paused and when Cooper did not respond, he continued. "Then when all this started again, when Robert found the hammer, she began to say weird things; phrases that made no sense unless …"

Cooper finished the thought for him. "Unless you knew what her fixation was about, what kind of visions she was seeing. I've had a couple of those free-association conversations with her."

He went on, very quietly. "You know, of course, that she's insane, dangerously so; that she needs professional treatment, in a locked facility."

"Yes. I have to deal with that."

Simon sat up straight in his leather chair, put his hands on his knees and leaned toward Cooper. His posture and expression conveyed that he was done talking, that he had made his confession and found himself less weighted down than when they had started, as though he had received some absolution. But Cooper was surprised by what Simon said next.

"So. Now that we've had this talk, what are you going to do with this newfound knowledge?"

And Cooper was even more surprised by his response.

"I don't know."

A Suspension of Disbelief

Two days later, Cooper still didn't know what to do.

The forty-eight hours had been marked by a flurry of events. Ellen filed a motion for dismissal, based on an "insufficient evidence" claim, and the judge granted it, surprising no one. For him, it was an easy call because the District Attorney did not object strenuously, even saying that she deemed a trial to be unwinnable.

Joan Martine did not relate the more important factor: that Simon could win an automatic ruling of "mistrial" by disclosing their prior relationship. It had taken a long time, but the threat to her career finally outweighed her visceral need for reprisal.

Simon immediately severed his attorney-client relationship with Ellen. "I've been fired," as Ellen wryly put it. He also told Cooper, "Thanks, but your services are no longer required." Both Ellen and Cooper were cut off from access to any of the Radners.

The question about the redevelopment of the historic Riverbend project was scheduled for a final hearing before the City Council with all parties expecting a rubber-stamp approval. Robert unveiled a very elaborate scale model of the envisioned project in the lobby of a downtown bank and announced the date for a ceremonial groundbreaking.

Dmitri retired from the Stanton Police Department. For the public, his retirement was couched as "long overdue, after years of meritorious service, etc., etc." Privately -- between Dmitri, Cooper and Ellen -- it was tacitly understood that Dmitri's decision was driven by his judgment that he had violated his self-imposed standards of professional behavior by withholding what he knew about Marcus's role in Rachel Radner's death. Cooper suspected that Dmitri was also regretting his shared responsibility for the humiliation of Tony Pastore. Cooper and Ellen agreed between themselves not to oppose his decision, even though they agreed that his standards were impossibly stringent.

Dmitri's retirement announcement had two important side effects. First, it triggered a series of organizational changes within the department hierarchy, including a significant promotion for Marcus. Second, it caused Ellen to wonder out loud about a partnership among the three of them, now that each of them was at loose ends. Once she planted the idea in Cooper's mind, the notion was becoming more and more appealing, to the point where what had started as a fantasy was beginning to take real shape in his head.

Cooper asked Dmitri and Ellen to meet him at Ellen's apartment. His invitation was simple and compelling. "I know who killed Edith. And I need your help deciding what to do about it."

When they were all seated, with Chardonnay for Ellen and coffee for himself and Dmitri, he began.

"I have a story to tell. Like most stories, it's about equal parts of facts and conjecture, kind of like the movie trailer 'based on actual events'. Some of it, probably only a small part, might be relevant to a court-of-law that decides on guilt or innocence. The rest of it is …. I suppose … for us. But I don't know what we're going to do with it."

Dmitri smiled and said, "Cooper! Such angst! I think you're becoming positively Russian. Today you sound a lot like Chekhov maybe?"

Ellen smiled also, in a private way that Cooper was still learning to interpret. "I feel sorry for you -- A storyteller saddled with an over-imaginative policeman and an unemployed attorney for an audience."

Cooper continued, as if he had not heard. "We have three … what shall we call them …. let's say 'incidents' for the moment, occurring over a twelve year time period. They are, in order, Rachel's death, Edith's murder, and the attempted murder of me. Each of the three involves an eerie – that's the only word that fits – combination of intent and accident. The perpetrators involved were opportunistic ... and very, very lucky."

Dmitri broke in. "Rachel's death was surely an accident? Unless you think that Nathaniel is lying about that sex romp in Edith's bedroom."

"No. I think he's telling the truth about the door slamming into Rachel. But that didn't make her fall. It's implausible for at least two reasons. First, we've all seen the gallery that runs around that ballroom. It's wide. I measured it at ten feet between the doorway where she was standing and the head of the staircase. There's no way – under the current laws of physics -- that she could have been propelled that far by Marcus slamming that door."

Ellen asked, "So how did she fall?"

"She didn't. She was pushed. She wasn't up there alone. There was someone with her. Remember, Nathaniel thought he saw another figure in the background, behind Rachel. He did; there was someone there. And they would have come forward if it had been a simple accident."

It was Dmitri's turn. "But what's the motive? And if you're trying to kill somebody, you don't shove them down a staircase, for god's sake! They break a leg. Or get a mild concussion. And then they get up, point at you and say indignantly 'You pushed me!' "

Cooper said, quite mildly, "You're right. It's not a premeditated act. It's a product of some spontaneous emotion. Think of the possible reasons – to stop her from telling anyone, to protect Nathaniel from exposure ... or maybe you're just plain nuts. But, at the end of the day, it looks like an ordinary household slip and fall. The killer was lucky."

Dmitri jumped in again. "And we thought Edith's death was an accident too. For five years."

"Again, dumb luck, mostly bad for the police, good for the killer. But these three 'incidents' have other common elements other than luck. The crime is committed among a crowd of potential witnesses, using a weapon that is convenient, taking advantage of circumstances that could not be predicted.

There is no elaborate planning, merely acting on impulse without much thought for the consequences. The killer simply doesn't care about being caught."

Cooper argued, "Think about it. Edith McKay was murdered. But it was the result of a series of random events, 'coincidences' if you will – the rain, the power failure, her going outside. All of these were fortuitous for the killer. Everything converged at precisely the right time, beginning with Dawkins arrival on the scene. He set Edith off on a course that the killer could not abide."

Ellen said, "Cooper. You think that all three 'incidents' were carried out by the same person, don't you?"

"Yes, I do. And I'll tell you why."

Dmitri was very quick to jump in. He said, "Can you prove it?"

"Not at the 'beyond a reasonable doubt' level that a jury would require. That's off the table."

He paused and then said, "But I think I can convince the two of you that I'm right."

He continued quickly. "First, let me get rid of some obvious contenders. Dawkins, for example. The mysterious guest. Marcus did a great bit of detective work to come up with him and at first I assumed that he was Edith's killer. But after seeing him in the flesh, I ruled him out, and you would too. He didn't and couldn't kill anybody. He wasn't within a thousand miles of Rachel and he has a partial alibi for Edith, just in case."

Dmitri broke in. "It's too bad he's dead."

The undertones of anger were very apparent to Cooper. He ignored the comment and went on. "Then there's Robert. Lots of potential motives – jealousy, humiliation, greed, among others. We can rule him out for shooting me. He wasn't there. In Rachel's case, he fails the irrationality/rage test. Robert hasn't engaged in a spontaneous, unplanned act during his lifetime. Plus he had no discernible reason to kill his first wife. And again, he has an alibi: He was at the bar with a dozen people when Rachel went down those stairs."

Dmitri spoke with some heat. "But he doesn't have an alibi for Edith. What about the fact that she was having an affair with his brother?"

"As to Robert being Edith's murderer: there's a compelling reason to eliminate him as suspect." Cooper said. "He turned in the hammer. He would never have done that if he were the killer. The case was dead and buried, along with Edith. Until he restarted it with the new evidence."

Ellen spoke softly, "Evidence that pointed to his own brother. There's one for the local shrinks!"

Dmitri said, "What about the forged document concerning Riverbend? That's a genuine motive."

"That's your 'greed' element at work. And I do think that he probably forged the Conservancy document. He had both access and a reason to do it. I think he planned to threaten Edith with the exposure of her affair with Simon unless she went along with it."

But that doesn't explain Natalie's signature as the second witness on a forged charter. And he thought again about how she stood too close to Robert Radner in her high heels on the lawn at Riverbend.

Dmitri said reflectively, "Just in the interest of covering all the bases, what about Nathaniel as suspect?"

"Kill Rachel, his aunt? I don't think so. But there's other reasons to eliminate him. Edith and Marcus were with him in that bedroom too, remember? I can't see them standing by. For an accident, maybe. But not for a deliberate murder. And Nathaniel's the one who told Dmitri what really happened in that bedroom. Why would he do that if he was the killer? As for Edith, he's no more or less likely a suspect than anyone else. But both of you have seen Nathaniel up close. Do you really think he could kill anyone and hide the fact?"

Dmitri and Ellen looked at each other, their silence confirming his reasoning.

Ellen said, "And so, we come to Simon ..."

"Yes, we come to Simon," said Cooper. "We always do."

"He was in plain sight – talking with James McKay -- when Rachel came tumbling down the stairs. We can rule him out there. And he's got a witness – Marcus -- that takes him out of the lineup in the case of my shooting … except on an aiding and abetting charge because of his subsequent handling of the gun."

"I still think he's the one who bashed Edith," Ellen said. "But you're going to tell me I'm wrong, aren't you?"

Cooper continued, "Under the Napoleonic legal system –where you're guilty unless you can prove that you're innocent – Simon would be convicted of Edith's murder. He's the single most logical suspect; there's strong circumstantial evidence; and he has no alibi."

Dmitri smiled, and said, "I like that system. Almost as simple as the old Soviet logic – 'You're not innocent unless I say you are'."

Ellen spoke, trying to get Cooper out of his lecturing mode, "Look, Cooper. So far, you've told us what we already know, including the merits of alternative schools of international jurisprudence. Why don't you just tell us who killed Edith and how you know?"

Cooper smiled at Ellen, then turned to Dmitri and asked, "Have you read any of the work of the English poet Coleridge?"

At this, Ellen rolled her eyes and glared at both of them.

Dmitri stood very erect, placed his hand over his heart, and with an excellent public-school English accent, recited, "In Xanadu did Kubla Khan a stately pleasure dome decree…"

He paused, then asked "Shall I go on?" He seemed to think very hard, and then said in an exaggerated manner, "But wait! Coleridge wrote that in 1798. He can't be Edith's killer!"

"Excellent deduction, Sherlock!" said Cooper drily. "But I was thinking of his contribution to literary criticism. He was, I'm sure you'll recall, the fellow who coined the phrase 'a willing suspension of disbelief', noting that such a state of mind was essential to successful storytelling."

Ellen lobbed a throw pillow from the sofa at Cooper. "I can't believe that I'm the one drinking! I feel like I'm in a BBC sitcom! Can we get back to the subject?"

Cooper caught her pillow in mid-air and pointed it back at her. "But think of it, Ellen. Isn't that the goal of the defense attorney arguing a case where the evidence is strongly against the client? When you have 'bad facts'? To induce 'a willing suspension of disbelief' in the jury? That easily morphs into the 'reasonable doubt' that sets so many villains free.

"What I've done so far is to use *facts* to rule out suspects in one or more of the 'incidents'. What I want you to do now is to accept four naïve assumptions as true – to suspend disbelief for just a bit."

Dmitri and Ellen looked at each other questioningly and then simultaneously shrugged and settled back with mutually skeptical expressions.

Cooper held up his hand with four extended fingers, and then ticked off the points one by one.

"First, all three incidents were deliberate acts with the intent to kill, not accidents. Second, they were carried out by a single person. Third, the motive is the same in all cases. Fourth, the killer is impulsive and irrational, almost indifferent to the idea of punishment."

Ellen was very quick to respond. "Each of those is arguable."

"I agree." Cooper said equally quickly. "But what if ...?"

Dmitri said, "Then there's only one candidate."

"Maria," breathed Ellen.

Loose Ends

"Let's talk about opportunity first," said Cooper. "She was there in each case. And she has no verifiable alibi for any of the three incidents."

He went on, "As to impulsivity and irrationality, each one of us has seen her in action – including those towering rages. Simon and Nathaniel cover for her in many ways, as much as they can. But I think Maria is losing her mind."

Dmitri put up his hand to interrupt. "But what's her motive? Aside from being insane, of course?"

"This is where I'm thin on facts. But my theory is that she wanted to protect Nathaniel from Edith in particular, and women in general. I'm no shrink, but I would diagnose a severe obsessive-compulsive disorder with violent outlets. Certainly not your everyday overstressed housewife. A flat-out psychotic."

Ellen asked, "So why did she shoot you? You're no threat to Nathaniel."

"She didn't shoot at me. You were the target. Happily, she's a lousy shot."

Ellen began to object again, but then a picture emerged in her mind, of her confronting Nathaniel both physically and emotionally while Maria sat watching intently.

Cooper knew what Ellen was visualizing and added, "It may also be the case that she actually saw you as Edith … some kind of transference thing."

Dmitri said quietly, "So it all starts with Rachel, twelve years ago?"

"Yes."

Dmitri continued, "Maria was the other person who walked in on the mini-orgy in that room, the shadowy figure that Nathaniel couldn't – or, more likely, wouldn't – identify."

"Yes. Although I think Nathaniel did recognize his mother but won't admit it. And I think he halfway knows that she killed Rachel. And Edith. And I think those few seconds while his mother was standing in that doorway have warped him as well. He's your classical innocent bystander in a lot of ways."

Ellen said, "That's a whole string of assumptions."

"Yes. But plausible assumptions. Especially if you watch the two of them together. Nathaniel is exceptionally tolerant of his mother's over-the-top behaviors, even when they involve him directly. I think he's afraid of her telling the world – either deliberately or in one of her manic phases – about that day."

Dmitri broke in, "And there must be a strong sense of guilt. He must feel partly responsible for what happened. It really is all that Greek tragedy stuff all over again ..."

While Dmitri talked, Ellen had acquired a sudden and dramatic stillness, marked by a rigidity in her posture and what war-weary soldiers labeled the 'thousand-yard stare.' Some new and dramatic thought-video was running, and Cooper thought he knew what it was. He remembered a recurring theme in what they had continued to call 'their catharsis sessions' over the last few weeks; a theme gently developed by Ellen, at first resisted but finally welcomed by Cooper. He thought that it worked as therapy because of the setting -- naked, in bed, after making love, creating a level of closeness and mutual trust that enabled them to talk about themselves in new ways. As he watched Ellen and remembered, he thought again about what a remarkable woman she was, in so many ways.

Dmitri was also aware of Ellen's stillness, and knew that it was about her and Cooper together. He knew himself to be irrelevant for the moment.

Ellen said just one word, "Marcus."

Cooper thought of all of the personal history and psychological freight that went with that single word, attached like a limpet mine to the hull of a blithely unaware luxury yacht. Dmitri immediately confirmed the metaphor for him by his swift and dramatic change of expressions, at first questioning and then troubled. As he watched them, he thought – for probably the hundredth time in the last few weeks – about how important these two individuals were to him, especially when the subject of "Marcus" arose.

Cooper held up both hands, palms out as though to deflect what they were each struggling to put into words. "Yes. I know. He was there too. But it wasn't his mother that walked in on them, and it was twelve years ago."

He paused and then continued in a reflective tone, "And Marcus seems to be one of the more well-adjusted folks around, including the three of us. I just don't see any guilt or the other kinds of emotions that goes with trauma like that."

After another pause, he added, "Other than the justified anger he exhibits toward me, which has nothing to do with Rachel's death."

Ellen said, "It is interesting how much influence he seems to have over Nathaniel. Maybe 'dominance' is the better word? Have you watched the two of them together?"

Dmitri responded. "No mystery there. It's your classic authority-based relationship. Marcus is a police officer and Nathaniel is your marginally law-abiding citizen."

"Maybe," said Ellen, clearly skeptical.

They were silent for about thirty seconds, with an obvious awkwardness. Dmitri broke the silence with a question to Cooper. "I think I know the rest of your story. Can I tell it?"

Cooper nodded. "You can write the script. No one was there to see what happened."

Dmitri begins, "The door slams. Maybe it knocked her off balance, maybe not. But Rachel stops short of falling down the stairs. She and Maria are standing closely together ... perhaps Maria even steadying Rachel. Each of them is shocked by what they've seen, but Rachel is slower to process it ... to recover. Perhaps they say something to each other, perhaps not. Maria's reaction – however it begins – turns into a pronounced fear for Nathaniel and – for the moment -- unfocused rage. Rachel turns to go downstairs ... maybe saying something about needing to tell Robert. Maria's unthinking act, her impulsivity,

as you put it, is to stop her. She does the only thing she can ...
pushes her from behind as she starts down ..."

Cooper claps his hands, three times, softly. "Bravo! A
riveting narrative! Only one edit to suggest: I think it was more
than a push. Rachel fell through an arrangement of clay
flowerpots near the head of the stair. The police report is pretty
sketchy, but it mentioned blood smears on a fragment of one of
those pots, consistent with hitting her head as she fell. I think
it's likely that Maria hit Rachel in the head with one of those
flower pots. That's what started the fall."

"If you want to kill someone, that leaves a lot less to
chance," said Ellen. "I don't suppose we'll ever know for sure,
will we?"

"Not without time travel. The evidence is long gone."
Cooper said.

Dmitri continued, "Fast forward seven years from that
night. Edith is back in town, but staying away from Nathaniel,
so no problem. Then Maria sees Edith confront him at the award
ceremony and once again acts impulsively, this time with a
hammer." He stopped and looked questioningly at Cooper, who
merely nodded.

"That would also explain another puzzle," Ellen said.
"Why the killer would put the hammer back in its case and
preserve all that evidence. An irrational act by an irrational
person!"

"One more thing," Cooper said. "I know that Simon –
and probably Nathaniel – either knows or strongly suspects that
Maria's done these things. And I think they've tried to protect
her." He went on to tell about his late night talk with Simon and
his explanation about picking up the gun.

"Sounds like a confession to me," mused Dmitri.

"It was, but not one that can be used. First, he'll deny
even talking to me. Second, it's all second hand observation. He
doesn't know any more than we do about what actually
happened. All we can do is make sure he gets Maria off the
streets and under some kind of care."

"It's a great story, probably even a screenplay in it somewhere," Ellen said. "I think it may even be true. But I don't like the ending – two murders and an attempted murder and there's no way to prove a shred of it! And don't forget about Dawkins! The whole thing stinks!"

Cooper said, "Nobody comes out looking very good, do they? Not even the victims."

"Oh. And there's something else ..."

Both Ellen and Dmitri looked at him with an almost-weary "what next?" expression.

"Cheer up. This bit may actually have some good news imbedded in it."

He went on, "It's about Dawkins. We know that the Dawkins boy is Edith's son, conceived in in Stanton about two months before Edith took off -- "

He was interrupted by Dmitri, "As somebody once said, probably in a paternity suit, 'Motherhood is a fact; fatherhood is a theory'. I gather you have a theory about the probable father?"

From the troubled expression on Dmitri's face, Cooper knew that he was thinking again about Marcus. So he quickly said, "I'm quite sure it's Nathaniel Radner, actually. For three reasons."

"First, the timing is right. Darren was born nine months after Rachel's death and Edith's little free-love romp in that upstairs bedroom."

"Second, when I met the Dawkins, I was sure that I had seen the boy somewhere before, but I couldn't remember where. I was thinking of a photo album, or in a newscast. But I now know where it was. Every time I see Nathaniel, I realize that the boy has to be his direct descendant! The resemblance is uncanny."

Ellen had become abnormally still. Cooper recalled that she had been friends with Edith during her first months of clandestine pregnancy, and he wondered if Ellen had some inside information about that time, or perhaps whether a story of abandoned children stirred some primal feminine emotions that were beyond a man's comprehension.

Ellen shook herself and asked, "You said there were three reasons … and that there was some good news?"

Cooper said, "Third, the boy's name is Darren…. "

And Dmitri finished the sentence, "… a six letter anagram of 'Radner'."

Cooper nodded. "These days, now that we have DNA tests, fatherhood has also become a fact, not a theory. If the Radner's want to find out, we can settle the issue once and for all."

The three of them looked at one another, until Ellen said, "That means Simon is a grandfather." Cooper was startled to realize that that idea had never occurred to him, nor had any of its major implications.

He said, "Oh, and the good news? Since Darren is Edith's son and regardless of who the father is, I think he's in line for a significant inheritance. Robert may not like it, but I think we can help poor Dawkins do what he tried to do that night – get some money for his son. And the boy's status as Edith's heir might mean that we could give the Conservancy movement some new legs. It opens up lots of avenues to block the development of Riverbend."

Dmitri said, "We?" It was a very expressive single word.

"I propose that we make Darren the first client of our brand-new three person firm." Cooper said the words very tentatively, as though voicing them would somehow spoil the idea.

Dmitri put his hands over his ears as though to block out further argument, then shook his head vigorously. He lowered his chin to his chest and looked up at Cooper over his reading glasses. "You *are* Russian! A sentimental fool … a schemer… "

Ellen simply reached over and took his hand, held it to her lips and kissed his fingertips.

Dmitri's and Ellen's reactions made Cooper think again about families, about the cobweb of needs and emotions that wove them together, about the centrifugal forces that must be overcome to keep them together. Most of all, he thought about the simplicity of love.   And then he thought about the dark side of those same forces and how they festered within the Radner family over the last twelve years. Finally, he thought about what he could not share with Dmitri and Ellen, at least not yet.

How it all started, what Rachel and Maria saw when they opened that door at the head of those stairs. As told to me in Simon's kitchen with Maria sitting in semi-darkness in the next room.

Nathaniel's original story, as told to Dmitri in the interrogation room, was deliberately misleading or outright inaccurate about two key factors. In that version, Nathaniel was near the door, watching Edith and Marcus writhing on the bed. Nathaniel failed to mention that in Edith's improvised and erotic game of "who's most valuable", she had started out with Nathaniel. He'd been the first on the bed with Edith; a wild, primal coupling, without any human language and over in seconds.   Then Edith rearranged the tableau so that all three were tangled together and, for a while, it was both unclear and unimportant who was doing what with whom. That was the misleading part, the lie of omission.

Nathaniel's outright lie was about what Rachel and Maria actually saw when they stood in the doorway. When the door opened, Edith was standing at the foot of her bed, watching Nathaniel and Marcus lying together naked and entangled, oblivious to everything except breathing, skin and pure sensation.

Maria

Maria was alone, sitting at her dressing table, staring at the dimly lighted mirror, but unseeing. The daylight was almost gone, absorbed in the shadows surrounding her. She liked being alone and in the near dark, in a world where she did not have to regulate her thoughts or words to stay within boundaries that she could not understand. Simon was the only one with whom she felt safe. She knew that he was sad because of her and what she had done, but he would not judge her. When Simon was there, she could let her mind wander and not worry about what she would say or do.

More and more lately, her thoughts were of their early days together – before Nathaniel, before what the psychiatrist called "her episodes," before the other woman came into their world, before Rachel opened that door. She and Simon were happy together. But always the thoughts of that other woman crept into her mind and blotted out the images of that happiness.

And the other woman was still there. That awareness fed a simmering rage that she knew she had to hide from everyone except Simon, especially from Nathaniel. Simon had told her over and over that she must resist the rage. He had given her some pills that would help; a sedative, he said. But they made her sleepy, and she didn't want to sleep.

She realized that there was another presence in the room before she actually saw in the mirror the dark shape approaching from behind her. In the semi-darkness, she could no longer tell whether it was Simon or one of those nightmarish visions that haunted her regularly now. She was not alarmed; she had come to accept the visits, even to look forward to them. She waited for it to speak.

It was a simple command. "Maria. You must take your pills."

She said, with no force to her voice, "But they make me sleep."

"Sleep is good. When you wake up, everything will be better. Like it was before." The voice was very soft and cadenced, almost a chant.

A gloved hand with three small white tablets reached around her right side and rested in her center of vision. From the left, another hand, this one with a glass of water. In the mirror, it was an intimate scene, Maria's still figure seemingly in the protective embrace of the dark figure encircling her.

She took the tablets, put them in her mouth and swallowed them with a sip of water. They were slightly bitter. She felt better; she had done something that would please Simon. Then the gloved hand appeared again with three more small white tablets. She swallowed these as well.

The tableau was stationary for a while; Maria seated, staring into the mirror, the dark figure looming closely behind her, its gloved hands resting on her slumped shoulders.

Maria spoke only once, "I'm glad she died ... not Rachel ... the other one ... in the rain."

"I know," intoned the figure. "I am too."

In a few minutes, Maria became drowsy. She was only vaguely aware of being supported to move from the dressing table to her bed, where she lay on top of the comforter fully dressed except for her shoes, which her vision – which was how she thought of it now – removed and placed carefully side-by-side beneath the bed.

More time passed. Her last semi-conscious hallucination was that her vision was helping her swallow pill after pill. After a while, they no longer tasted bitter. She slept deeply.

When the white vial of small white tablets was empty, the dark figure placed it and the water glass on the bedside table and stood quietly alongside the bed – like an honor guard of sorts – until Maria was no longer breathing.

Then the figure left, turning out the lights around the mirror, leaving only the blackness and a complete and utter stillness.

Simon

Simon stood at his floor-to-ceiling office window, watching a spectacular sunset. Its dramatic colors emphasized both the downtown skyline and the transition from daylight to dusk. It was a visual effect that Simon felt as a vague and expanding foreboding, a feeling that his life would change in some inalterable way once the color faded.

The dead bird was still on the ledge, his feathers rippling in the light breeze as though thinking about flying. Simon again thought of omens, and shuddered slightly.

His office door opened. He turned and smiled. "You're late."

"Things to do, places to go ... "

Simon said, "Tell me that we're done with trials, and courts, and lawyers, and reporters. Tell me that you love me."

"We are. And I do."

They stood together at the window. They kissed, lingeringly.

Simon leaned back in the embrace and asked, "And Maria? There's nothing they can do to her for Edith's death?"

"They're done. They have no case against Maria. It's all circumstantial. There is no way that she can be harmed now."

Simon thought for the thousandth time about the chaotic, irrational nature of passion. How Maria tried to protect Nathaniel from imaginary threats, how in her demented way she fought to erase the sight of her naked son interwoven with another boy. How she demonized Edith, killed her, only to see her reincarnated in Ellen.

He recognized that he suffered his own unique form of dementia. He could neither control nor understand his need to protect Maria from her psychotic rages and acts. Even if it meant exposing himself to murder charges. And beyond any definition of reason, this insane partitioning of himself, each part bound to a different person. He loved Maria, in a paternal fashion shaped by common history and duty. He had loved Edith, driven by an unsustainable mad sexual need. And he loved this person within his embrace, for reasons he could not begin to name.

Now that it was over, he could say, as though talking to himself, "If only she hadn't killed Edith!"

"She didn't. I did."

Simon heard the four simple words. At first, they were merely disconnected sounds, lacking syntax or meaning. Then came disbelief, then shock. And then, finally, they were irrevocably real, hovering in the silence around them. Simon tried again to believe that they could not be true, and failed.

Finally, he asked, "Why?"

"Because you loved her."

"I didn't!" And then, because he knew that he had lied, "Not like I loved you!"

"Then let me say it another way: Because I wanted you to myself. It's important to me that you not love anyone else."

Simon reached out to touch the glass, needing to find something real, a tangible sign that he was here in this time and place. He addressed himself, silently. *You're a coward. You knew!* His next thought was that he was thirty stories in the air and could step out for a long and final fall, if only the windows opened. But he knew that vision to be false, a wishful vestige of the person he had been a long time ago.

He turned and asked in a wondering tone, "The hammer? You had it the whole time … Why?" But he knew the answer.

"Actually, I waited until the police search was over and then buried it in the riverbank. It would have been useful to me if you --"

Simon finished the sentence "… if I got tired of you." He felt enormously tired, wanting only to lie down in a small dark space. Instead he said, "And Dawkins…"

"A mistake. I thought he could be made to look like the killer ... and you'd be off the hook for Edith ... the story worked better if he was dead."

Simon heard the words as though from a great distance. He also heard the absence of feeling underlying them, as though running through a checklist. He wondered at his lack of surprise. Both the words and the casual manner with which they were spoken confirmed for him the extent of his willfully blind complicity in his own manipulation and the crimes inflicted on others. Simultaneously, he realized that it was a deliberate choice; that his insatiable need for this person made him as guilty as if a jury had sentenced him in a court of law. Finally, he wondered – without any real curiosity -- whether this newfound self-disgust would make any difference. He thought not.

"There's one more thing." The other spoke very gently, but Simon knew that one more crime, the worst of all, was to be added to his legacy.

"Maria committed suicide thirty minutes ago."

The brilliant colors of the sunset had suffused into an orange glow that radiated from below the horizon, leaving the office in semi-darkness. Simon pressed his whole body against the window and repeatedly struck his head softly and slowly on the cool glass. He thought of what he had said to Cooper that first day, "that we all need atonement." He knew now, with absolute clarity, that he would not receive it.

He felt Marcus's hand on his neck, gently pulling him back into an embrace. From the doorway of the office, the two figures silhouetted against the dying light moved together slowly, finally merging into a single unmoving shape.

About the Author

Thomas Hofstedt is engaged in approximately his fourth career, each of which is partially reflected in this book. He has worked as a professor, an international banking consultant and as advisor to not-for-profit organizations. He is the author of two other books -- *A Conspiracy of Patriots* and *A Convergence of Evils*, both available on Amazon.Com. He lives in San Carlos, California with his wife and most diligent critic, Sharon.

CPSIA information can be obtained
at www.ICGtesting.com
Printed in the USA
LVOW04s1617091215

466131LV00022B/1124/P